Near Misses

S. E. Finken

Steve Finken

authorHOUSE®

AuthorHouse™
1663 Liberty Drive
Bloomington, IN 47403
www.authorhouse.com
Phone: 1-800-839-8640

First published by AuthorHouse 5/5/2011

ISBN: 978-1-4567-0068-3 (sc)
ISBN: 978-1-4567-0067-6 (hc)
ISBN: 978-1-4567-0069-0 (e)

Library of Congress Control Number: 2011902128

Printed in the United States of America

Cover designed by Bill LaFever

This book is printed on acid-free paper.

Chapter One

On the Friday evening of a Memorial Day weekend I was sitting at a little round table in a coffee house in central Kansas City. A giant cardboard sunflower on a string hovered above me. I had put down my paperback account of the life of Madame Bovary. Its slick cover was worn dull and veined. I was remembering summer, being thirteen and drinking from a park fountain after playing tennis with a friend. He was fun on the court, didn't stop joking if you were beating him. After drenching our heads and shirts, we sat in the shade of a stone shelter. Two older girls from the neighborhood came by and talked to us. I was recalling how good it was to be cooled by water on a hot afternoon, to be laughing with pretty girls in pastel clothing, to have one swing my racquet while the other smiled at something I said.

A female voice brought me back to the coffee house. "I can't possibly eat all of this. I don't know what I was thinking. Want some?" A woman of around thirty in a pink sweater and hospital whites was holding a plate with a large golden pastry on it.

"Well, Carrie," I said, my forty-six-year-old eyes squinting at the name plate pinned to her uniform pocket. "I never overlook a gift course for my mouth." I lifted my reading glasses from the table and put them on. Good-looking woman. "I'm Mitch Hamilton."

1

"Clever line, Mitch. Is it rehearsed?" Her curiosity seemed genuine.

"More like a reflex. I work with so-called clever copy. Gift books, greeting cards, calendars, things like that."

"Must be a fun job." She set the plate on the table and sat down across from me.

She used a plastic knife to cut the scone in two, then put one section on a napkin and slid the plate over to me. "I'm a nurse."

"Just like every other woman on the planet earth."

Her eyes opened then almost closed. She looked above me and said, "That paper flower has a pine scent."

"A happy reminder perhaps that winter's truly over and summer's starting."

"Happy holiday weekend." Carrie raised a ceramic cup.

"Only three coping days left."

"Tell me about it," she said softly. Her shoulders slumped and she looked down.

"What's a nurse girl like you doing in a mood like this?"

"I didn't feel like going home after work. I'm with a doctor's office on the Plaza. I'll just tell you I've had a recent break-up. Not fun. I did not see it coming. Just wham, you know."

She looked hard into my eyes with a quick flash of anger.

"You're beautiful when you're angry," I said, hoping to lighten things up a bit.

"Only when I'm angry?" She pressed her lips together. She was on the verge of either laughing or crying.

"Let's see if we can drown your sorrows with demon caffeine." I took our cups to get refills. When I got back, she told me she was getting over a relationship that had lasted almost a year. Her hurting was as obvious as a child's. I told her I could somewhat identify with her feelings.

"Divorce?"

"A few years ago."

"Ouch. Children?"

"A daughter. Megan. She's in college out west."

"You shouldn't be in a dark coffee house by yourself," she said, more composed as her attention shifted to me. "You should be in a sports bar with your buddies, screaming at a big screen ball game."

"I might scream anyway."

Carrie laughed and shook her head a little. She put her hand on mine and laughed again.

"Tell you what, Carrie. I'm on my way to our company's anniversary party. Crown Center. I can bring a guest. Be my guest. They're fun people. No pressure."

"I'll need to change." She opened her sweater wide.

"Won't we all?"

I drove behind her silver compact car to an apartment complex on the Kansas side of the city and waited for her in my unquestionably reliable sedan. She came out in twenty minutes wearing a modest red dress and black high heels. Fresh lipstick and invisible touches of makeup had transformed her from pretty to gorgeous. Nice start to a long weekend.

As we headed towards downtown I gave her a rundown of my workplace. We're not a large company. Somewhere over three hundred people. Besides publishing, we do some work for local advertising companies. We have a dozen in-house artists. The copy comes from a few of us inside and a network of free-lancers. Employees and guests at the annual shindig fit easily into a large hotel ballroom where a disc jockey plays the kind of music you hear at wedding receptions.

Inside I introduced Carrie to Eunice, the widow of the founder of Punchline Press. In her late fifties, she's a trim handsome woman with untouched gray hair that she wears in a short athletic cut. That night she had on a glittering silver dress and dark smoky pearls and multiple metal bracelets.

"Eunice is owner and CEO," I explained to Carrie, who listened and raised her eyebrows and nodded. Eunice put a hand on my arm and leaned towards Carrie with a sly smile and said, "More accurately, meddler in everyone's personal life when I'm not blatantly pursuing hunky creative types like his royal cleverness, Sir Mitchell."

"Oh, really?" Carrie responded, her lips pursed in feigned coolness.

"Sometimes we jog together," I explained. "And it's me trying to keep pace with her. She's in great shape."

Ted Sorenson walked up with a cocktail in each hand. He was wearing a thin black t-shirt beneath a gray sport coat. He's ten years younger than I am, taller than average, stays in shape. He'll change his look to keep up trends. He'd just started wearing his dark short hair in small spikes with lots of gel. I pointed to his head and said, "That reminds me. I've got to get my car in for a lube and oil change."

"Oh, good, Mitcheroo," Ted said flatly. He held up his drink glasses. "Look, I'm taking this year's bonus in booze."

"That's too much then," Eunice said, grabbing one of the cocktails.

"Not for a hardworking genius, not for the king of copy," Ted protested. "I'm always working, always looking for fresh ideas, always thinking. Just a minute ago I got an idea for a Christmas card. Two wise men. Frank Incense and Murray. Actually, they're wise guys. Mafia types. One says, 'A gift for you?' The other says, 'Fuggetaboutit.'"

Carrie laughed sweetly. Eunice and I exchanged looks. I took Ted's remaining drink.

"Okay, okay, adapt, change, revise," Ted said, pretending to be frantic. "How about they offer to give the card recipient a ride to a Christmas party, then find out there's no room in the trunk? Something like that. Huh? Work with me, people."

"Nice try," Eunice said. "Maybe you should take a break and just enjoy the party."

Ted turned to Carrie. "And you must be the Virgin Mary."

"Carrie," she said and held out her hand. He grasped it and held on.

"Virgin Carrie then. Close enough. Divine, I'm sure. I have to tell you here's no room at the Holiday Inn. You'll have to spend the night at my place."

"She came as my guest," I said.

"Oh, Mitch, you can have one of my old girlfriends," Ted said with a dismissive hand wave. "I've had so many, Carrie. Someday maybe you can be one. I treat 'em like disposable lighters. Use 'em up and throw 'em away."

"He burns hot, he burns fast," I said.

Carrie gingerly touched Ted's arm as though it were a plugged in iron. "You must be quite a man," she said, her eyes wide with amusement.

"A literal hottie," I said.

"Wait till you see me dance." He took both her hands. "I can twist and shout at the same time." Carrie looked at me, hesitated.

"Go ahead," I told her. "It'll give Eunice and me a chance to discuss the direction of Ted's so-called career."

"Ah," Ted sighed as he laid his head lightly on Carrie's shoulder. "Many are so-called but few are chosen for the big jobs." He and Carrie moved quickly without seeming self-conscious to the open area where a dozen people were dancing in front of the d.j.'s table. The current song was lively with heavy rhythm. The pair moved well together and appeared to know what they were doing. I actually enjoyed watching them.

"She's very pretty," Eunice said. "Striking really. That red dress and auburn hair.

She moves very gracefully. I might say alluringly."

"Pretty as in pretty young. She recently broke up with a guy. I met her at the Coffee Horse."

"What were you doing there, reading or writing?"

"Reading. Flaubert."

"Glad to know you're keeping up with the latest trends in nineteenth century foreign culture. That will keep our copy fresh and current." She took a small gulp from her amber drink, a gesture I remembered from childhood when an older generation always seemed to be holding mixed drinks in social settings.

"I thought coming here would take her mind off things, give her something to do. I talked you all up as fun people. I guess I didn't need to say too much about Ted." The music had switched to something slow and the new couple was touching lightly as they swayed and chatted.

"You should ask her out on a real date, Mitch. You've been alone long enough. It's time, dear boy."

"Great. Then Ted could point out the age difference by saying dinner and a movie would be a Happy Meal and a cartoon."

"Mitchell," Eunice said as stared hard into my eyes. "The problem with running away from life is that there's no place to run to."

Ted and Carrie were still laughing when they rejoined us. The four of us spent most of the evening at a table together. We all got up for some of the goofy dance numbers and made small jokes as door prizes were announced and handed out. When I won a metallic toaster that worked for bagels and muffins, Ted said, "Hey, Mr. Technophobe, want me to show you how to use it? It's pretty complicated. I'll stop over. We'll tackle that bad boy together."

I had the sugary experience of finding a woman more attractive as the night passed along. Carrie employed the not uncommon female talent of holding her head with upturned chin and smiling to show display of bright teeth that showed off beauty at its best. I felt a lot older than she and tried to refrain from looking at her too long or too often. I took her straight home after the last song and nodded when she turned down my offer to walk her to the door. I hadn't asked for her phone number and she hadn't asked me to call her. The only overtly positive sign she gave was humming that final song as she walked away. Great legs.

The next morning I showed up a little before nine to play tennis with Ted at his racquet club after years away from the courts. While I was waiting for him in the food court I caught a glimpse through a doorway of a woman with short blonde hair wearing a multicolored leotard over white tights and a thick towel draped over her shoulders.

Scientists can determine a lot about a long gone dinosaur from a single fossil tooth. The size, shape and wear of an incisor tells hem the scope and curve of the jaw, which give them the dimensions of the head, which informs the configuration of the neck and so on and so forth until they have completed an entire skeletal structure. Then it's possible to theorize with a high degree of certainty the layers of muscle and skin along with diet and level of ferocity. Three-dimensional computer animation shows the virtual beast moving and making some approximation of the grunts, growls, roars and sobs that would come from the chest cavity and throat.

Similarly, men believe they can assemble the same fairly complete picture of a woman from a quick glance into a passing car or a brief look at a jogger. While I was seated at a light beige wooden table with a cup of coffee, before Ted showed up, I put together a fast mental profile of the woman in the leotard of many colors. I imagined her briskly heading off to lead an aerobics class with women would appreciate her constant smile and perky encouragement. She would keep the towel near her on the floor and pick it up frequently to lightly rub herself because the vigor she brought to her job would cause floral scented perspiration to trickle down her high cheekbones and long graceful neck. She kept her compact body toned but she wasn't obsessed. She'd drink a light beer at dinner while she chatted with her dining companion about what she was reading, a tome not overly literary but one the high end of popular fiction.

Ted came through the doorway that the blonde had just passed through. He paused and looked backwards before coming to my table.

"I may sign up for an exercise class," he said as he set his athletic bag on the floor. The frame of his racquet was much larger than the one on my older metal model.

"I don't think they'll let you just watch."

Ted cringed and held his hand to his heart. Then he took a puzzled look at my racquet. "Mitch, if you're worn out from beating rugs, we can skip the tennis."

"I haven't hit a tennis ball in a long time. I don't now if I can get back in the game. I may not be able to remember the moves, the strokes, the trash talk. Maybe we should just sit and sip cranberry juice. Good for the kidneys."

"Hard to get tanked on that stuff."

"Not at my age."

"Yeah, right." Ted breathed a light laugh. "A guy in his mid-forties has to watch it." A tall woman with a pony tail, white shirt and black shorts, took his order for orange juice.

"You're still jogging, aren't you."

"That's a generous word for it."

"How fast do you go?"

"Beats me. About as fast as I can. I stopped timing myself about the same time I stopped stepping on scales. Ignorance is bliss."

"Knowledge is nothing," Ted pronounced with a professorial air.

"Exactly."

"Unless it's carnal."

I picked up my racquet and faked hitting him on the head. "You've got such a one-track mind, your parents should have named you Amtrak." Ted pumped his arms and said in a muted shout, "The little train that could, baby."

We played two sets on an indoor court. During warm-up I was able to get into an effortless rhythm of taking the racquet back a ways and hitting low hard shots that dipped from topspin after crossing the net and accelerated upon hitting the surface. Ted's shots came back in a similar way, usually within a step or two of me, and we had many long rallies. The pleasant thwack of the ball on taut strings and the oblivion of concentrating on a simple synchronized task gave me a mild euphoria. I was more than willing to continue until Ted gathered the balls and hit a mild underhand to indicate that we were volleying for serve.

I served surprisingly well and moved okay, managing to win a few games in each set before Ted beat me. I didn't go all out in chasing down sideline shots and I was ready to quit when our court time was up. We stuck around for lunch, turkey and cheese sandwiches and chips. We sat near a railing where we could look down on three courts below. Four men with gray hair, two with those raggedy beards that older men find attractive when they look in the mirror, were playing doubles in the center court. They wore shorts in earth tone colors and knee braces that surely contributed to their stiff semi-running.

"So what's with Nurse Carrie?" Ted asked as he brushed crumbs from the fresh white shirt he'd changed into.

"What's what with her?"

"Well, let's start with great-looking and leggy, and we'll go from there. Are you going to be asking her out?"

"She's very sweet," I said. "And young."

"Sure, for you."

"You really think so?" I tried to sound unconcerned. Ted took a slow swallow of juice and mouthed a silent "No." He leaned forward, his usual smirk nowhere to be seen.

"Look, you're not an old guy," he said. "You're in good shape, nice-looking in a strange weird kind of way. Hairline's not moving back too fast. Not a big deal. Just enough gray to make you look wise, quasi-distinguished. You don't see the way women look at you. They're sly about it, but I see it from the side. They're definitely interested in the Mitcheroo."

"Okay, now you're messing with me, making things up."

"I'm serious."

"It's really okay. I can take it. Thick skinned. Wrinkly, but tough and thick."

"You may feel like an old guy, resident of Geezerville. I don't know. You married young, stayed married for a long time, got a daughter in college. You're just now waking up to how much time has passed. You've been busy, head down, making a living, paying the bills, picking up disposable diapers then mailing tuition checks. Happened so fast. Taking care of personal and company business. Now that you've had a chance to slow down and look up, you have a sense that it's too late for you to start something new, that maybe life has passed you by."

I was genuinely startled. It was a few seconds before I could say, "Ted, that's thoughtful, almost insightful."

The smirk came back to Ted's face, "That's what I thought when Eunice said what I just repeated verbatim." We both laughed and I turned to watch the seniors go at each other down below. A man with thick black wrist bands and a sleeveless shirt hit a feathery serve into the net. "That oughta scare ya!" he shouted in self-disgust.

"So," Ted said. "About the nurse."

"She just broke up with some guy. Medium length relationship. We talked in the car. Both of us laid out that we weren't looking for a relationship but that it had been fun to be in a festive setting for an evening. I'm not planning to pursue anything." I didn't mention that I had not experienced the early physical manifestations of romantic interest. No fluttering in the stomach, no excited chattering, no urge to phone her as soon as I got home.

"Hmmm," Ted mused, finger to lips, eyes looking to ceiling. "So what I'm hearing is that this hot redhead is, how you say, available. Unattached, as free as the proverbial bird."

"You can call her if you want to. She's a lot closer to your age than mine. She's a nurse. Seems like a good thing to be. A profession that a good person would get into."

"I do like goodness," Ted said, the smirk now aroused to a grin. "I've got a poster of Joan of Arc over my bed. Burning at the stake. Talk about a hot babe." This time I really did pop him on the head with my racquet.

"How ironic," Ted observed. "If I were wearing a toupee, that really would be a rug beater."

"That does it. I'm outta here." I gathered my stuff and stood up. "What are you doing the rest of the day?"

"Don't know. No plans yet. Might go to the do track tonight. Interested?"

"I'll see how long I nap. Don't wait for me. I'll call if I'm going."

Several days a week and sometimes at night gray hounds race at a track north of Kansas City. After Kim and I split up, I would drive there once in a while, traveling the fifteen miles of highway that rose and fell in long slopes. I rarely bet on the dogs. I preferred to put the minimum two dollars down on horse races that were televised live from various cities around the country. Horse races had a higher degree of predictability than the hound events. Unlike dogs, a heavy favorite never tripped and rolled wildly on the first turn and then popped up to trot with flagging interest in the general direction of the finish line.

Horse races last three times longer than dog races. The outcome remains in doubt down the stretch. You get a more sustained and intense adrenalin rush for your two bucks. I seldom laid out more than twenty dollars in total and I could usually win at least a few races. The entire experience would end up costing no more than a single movie ticket. And sometimes I came out ahead.

The track was a bridge of diversion between errands and jogging, household chores and reading, golf and solitary or group entertainments in the evening. Like a shark requiring constant gliding through salt water to maintain a flow of oxygen to the gills, never stopping to rest and risk deep thinking, I drifted through the leisure hours, chomping down one morsel of activity after another without really considering how much pleasure I was experiencing.

I almost always went to the Woodlands track by myself. That way I could leave whenever I wanted, after a few races or a few hours. I didn't lose more money than I felt comfortable about because I was sticking around to keep someone company. I bet on horses that paid roughly even odds, those destined to win regularly and pay about what was wagered. No long shots. No miracles in the mud. I couldn't expect to win big, but I also wouldn't be hurt too badly when it was all over.

Beamed electronically from hundreds or thousand of miles away, the colorfully shirted jockeys on the television screens in large hope areas next to betting windows look like glittering passengers on bulbous rafts bobbing smoothly in a tight pack on a swift current until the final turn when one or two of the horses pull away and sprint to the end.

For six weeks in the fall there is live horse racing on a track across from the one where the dogs run. I only went on those afternoon events a few times, placing my inconsequential wagers and wandering down to the finish line where I could see the races end just a couple of yards away. Up close the picture hanged quite a bit. Tons of straining animal muscle bounce chaotically on the nearly lumbering beasts. The bright shining shirts and goggled faces of the jockeys have a thick splattering of mud on them. By the short oval journey's end the faces of horses wear expressions of pain and panic.

At the time, in the first year of divorce, I saw similarities between the horse racing and romance. The picture is pretty on the stylish Country Club Plaza shopping and dining district where couples hold hands in horse drawn carriages or a woman in a short skirt rises on tiptoe to kiss her boyfriend or lovers smile in the serene glow from a candlelit table. Love appears to be a thing of many splendors.

Get closer and it can be a different thing. In a movie theater ticket line you might overhear a woman giving a detailed account of her frustrating work day to a man whose single syllable responses are desperate pleas for silence. At a marble topped bar a man in a funereally dark suit is giving opinions on everything from politics to pin stripes for a female companion whose voice you never hear but only presume from the pauses in the gas bag's cadence. Not so good.

And yet. It is hard not to feel a sharp longing when I see a live romantic snapshot. I observed one at a stop light alongside Loose Park, the city's ten acre rectangle of rolling grass hills and tall trees where joggers run on an asphalt track past young parents with strollers and toddling children carrying sacks of bread crusts to the duck pond. On Saturdays in warm weather marriages occur hourly within the stone walls of the rose garden. In front of me at the red light while the first summery breezes brought warmth and memory through the open car window, there was a newer white convertible with red leather seats. The top was pulled back to admit the abundant sunshine. The front seat held two sweetly pretty young women, a bight yellow blonde and a strawberry blonde with similar cuts of thick clean hair. The passenger leaned over lazily to stroke the driver's neck and deliver a small smiling kiss. My heart sagged with envy.

Chapter Two

Like any American city of any size, Kansas City has an old and central area that's been renovated to house trendy shops, bars and restaurants. There's a small theater complex that shows independent films and documentaries. The eating places are non-franchise. The lack of familiarity with the fare adds a refreshing deliciousness. There are a couple of older bars where you can get an inexpensive drink. Like beat-up couches in a college apartment, the cheaper joints have a homey, comfortable feeling that's become embedded over the years into the rough beamed flooring, ornate molding and high panes of distorting glass.

In the last few years coffee houses have taken over the spaces of gift shops and hippie clothing stores. They're nice places to sit if you want to read or write or kill time before seeing a small film just down the street. The regular coffee, without syrup and candied whipped cream, isn't priced outrageously. They play good recorded music at just the right volume. You can listen easily if you want to or just as easily ignore it. Drinks and pastries and sandwiches heavy on vegetables are served by kids of college age in black t-shirts and baggy pants who've spent a lot of time doing things to their hair. They're constantly happy and friendly. Being around several of them at once used to give me some of that remembered feeling of late adolescence when I relished the near future.

Sometimes I'd see a guy about my age come into one of the coffee places and I'd get an unsettling feeling about the close-in future. One breezy fall afternoon I had stopped at the Broadway Coffee Horse to re-write some copy from work. A man was waiting at the counter for his order. He had fairly long hair faded from its original color to a graying version either brown or black. Thin pales legs stuck out of his shorts that went below his knees.

The guy wore his shirt loose, probably to obscure a bulging mid-section. Next to him there were two really cute little dark-haired girls in bib overalls and pastel shirts. Their ages couldn't have been more than a year apart. I guessed they were his children from a second or third marriage to a beautiful younger woman. She had no doubt initially riveted his gaze as intensely as it was now fixated on the slender young lady in the long print skirt who was talking into her cell phone while she stood by the front door and confirmed her allure by scanning the room for admiring looks.

The tiny girls teased each other with subdued giggles and never spoke to the guy. I wondered about being a middle-aged man whose haircut was something other than practical and whose marriage to someone half his age would produce an afternoon of taking the kids off her hands while she was off spending a hundred dollars at a hair salon that served espresso to its clients.

One night I was dining with Eunice just a few doors up from the Coffee Horse at one of the Westport restaurants whose Mid-East menus grudgingly list one, maybe two, dishes involving meat.

"So did you make a date with Carrie?" Eunice asked as soon as we ordered wine.

"Ah, the Question. Every woman wants to know the answer to the question of whether you're seeing anyone. Nature abhors a vacuum, women abhor a vacancy, an unfilled space next to a man. The answer to the Question is No. I didn't ask Carrie out. She just ended a relationship and I'm not looking for anything long-term."

"Okay," she said brightly as she shook out her napkin. "Fine. Forget about Carrie. Let's talk about Linda."

"Your friend from Texas. Annie Oakley type? Shoots glass balls out of the air while riding a horse? Yee-ha."

"My pretty, athletic, fun, interesting, not desperate, has a good job, independent, dresses well friend from Texas. She reads."

"All that and book-learning, too? Wow. The complete package."

Eunice tried to hide her pursed smile behind a napkin dabbing her lips. She made her voice a little stern. "Mitch, you've got too much to offer to spend your evenings alone at home or having dinner with the widow of your company's founder. There's absolutely no reason for you to be avoiding women."

"It's not women I'm avoiding."

"Well, commitment then or relationship heartache or the possibility of a wrenching break-up. Whatever you want to call it, it's worth another try."

I reached across the table and lightly touched her wrist. I told her that I would be happy to take Linda out for an evening. And I was thinking to myself that this was actually a pretty good situation. If it turned out to be less than a circus of fun, it was just one evening, and it had to be at least mildly engaging to converse with someone from a different city, with a different background and set of friends. If we did enjoy each other, there was still no inevitable second date, which would pretty much force a third and fourth date, and on and on and on until the dominoes falling in a serpentine line ended in a big fat relationship.

During our dinner of roast chicken, oddly yellowed spicy rice, steamed vegetables and soft, warm pita bread, Eunice and I talked about a few current movies, a recent non-fiction best-seller on the global economy, and nostalgia for cars with styling that made our parents dressed up and departing for an evening look like royalty.

Chad the Friendly Waiter failed to persuade us to have dessert. We gave him a partial victory by asking for two de-caf coffees.

"Thanks for not ordering the thirty weight stuff that comes in a thimble and costs four bucks," I said. "It freaks me out. I don't understand the concept. It's like getting a twenty dollar cigar that's a half inch long. Two intense puffs and you're done. What's with that?"

"Don't you believe in romance, Mitch?" Eunice asked, her shoulders slumping

"Don't know, at least for me. I'm a romanostic. I'm uncertain about the existence of true love. As I said, that's just for me. For others sure. I recently saw a large couple, young and large, huge, and sweet-faced. Smiling. They were getting into a car, probably to go eat. They looked very happy. Neither will nag the other or look disapprovingly at the ice cream scoop on the pie. Three times a day they think to themselves how glad they are to be married to each other and able to enjoy together something that means so much to both of them."

"Be serious, Mitch." A quivering stream of emotion flowed through her quiet voice.

"I am, Eunice. I just used a lighthearted example."

"I should leave you alone. I'm meddling."

"You're just a good and caring friend."

When we left the restaurant, a cold wind was blowing steadily down the red brick street. The few couples on the sidewalk held each other close and hurried to their cars for the drive home. I replayed in my head an incident that occurred to me at dinner and that I had decided not to tell Eunice about. It had happened a while back, on a street in San Francisco in Union Square. I had been in town for a book convention and had gone to dinner with an old friend from Punchline who had moved out to California and done okay as an artist working on her own, some years great, and others a struggle. She's a beauty. Supplemented her early west coast years by modeling. She has the classic high cheekbones, big expressive eyes and sensuous lips that agencies look for. She's smart and informed and a good listener, appreciates a witty line, talks neither too much nor two little during conversations.

When she and I parted, her to walk up the steps to her apartment and me to get in a cab and go back to the hotel, I gave her the we-re-close-friends-it-was-so-good-to-see-you hug that last a few seconds longer that a regular hug. She leaned in and kissed me full on the mouth, her hands reaching up and pulling me forward by the shoulders. I pulled back after the kiss, still holding her. "Well" was all I could think of to say as I tried to create a smile composed of surprised delight. We parted awkwardly. I got into the waiting cab too hastily, looking like I was running away. Maybe I was. Many times since then I've thought if that kiss from Angela didn't light a fire, there's no hope. As Ted might say, "What the hell do you WANT, man?"

Chapter Three

On a Saturday night I was nearly asleep in front of a televised baseball game, Kansas City against Cleveland. Local channel. I don't have cable, which strikes me as a way to spend time and money to find out there's not much to watch. John Cheever's hardcover collection of short stories lay soothingly heavy on my chest and my reading glasses were dangling from my hand. Stranded in the standard position of the non-scholarly reader, I dozed beneath the weight of this elegant prose with its depiction of middle class life in the suburbs of a faintly exotic and romantic New York City.

I subscribe to the various magazines that publish fiction, but I stopped reading the stories some years ago. They don't seem to measure up to the years when Cheever was showing up regularly in publications. I remember his time as a kind of golden age of short fiction, when you put off reading the stories until you'd been through the essays and reviews, in effect not having dessert until you'd finished your vegetables.

That perception was reinforced a few years ago when I was staying in the guest room of a college friend while visiting him and his wife in Minnesota. After a stimulating evening of conversation, I was unable to get to sleep and I pulled a book of older magazine fiction off a bookshelf in the living room. I read several entries. They were all pretty good. One was a matter-of-fact telling of the daily life of a childless housewife in a new development as she slowly went mad. Another was about a doorman who worked at an expensive apartment complex day in and day out across from a newly built aquarium that featured an enormous octopus, and he kept putting off a visit to the attraction, so long that he retired and died without ever seeing the sea beast. The most memorable story concerned an older gentleman who gets picked up in Manhattan and driven to spend Thanksgiving with his son's family in an outlying area where he gets confused about the location of his bedroom bath and walks in as she's dressing for dinner. Her outraged screams are the last sentences of that story. They all packed an emotional punch that made the reading engrossing and memorable.

What a treat it would be to pull a magazine out of your mailbox and come across a story like Cheever's "Chimera," about a executive with an ethereal mistress who appears from time to time and seems real, giving him an extra and totally separate life. One evening she's on the patio where he's firing up the barbecue and he looks across the neighborhood backyards and sees neighboring men on their patios with smoking grills and their own chimeras.

The phone rang. It was Ted. "Come out and shoot some pool," he shouted over brittle bar noise. "I'm at the Riverfront Brewery."

"Why me? Couldn't meet any women?"

"Hey, no problem there, my friend. Just looking for a little manly competition. Come on down."

"I don't know. Kinda late." I was planning to go in to work early to finish editing a book of humorous fishing tips before morning meetings started.

"Come on, be a sport. I'll buy you some geezer treats. Non-alcoholic beer, really soft drinks, chewy nachos."

I was pretty much awake by then. I figured what the hell, something to do. "Thirty minutes," I said. It's about seven miles from my house to the brewery and bar near the Missouri River. The beer is fermented in enormous copper tanks set between customer tables. It's served in pint glasses. Per serving cost is about the same as a six-pack in my refrigerator.

I showed up about ten o'clock. Prime bar time. The place was packed solid. I spotted Ted wedging his way through the denim and khaki clad natives of the social jungle. A new dark brown goatee made his jaw look big and square.

"Women," he mouthed excitedly from twenty feet away.

When I reached him, he put one hand on my shoulder and pointed with the other to a side room where a blonde and a brunette in blue hospital scrubs were shooting pool at the farthest of six tables. The woman with dark hair was rapidly firing off practice shots. The blonde's swaying body twitched in time to blasting rock and roll. Two nearly empty pitchers of beer sat on a tall round table between them.

Ted gave me a "Pretty good, huh?" grin of self-satisfaction. "I just made contact a few minutes ago," he said loudly into my ear. "They appear friendly. They do not fear our ways."

When we got close to the women, they both looked at me. Their eyes were at once wild and sleepy. They wore their hair loose around pretty faces.

"Ladies, this is the famous Mitch," Ted said. He gestured towards the blonde. "This is Julie."

"Hi, Julie."

"And her friend is the famous Minnesota Cathy."

"I'll call you Minnie," I said.

Cathy laughed easily and said, "You can call me anything. Just call me for beer." Stumbling a little, she went to the round table and picked up her glass. "I'm the designated drinker."

"These ladies are nurses," Ted pointed out.

"I could use some intensive care," I said.

Cathy laughed again and looked at me. A red polished forefinger twisted the gold chain around her neck.

"Mitch," she said slowly as she leaned into me, spearmint breath brushing my face. "Let's show these two losers how to play eight ball."

Cathy and I were good enough to win almost every game. Each victory brought out a little livelier celebration dance from her, a tighter hug after the high five, a further migration from the middle of my back up to my neck and hair.

We played until after midnight. I was the only one not drinking steadily. I've been Two Beer Guy for a while now. Ted and Julie had put two long-legged stools together and eventually lost all interest in the game. While Cathy and I played nine-ball, the two of them sat side by side with her leg across his lap and her face pressed against his neck.

Cathy and I decided to play a game for one of her skinny cigarettes.

"This is like prison gambling," I said. Her break shot exploded the balls. "Cigarettes as currency. You'd be asking if someone had change for a carton. The slot on your piggy bank would be a little round hole."

Cathy started laughing really hard. She started to shoot, then doubled over and walked away from the table. She lined up a new shot, then bent over again and walked away. Then she walked over with gliding steps and put both arms around my waist.

"I think we've shot enough pool," she said.

Suddenly the Julie's blonde head lurched up away from Ted. She hurried through the thinned out crowd in the direction of the rest rooms.

"Right on time," Cathy said calmly. "Girl cannot hold her pitcher." She picked up her purse from the table and followed her friend. A few minutes later she came back and told us Julie was fine, throwing up at the moment and probably for a while longer, feeling embarrassed, we should call it a night, we'll see you here again, we're regulars, it was fun, we'll look for you. She gave me a wink and a light kiss on the lips.

"Surprise ending," I said to Ted as we walked out.

"Not totally. She was asleep, snoring a little, before she ran off to hurl. You were doing okay. Cathy was digging the old boy."

"Ted, are you okay to drive?" I looked into his eyes. "I can take you home, bring you back in the morning before work."

He waved me off, touched his nose briskly with hand and then the other before quickly walking heel to toe along the sidewalk. He gave me a brisk farewell salute and exclaimed, "Jober as a sudge!"

On the drive home I smoked the thin cigarette won in nine-ball, my first in years. The air from the open window was cold and sharp, the tobacco smoke warm and nostalgic. I felt young. I thought about how Cathy was the kind of woman people call a party girl, someone who laughs freely, a little loud, who drinks quickly and leans her long body across a pool table to reach a corner shot. She'll kiss a stranger and dance seductively in front of him in a bar as the rock and roll thunderstorm moves through. She's a short term girl, interested in a few hours of foggy pleasure that's forgotten in the morning. Not a bad way for a geezer to spend an evening.

The people in the brewpub reminded me of my neighbors around the townhouse in Midtown where I'd lived right after the divorce. I had a place where the interior walls were faded red bricks with fresh seams of mortar. It was near Crown Center, almost downtown. The building's old, but the inside is all updated. It's a little pricey for what you get, but I didn't mind paying during my transition to something more permanent. I had two bedrooms and a bath and a half. There was a gas fireplace that I didn't use. The flames on those things always give me an image of quickly burning money that generates basically no heat. The mantel was a nice place to keep photographs of Megan as a child and more recent pictures of our dad and daughter vacation trips out west.

There were about fifty units in the complex. The residents were mostly in their late twenties and thirties, singles and couples who leave for work in suits and drive expensive cars. A few boats sat on trailers in the outer parking area. The men were relaxed and friendly. They greeted me with "Hey, Dude." at the dumpster and communal mailbox. The single women tended to be wary, offering little more than a silent smile with eyes averted. No doubt they'd encountered divorced men my age at fitness clubs, guys who work out briefly and stand near the entrance to the locker room, greeting women as they pass by.

I should have felt out of place, like the small town kid who stays behind when all of his friends head off for college or the military, but I didn't. I found the environment pleasantly reminiscent of in other summers when small scenes unfolded outdoors. Couples kissed as they leaned against cars. Shirtless teams of lean young male athletes played basketball at temporary hoops set up on the asphalt. Unfamiliar women in short skirts and high heels slipped out of doorways on Sunday mornings. Empty beer cartons piled up in the dumpsters on weekends.

Sometimes very late at night my open bedroom window would admit the sounds of people being dropped off after a night at the bars. Even though they were in a totally silent setting, the participants in lingering conversations would speak over each other about mundane matters in voices whose volume had been turned up by alcohol and the recent din of the club scene. "So are you coming over to Shawn's tomorrow?" someone once absolutely shouted without emotion. After a brief silent pause while the person inside a car responded, the guy fairly yells, "I'll tell Jesse. Maybe we can shoot some hoops." It made me smile as I remembered my college roommates coming back from a night of beer and thundering on as they talked such exciting events as setting the alarm and making sure to pick up toilet paper before the weekend.

The thick old walls separated me from the radio and CD music of my younger neighbors, but I would occasionally hear their listening preferences from cars being washed and from portable players on patio tables during sunbathing or small outdoor gatherings. This intermittent exposure to songs and singers of a younger generation made me curious and in the car I sought out radio stations that play the newer stuff.

Very little attached itself to me. I didn't listen for long. I've been at stoplights while in cars beside me, young women tap their steering wheels and sing open-mouthed to the same song I've come upon. They're grooving and I'm not moving. Maybe there's a relevance to them that is lost on me. Perhaps I'm not open enough to new things, although occasionally there's something I like a lot.

I used to think that the reason I don't appreciate and enjoy new waves of modern rock and roll is because of a phenomenon common to all musical forms, that they reach their pinnacle, scaling the tallest peaks in their particular range, go as high as it is possible to go. Symphonic music climbers Mozart and Beethoven still outsell everyone on the classical shelf. Intrepid jazz explorers Louis Armstrong and Charlie Parker planted lofty flags that others can only gaze at from an impossible distance.

The 1960s innovators took rock and roll about as far as it could go. Dylan brought poetry to the irresistible rhythms and raw energy. The Rolling Stones unleashed as much sexual power as the genre could generate. The Beatles infused a kind of startling beauty that no one since has been able to approximate. On a New Year's eve I was walking a sleepless infant Megan and halfway watching a midnight special countdown on that year's most popular musical artists. The number one spot went to the Beatles. The had broken up years earlier.

I had a friend who bought a used upright piano and had someone teach him five of his favorite rock and roll songs. That's all. Just the fab five. He had no desire to learn more. He said the when he sat down to play, he would perform each two or three times, never tiring of the ritual. Each day he would sit down with anticipation and thoroughly enjoy the experience all over again. He would stay wedded to those tunes forever.

I've wondered if it's possible for me to unearth a rich new vein of musical wealth, a mother lode of rhythm and views, that would excite me as much as Bob Dylan's first albums and entice me to listen to the same songs thousands of times. I don't know. Maybe the old music isn't really any better. Maybe the new music's just fine and I'm just too old. This isn't a pressing question. It's more of a curiosity. I have plenty of music to listen to. So when I look across at the young women who lip sync to radios in untidy cars, the tinge of urgency I feel comes from wondering whether I'll ever again experience the sharp visceral tightening and noticeable jellying of the knees at the first sight and countless subsequent sightings of a particular woman, the romantic equivalent of repeated exposure to Blonde on Blonde. Could it start with the acceptance of an invitation to have a drink, then continue as fresh excitement each time she put on a new flattering outfit or did her hair in a slightly new way?

I'd pretty much given up any real hope of the earthquake of infatuation, a singularity of desire, like that of the young men in romantic comedy movies who are willing to go anywhere and do anything to be with the objects of their desires. Works for these young guns on the streets of Loveland, but doubtful to say for the men who have been around a long time and may have grown to see romance as merely an O.K. Corral.

Two things came to mind last time I saw a lovely pony tailed brunette pulling away from a stop sign and singing along with the car radio. First, a huge appetite for the sweetness of romance is probably something you outgrow, like the childhood love of breakfast cereal that is just solid colored sugar pressed into fun shapes. Second, romance would probably lose out to more practical considerations like a steady paycheck with health benefits and a very simplified life style and routine.

Chapter Four

On a Thursday afternoon I got up from my desk to get coffee refill and walk down the hall to chat with Charlie Flanigan. He's a little older, a bit heavier and a lot balder than I am. He's the head of the design department and a longtime friend. We shared a phone line when I started at Punchline twenty years ago. His wife Margaret is close to my age. For many years the Flanigans were frequent weekend companions of my wife Kim and me as we looked for happy diversion in our days of abundant time and scarce money. We made the rounds of lakes and camping areas in warm weather. We spent wintertime eating inexpensive home cooked meals and playing cards and board games. After our daughter Megan was born, we kept up the routine, driving to familiar destinations with a car seat and toddler treats in a grocery sack.

When I looked into his office he was shaking hands with a willowy woman in navy business attire. She was young, no more than thirty. Her jacket and skirt and black shoulder bag looked more relaxed than brand new. She probably wasn't interviewing for her first professional job.

She put the bag strap on her shoulder and turned to leave. I guess she was startled to see someone in the doorway because she opened her eyes wide and she flinched. I didn't look at her in a lingering way. She was clearly a beauty. I didn't want to look like an old letch. And I didn't want to show a lack of self control. Inwardly, though, I emitted a long, low whistle of amazement at her big brown eyes and perfectly white smile framed by a thick mane of shoulder length brown hair.

"Hi," I said, making brief eye contact. "Didn't mean to sneak up on you. I was just coming by to rouse Charlie from his afternoon nap. If he sleeps more than an hour, he wakes up cranky."

The young woman kept smiling and nodded awkwardly before walking past me.

"Chatty," I said to Charlie after she'd gone.

"She was with me. In a smart way. Poised. I liked her."

"What's the deal?"

"Interviewing for a job in Finance. Eunice wanted her to talk to a creative person, give her a general feel for the company."

"Think Harper will hire her?"

"Don Juan Harper? Oh, hard to say. Smart. Beautiful. Big Eight accounting firm background. Did I mention beautiful? I'd say she has at least a fair shot."

On a drawing table against the wall there was an illuminated light box with slides scattered on it. I scanned them and picked up a few. There were various shots of a pan with frying eggs and bacon making faces with different expressions. On some of them red drops on the yolks looked like pupils. Added a lot of expression.

"Tabasco sauce on the yolks?" I asked. Charlie nodded yes. "Nice touch, Mr. Big Shot Art Director."

"It's what I do, Mitch. We're looking for a cover for that cookbook with jokes relating to each dish."

"Sure, <u>The Joke of Cooking</u>."

"Egg faces make sense?"

"Want to make them clown faces?"

"I would have but we don't have an Over Design Department." I put up my hands in mock surrender.

"Mitch, speaking of food, Margaret's trying some new dish tonight. Savory loves company. Join us."

"Well, I know whatever Margaret cooks will be great, but I don't know. Pretty short notice. I don't want to impose."

" Not at all. She'd love to have you."

"Well, I'm a pretty high level guest. Won't Margaret feel like she needs to go to a lot of trouble? You know, polish the chandelier, order up fresh flowers, fatten the appropriate calf. Maybe I should take a rain check."

"Nonsense. Done deal. I'll just let Margaret know. Stop by around six-thirty."

I arrived at precisely six-thirty. I brought a bottle of wine that cost a few dollars more than the everyday stuff. Merlot. I figure it's the ketchup of wine, goes with everything.

Charlie and Margaret live in a square two-story stucco surrounded by thick, neatly trimmed greenery. Tall elms and pin oaks stand comfortably along the block. I stood on the steps to their screened-in porch and rang the bell. Charlie came out of the house with their eager golden retriever on a leash.

"Go on in, grab a beer, grab a snack," he said jovially. "Hands off the wife though." Outside the office Charlie tended to really loosen up. He made repeated motions to me to go inside like I was a dog. "Go on in, Mitchie, that's the boy, go inside, that's the boy."

I stuck out my tongue just a bit and did an extremely half-hearted imitation of a panting dog.

"Really, Mitch, go on in. Ogilvy's got to do his thing." He held up a plastic grocery bag. "I'll be back with a gift in fifteen or twenty minutes."

Margaret was standing near the fireplace in the living room where ex-wife Kim and I had spent so many evenings after movies and dinners, more than a few holidays, opening inexpensive gifts after simple meals and jug wine, talked long and laughed often. It was the epicenter of our long friendship.

Early spring and Margaret was already tan. Her naturally dark complexion needed almost no time to turn a summery golden brown. Her brown hair was tinted with highlights and cut short for swimming and tennis. She was wearing a sleeveless dress, lavender with a floral print, tight against her curvy hips. As she walked over to greet me, the heels of her pumps clacked against the hardwood floor.

Margaret's tight smile and outstretched arms communicated welcome and wistfulness. As we hugged her lips pressed lightly against my cheek before brushing across my lips. Holding her sturdy body close to me and inhaling the familiar scent of her signature perfume and the smell of her house and furniture, I felt an ache for a time when summer weekends were long and perfect, and future problems seemed to sit on a very distant horizon.

"Mitch." That was all she said. Her eyes were closed.

"I brought wine," I said, fumbling in my mind for a small off-hand joke. I didn't come up with much. "It's for all of us to share."

"It's really good to see you." She accepted the wine and I followed her to the kitchen, reliving backyard picnics when I spent evenings trying not to stare at the backside of her short and fraying denim cutoffs.

The kitchen is like the rest of the house, clean and spacious and practical. Not much clutter. Decorations are fresh flowers here and there, framed pictures of family and friends on walls and end tables, a clock in every room. One thing I've always liked about their home is the casual and occasional incongruity. You might see a claw hammer on the fireplace mantel. A basketball might sit in an easy chair. Glass jars, one holding rice and the other containing tea, might sit on the kitchen counter with a magazine stuck between them. The house is neat and clean, not too fussy. You can relax there.

"How's Megan doing out in Arizona?" Margaret asked as she put the wine on the counter.

"Great. Top grades. Enthusiasm for everything. Still majoring in English and Advertising."

"Following in your footsteps."

"Big creative shoes to fill. Let's see her beat <u>101 Uses For A Bent 5-Iron.</u>

"Still sarcastic after all these years." Margaret sang the words.

"I didn't mean to put myself down."

"That's Charlie's job."

"And he does it so well."

Margaret opened a drawer and found a red kitchen tool with a corkscrew attachment. She went to work on the bottle of wine.

"How are you holding up, Mitch?" she asked, looking down at the task before her.

"Peachy."

"Honestly?"

"I'm staying together for the kid."

"Clever old Mitch." She concentrated on twisting the red handle. "We used to laugh a lot, didn't we?"

"Often. On the way over I was almost laughing out loud remembering the picnic the four of us had at Clinton Lake when Charlie was in charge of bringing the burgers."

"He brought hamburgers all right," Margaret said, giving a small laugh that was a kind of sniffle.

"Yeah, two pounds of ground beef. No ketchup, no mustard, no pickles, no onions."

"No buns."

"No buns. No charcoal or lighter fluid. Just a mound of raw meat."

Margaret laughed silently, shaking her head slowly as she tried without success to pull out the cork. She handed the bottle to me.

"You'd never make it in the Swiss army," I told her.

"Too weak, huh?"

"Poor yodeling skills."

Margaret bent at the waist and cupped a hand over her mouth. Her shoulders shook and she wiped away a tear.

"Funny," she said.

While Margaret stirred and basted and fluffed in the kitchen, I set the table and poured the wine. We were having stuffed Cornish game hens, lemon rice pilaf, steamed asparagus, French bread, salad. I've always liked Margaret a lot. She's very tender of heart. When she asks you about yourself, she really listens to what you say. In the early years it didn't matter what anyone wanted to do, she was glad to go along and be part of our foursome, just happy to have us all together.

Margaret and Kim were similar physically. Margaret had a darker skin tone, but both were taller than average, slender and willowy. They maintained young girlish looks. When the four of us went to the lake to swim and water ski from a rented boat, part of the true enjoyment was seeing their nearly nude bodies, trim and perfectly proportioned, moving with grace and coordination as the breeze blew their long straight hair across their smiling faces.

"Okay, you two, out of the bedroom, break it up in there," Charlie shouted as he came back in with the dog.

"If we give you money, will you go out and get yourself an ice cream cone?" I shouted back.

No answer.

"Well?" Margaret called out.

"How many scoops?" Charlie finally answered.

It was a warm enough evening that we could eat at a card table on their screened-in porch. Charlie heard a retelling of the hamburger story. We talked about other inexpensive outings we took when money was scarce and time was abundant. Margaret recalled the time the four of us slept in two double beds in a tiny cabin room at Table Rock Lake in southern Missouri. It cost sixteen dollars a night. Eight per couple.

"Remember, Mitch?" Margaret asked. "We turned out the lights and laid there for a little while, feeling awkward. And you said, 'Good night, John-Boy.'"

Margaret's sharp laugh sounded like a sob.

Chapter Five

I don't eat a lot of fresh fruit. I used to, years ago, but I don't anymore. When it's perfectly ripe, there's nothing better than fresh fruit. Crisp sweet apples in the fall, firm and juicy melons in summer, golden pears whose delicious pulp melts in your mouth. The problem is that it's almost impossible to find perfectly ripe fresh fruit. I end up throwing away time and money. Over time I've lost my tolerance for fruit that is less than perfect. An apple that has gone just a little bit to the mushy side gets tossed into the garbage with two bites out of it. A navel orange with any touch of bitterness is gone. A mouthful of pear just starting to brown, carrying the smallest harbinger of being too ripe, is spit like a sneeze into the garbage disposal.

I'm afraid I've developed the same super perfectionist attitude about women. I fear I cannot bear even a minor deviation from the ideal in physical appearance, basic goodness, pleasant temperament, sense of humor, compatible interests, ability to maintain interesting conversations. I want to gaze upon a well-proportioned body. I don't want to bear witness to rudeness, even impatience, towards the actions of a waitress with good intentions. I don't want to find myself on a long car trip listening to her music.

This all became apparent to me after Eunice tried a few times to partner me with a local television newswoman she knew through a women's business club. The anchorwoman is quite the beauty, with auburn hair around an angular face that will remain attractive for many years. Her banter on the air with the other personalities is a notch above the typical inanities you expect on local television news.

Eunice first talked to me about TV Girl just after I moved out of my family house. I was too numb from the separation to even think about her. About six months later she tried again, saying that the woman had asked casually whether I was still uninvolved and would I ever be interested in the three of us having lunch just to get acquainted. I apologized for unfounded reluctance and said I'd think about it.

Sometimes I watched the newswoman while I ate supper at the coffee table in my living room. I started thinking that I wouldn't initiate anything but if Eunice mentioned her again, I'd agree to lunch or drinks. At the very least, I'd probably hear some interesting things about reporting on television and the people she appeared with on screen.

While this was all floating around in my head, I went to an art festival in Westport. I went three times, always around mealtime. The paintings and pottery and sculptures were fine, but I was there for the food. I could get a sandwich or trendy pizza from booths set up by the better restaurants for around five dollars. You can't beat that.

Artists booths were in the barricaded streets. The sidewalks stayed relatively free of people. The May weather was warm and still. A big crowd was always milling around. On a clear evening just before the sun disappeared I was leaning against a storefront and eating grilled salmon on a soft seeded bun when the newswoman appeared in the flow of strollers. She looked anxious, nothing like the poised and smiling woman I saw on my TV, as she talked to the guy she was with. He had an expensive haircut and pricey patchwork sweater. His face bore an expression of firmly set annoyance. She and I made eye contact for a nanosecond before she turned her attention to a display of cityscape paintings rendered with photographic realism.

I had only seen this woman from the waist up as she sat behind a news desk. She always wore a jacket and a bright scarf or heavy necklace. On this night she had on an embroidered blue work shirt tucked into black jeans. As she turned and eased back into the milling crowd, I saw her completely. The lower part of her body had a slight thickness that I didn't expect from seeing her slender arms and face with its angularity and high cheekbones as she reported the news of the day. The minor heaviness of her figure was emphasized because she was wearing moccasins. They were a dirty gray with small multicolored beads stitched onto the toes and along the sides. Any trace of squatness in her figure could have been eliminated by the wearing of shoes or boots with just modest heels. If I were to pick her up for a movie date or to take a walk along a river, I would be disappointed to have her come to the door wearing the moccasins. And it would be of course petty of me to say anything negative about something as trivial as choice of footwear.

So I crossed the newswoman off of my mental list of potential dates and added moccasins to my list of reasons to immediately reject bright, attractive women. On a golf course later that month I found another one.

I was with Jack Buckley. We play a similar game, decent length and accuracy off the tee, not bad from the fairway, a little shaky around and on the greens. We both walk and carry, leaving plenty of riding carts for lanky guys in their twenties who seem to have plenty of loose cash to throw away.

The Friday that we played was one of the first summer like days of spring, when you no longer detect any remnant of winter's stale coldness if you're standing in shade. The course parking lot was almost full. On the driving range each little square island of artificial fairway was inhabited by a golfer trying to rediscover a close approximation of last summer's swing. Sunlight was a warm yellow blanket on your back. Several hours of tree lined greenery lay ahead of you before you sat in the clubhouse in the golden glow of a second beer with happily aching legs.

On the practice green I rolled in a thirty foot putt. "Nothing to this game," Jack said as he watched me take the ball from the cup.

"Not for me," I said.

"With your natural athletic ability, you could quit your job in a few years and join the Senior Tour," Jack said with mock solemnity.

"Golf or bus?"

Jack's laugh was almost a bark and he took a few steps back from the force of it. Over the loudspeaker the starter announced that the Buckley twosome was due up on the first tee and would be joined by the Turner twosome.

Two women in a cart pulled up alongside us. "Hi, we're the Turner twosome," the driver said.

"Ike and Tina?" I asked.

"Sam, short for Samantha," the passenger said, pointing to herself and flashing a killer smile. "And my friend is Sherri."

"Mit, short for Mitch," I said. "And this is Jack."

Both women had carefully frosted brown hair and huge diamond wedding and engagement rings. Their sleeveless pastel blouses exposed the thin muscular arms that you see promised by health club ads. Samantha was the taller of the two. She was just beginning to acquire the tan that she would maintain for the summer. Only a small abdominal bulge beneath her pleated khaki shorts revealed that she had given birth to the two children she mentioned having to pick up at middle school after golf. Sherri was more fair skinned, shorter and more voluptuous. Both of them seemed very much at ease with themselves and smilingly eager to have a good time.

The warmth of a perfect afternoon, Jack's ready laugh and the ongoing conspiratorial giggling of the ladies in the cart put me in an almost goofy mood. I bragged about my game. "Heads up!" I yelled at a foursome almost four hundred yards ahead of us on a long hole. I belittled the accomplishments of my playing partner, "Nice par, Jack. You must have five in the last six months." I teased the women. "Does it kill ya that they don't put golf spikes on sling back satin pumps?"

Suddenly, surprisingly, pleasantly, I experienced an awakening physical desire for a woman. Samantha's bright white smile had me. I produced and directed brief mental movies as we moved around the course. Me with Samantha in the tall brown grass out of bounds and behind a stand of trees, under the pretext of finding an errant ball, the wind blowing her golden glinting hair in a veil across her face while she looked at me with longing upturned eyes. Another time I imagined Samantha offering me a ride in her cart to hit my ball in a distant location and shifting suddenly to expose the skin beneath a suddenly open blouse and later opening her car trunk in the parking lot just a few spaces away from me and taking off her slightly soiled top to briefly pose in a white lacy bra before putting on a large soft pink hooded sweatshirt. All in all, a good day.

By the end of our game, a chill had found its way into the breeze that was blowing harder. Our play on the last few holes got kind of ragged. I was ready to wind things up and buy Jack the beer he'd won from me. He paused in front of the clubhouse to get his cell phone from his bag to call somebody at his office and Sherri was around the back of the clubhouse returning the cart. I was thinking about whether to get Jack a beer in the course bar or stop at some neighborhood place on the way home and get a sandwich.

On the sidewalk leading to the parking lot Samantha gave me a direct expressionless look that I hadn't seen all afternoon. "My husband wants me to play in a golf tournament in Wichita next Monday," she said flatly. "He leaves early in the morning and won't get back till after nine that night. What do you think I should tell him?"

"Oh, I think you should go. It's probably at that nationally ranked course down there. Beautiful place where they hold occasional tour events. Dub's Dread or Fudd's Head or something like that. Especially if this weather holds and you keep hitting the ball well. You have a nice swing and your attitude…" I kind of blathered on, knowing I wouldn't be seeing Samantha again on Monday and noting that my list of things that would prevent involvement with a woman had grown by two. Moccasins and wedding rings.

Chapter Six

Ted and I were having a drink after work. We were in a Westport place with thickly veined reddish brown wood and cigars sold out of glass cases with controlled humidity. The cheapest drinks aren't cheap. The waitresses in semi-sheer white cotton blouses and short black skirts, bare-legged and wearing black pumps, are dark and exotic. They wear sullen lipstick on mouths that carry accents and slight formality ("What would you like to order?"). They're too beautiful to risk any attitude with the male customers other than aloof courtesy.

Jazz was playing fairly loudly, but that was okay because it was the kind of jazz I like, with a familiar melody getting an improvisational treatment, lots of solos. Ted was holding a fat cigar like a big dart and puffing thoughtfully while I talked about Joe Montana.

The San Francisco quarterback came to Kansas City after winning four Super Bowls, joining the Chiefs because he thought they were good enough to guide to another championship victory. At the time Montana had an elbow injury that looked like a bulging grapefruit. He couldn't throw the long ball. He hopped and limped in efforts to escape the rush of opposing defenders.

Well, Joe Montana didn't get a fifth Super Bowl ring. Close but no metaphorical cigar for him. "But he's a better man than I am, that Gunga Joe," I was saying.

"How's that?" asked the puffing gourmet of hand rolled tobacco.

"Willing to take the hits that are inevitable, okay with waking up to a world of personal pain, fine with taking the bruising, the sprains and strains, contusions. Contusions, man! Even knowing the repeated conquest would never be as thrilling as the first one, and not even getting that. Still, he went back on the field. Kind of like you, young Theodore."

"Like moi?"

"You've been on the field many times, sort of settled down and settled in, had it all turn bad. Many times. Yet you keep getting out there onto the playing field. You keep getting back at it."

Ted's eyes floated towards a dirty blonde in a mini-skirted business outfit at the bar. She was smoking in fast, deep drags. The multitude of silver bracelets on her wrists clattered as she kept running her fingers through her streaked hair. I was guessing she'd had a tough day at the office.

"I'm back at it," Ted said absently, his eyes now aimed squarely at the woman at the bar. His voice lowered, slowed down. "Back in the saddle again. Right at home on the range, baby." Ted was transforming himself into the stealthy predator, intent on conquest, eyes narrowing as he waited for the opportunity to pounce. He was a hawk hovering languidly over a brown farm field, hungry and alert, reflexive, unthinking.

When the object of desire held an unlit cigarette in one hand while she used the other to dredge through a black purse the size of carry-on luggage, Ted slid quickly from his chair and pulled a box of matches from a basket on the bar, then struck a flame as he moved towards her.

She didn't look at all surprised to find a hand holding a small burning stick inches from her face. She put a cigarette tip to the small orange blur and watched it flare as she inhaled deeply before looking up to see who her benefactor was. I could see Ted's mouth form the words, "Come on, let me light your fire."

With half a pint of overpriced beer to finish alone I did this thing I do sometimes where I mentally tell an anecdote to myself like I'm talking to someone who's never heard it. It's kind of a strange thing to do, I suppose, and sometimes I get noticed moving my lips and making vague hand gestures. But I see it as similar to humming a favorite song or remembering a happy time. Essentially, it's just killing time.

So I was telling my imaginary drinking companion about Ted's involvement with a woman a few years ago. She also wore mini-skirted and matching suit jackets, with blouses opened low, and lot of jangling jewelry. She was an employee of a company that we had recently gotten involved with to distribute a series of humor books about professions such as medicine, teaching, computer science and others, all the widely held areas. She was down from the home office in Minneapolis for a few days to work out the details of our new working arrangement. We worked with her during the day and some of us went to dinner with her in the evenings. After dinner each night Ted drove her back to a hotel on the Plaza.

At the office and in the restaurants Ted and the lady treated each other with professional distance and businesslike courtesy. But something must have gone on. Whatever it was had created certain expectations in her about Ted. He didn't talk about her after she returned to the frozen north, and once the distribution policy was finalized, there was no reason for her to come back to town. But a month later as Ted and I were walking to his convertible in the lot adjoining our building, the girl from the north country came at him full bore in a rental car, mascara and tears forming dark streams of rage on her face. She swerved at Ted and then shot around him while screeching an obscenity.

"Was it something I said during sex?" Ted asked a few moments later as we assessed what had just happened.

"I don't know. Maybe it was something you didn't say. Have you been calling her?"

"Left a few voice mails."

"Oh, so you were making impersonal phone calls."

"You could say that."

I finished the story to my invisible listener by saying I was reluctant to be a Joe Montana, taking the brushings that come from playing the game. And I also didn't want to be the crushing lineman who hurts someone else, without intention, sometimes permanently, just following the rules of how the game is played.

I started to think about Lolita in Nabakov's novel and how the young teen girl travels from motel to motel with the narrator, a middle-aged man, while she's on the threshold of womanhood. I was remembering that literature isn't literal, that Nabakov isn't writing about a literal man driving about with a literal girl. My reading of the book is that the author is talking about the journey part of life, the becoming section as we transform from children to grown-up with all kinds of possibilities sitting tantalizingly in front of us, kind of where Ted was with the woman in the bar, before a finalization brings the inevitable deterioration, that delicious time when each morning brings figurative motel sheets and soap and towels that are fresh and clean and fragrant.

The literal bar was filling up. Time to go. I walked by the tall stools where Ted and the blonde were almost touching foreheads while he looked hard at her as she was doing an intense monologue with a fair amount of swearing. I patted Ted on the shoulder as I walked by. "Mind if I leave?" I asked. He gave a half-hearted wave without averting his gaze.

Near the door I took a panoramic view of the room to get a last glimpse of the comely foreign waitresses. At the front of the bar where tall panes of glass look out onto the street of red cobblestones, I saw the slender woman Charlie had been interviewing in his office. She was with a group of people her own age at a couple of tables pushed together. Some were crowded around in chairs and she was standing with some others. I recognized the sweep of her thick brown hair and I could detect in her big brown eyes that she was glancing at me sideways, trying to disguise the looking. Her mouth was hidden by the head of a shorter woman standing in front of her, so I couldn't detect her expression. My guess was a slightly puzzled one as she tried to remember where she had seen me before. Her attention went back to her group as soon as I looked her way with two brief thoughts: Too Young and Out Of

My League.

Chapter Seven

We start shipping Punchline calendars to retail outlets in the middle of summer. On a yellow May morning I was looking at finished samples from the manufacturer. Some of them are collections of cartoons from a place in Manhattan that collects and licenses magazine cartoons. We've had an agreement with them for several years. Our current calendars carry the themes of Cats, Romance, Office and Computers. A fifth calendar features a female cartoonist who depicts various aspects of modern culture.

When I first went to New York to make selections for calendars, I reviewed decades of cartoons grouped by subject matter. Their system for organizing and filing had not advanced much beyond that of a moderately efficient fourteenth century monastery. Binders were on shelves in a basement. Aspirants to editorial offices at magazines in the city and college students working part time toiled in shoulder hunching confines. They made photocopies of the cartoons that were published each week and glued them in three-ring notebooks.

Groupings were according to author and theme. Some of the binder labels were Couples, Dogs, Cats, Drinking, Office, Children, Kings and Queens, and Politics. One of the tedious parts of my task for sorting through the files was that the same cartoon could be found in more than one themed group. For example, one drawing depicted a man in a ragged business suit who was dragging a briefcase as he crawled across a desert landscape. He had come across an open air bar and bartender. The caption read, "Martini. Not too dry." I came across that cartoon in Drinking, Desert and Business.

Likewise, the same piece showed up under Cats, Lawyers and Fitness. It depicted two anthropomorphic cats in suit coats and ties. They had athletic bags on their shoulders. One is saying, "Workout time is no problem. It's licking my entire body afterwards that cuts into the billable hours."

Of course, many cartoons appear only once, under a single theme. Some cartoon set in bars are just about drinkers in a bar talking about drinking. As I sat in the office on that morning in middle spring with the newly minted calendars, I had the thought that if life resembles a series of sophisticated cartoons, funny and sad and poignant and occasionally profound, it's better to have an existence that can be grouped under several themes rather than just one.

The clearest instance in my mind of a singly themed life was a woman who lived next door to Kim and me in our old midtown neighborhood, before our move to the reliable public schools in the receding farm fields of suburbia. It was back when Megan was toddling around in disposable diapers. The elderly little woman lived alone in a two-story stucco home with a screened sun porch and an enormous dining room.

The neighbor had been a concert pianist. Now she lived on some sort of barely sustaining fixed income supplemented by very occasional music lessons for children in the immediate area. She mentioned having a grown daughter somewhere, but we never saw her. The very distant relative had been raised mostly by nannies and a sister while her musical mother practiced all day at pianos in nearly unfurnished rooms that admitted no outside sounds and very little sunlight. She traveled worldwide, went everywhere and saw nothing.

On holidays and Megan's birthdays, sometimes on a random Saturday night when we made our own pizza or cooked chicken outside, we invited the concert lady over to share dinner. She ate sparingly and said little in response to our attempts at conversation. In answering to our questions, she had a few interesting things to note about her musical odyssey, personalities encountered and quaint customs of foreign lands, but she was at a total loss at beginning conversations on her own.

It was during her attempt to reciprocate our hospitality that we learned just how narrow her life had been. Her comments on the prices of minor repairs to her sagging house indicated that it was easy to overcharge her. The biggest indicator of a sheltered existence was her attempt at cooking. She merely stuck food into a pan and placed it in a hot oven for a while, then took it out without inspection and served it. She had the culinary knowledge of a kindergartner. On those occasions when we couldn't get out of going over for a meal, our dinnertime activity consisted mainly of consolidating nearly raw meat and overcooked vegetables on the plate to give the illusion of an amount growing smaller. We brought a lidded plastic bowl of our own food for Megan and made claims of a need for special diet.

In the Great Cartoon Binder of Life the elderly lady next door would show up only in Music. You wouldn't find her in Sports, Parties, Camping, Dating or much of anything else. I found it interesting as I was going through the decades of illustrated humor to compare those endeavors to my own at a company that creates and sells greeting cards. The format has a lowly reputation among readers and writers who swim in a sea of fiction and poetry, even if it's only at the middle brow level. Although printing houses glue and bind pages of books containing ludicrous plots, ungrammatical prose, laughable dialogue and inaccurate depictions of human nature, no one disdainfully compares weak, uninspired writing to "something you'd find in a *book*." Greeting cards can contain quotes from Shakespeare or cornball jokes, rambling idealized sentiment with singsong meter or elegant, stately lettered expression of empathy. Yet the entire format has a negative reputation in many circles and functions as the low bar in the hierarchy of writing.

I have seen coffee tables in private homes that prominently display books of supposedly sophisticated cartoons, drawings and captions widely considered amusing and insightful, sometimes esoteric, typically related to modern life. Dog lovers who walk their purebred canines on long retractable leashes along the grand avenues of New York City might have a spiraled day planner filled with dog cartoons. Their homes might contain poster sized prints of fine art with large lettering across the bottom listing the dates of a traveling exhibit at a particular museum. I assume some of these residences house people who would not similarly put out greeting cards on the mantel except during the Christmas holidays even if they were Punchline products containing the very same cartoons that sat on the coffee table or the desk in the den. There could be exceptions if the back of the greeting cards listed the printer as the Metropolitan Museum of Art. Cards that originate entirely on the wrong side of the publishing tracks perhaps get stored away in a bedroom closet on a shelf next to the good shoes, stored away for sentimental rather than artistic reasons, like ceramic, keeping company with the ceramic and string wind chime molded and presented as a gift by the naïve and innocent hands of a first grader.

Purveyors of expensive cups of coffee occasionally print poetry on their to-go containers. Odes on a caffeine urn. If those same places start sticking jokes or sweet rhymes on the cups, you may someday see an unfavorable book review where the writer puts down the examined work as "coffee cup drivel."

I saw a movie in which the unattached male lead lamented to a friend, "I haven't been inside a woman since I toured the Statue of Liberty." The film received an Oscar nomination for Best Script. A few years before I had concocted the same joke for application on a greeting card. I don't recall getting nominated for any writing award for that one. And I will say that while I've never seen anyone laugh out loud during a scanning of Manhattan's cartoons in an airport or moderately priced cafeteria, I have seen numerous browsers laugh audibly at the jokes delivered inside our greeting cards, and those individual cards often sell in the hundreds of thousands. Well, no need to get defensive, no point to it and nothing to be gained. And no need to get too worked up over an abstract like reputation or perception among strangers.

A noted American poet was criticized in recent years for allowing her work to appear on products from a company similar to mine. The critic was at the time the nation's Poet Laureate and he was promoting the reading of poetry as an everyday activity. So in essence he objected to the format and the name of the publisher on it. He didn't have a problem with the content. I wondered if he ever got nose bleeds from being so far up on his high horse. And the guy was a practitioner of prose poetry, the kind of thing that Robert Frost called playing tennis without a net.

It was under the influence of this realization of a desire not to live the one dimensional life and to be open-minded that I agreed to Eunice's pushy suggestions that I go out with Linda, the visitor from the Texas. I went to pick up Linda at Eunice's condominium halfway up the fourteen floors of San Francisco Towers, a high-rise in the Crown Center hotel and shopping complex near downtown. From Eunice's westward looking balcony you can see the bluff from which Lewis and Clark could look across the Missouri River to the threshold of a shining new frontier.

Linda and I had spoken briefly on the phone. She had a tinge of a Texas accent, spoken a little slower and softer that what you find in the Midwest. She didn't sound at all nervous or desperate. She laughed easily.

Driving over for the date I tried to rid my mind of the beer poster image of a Texas woman: Achingly bright blonde hair, huge white smile, cocked white cowboy hat, leather miniskirt and vest, no blouse, calf hugging white boots. I attempted to replace that image with the vision of a casually dressed couple engaged in the most dreaded of all first dates: The three hour small talk marathon concluding with the kiss as brief and unexciting as a curtsy.

I decided to propose a drive in summer's evening sunshine to Weston, a town of a few thousand residents, forty-five miles north of the city. Advertising itself as The Town That Time Forgot, Weston has a well-preserved Main Street consisting primarily of antique stores and eating places surrounded by accurately restored homes that date back to the Civil War. We could stroll in and out of storefronts and eat at a restaurant attached to a winery housed in an old brick barn that had once served as a hospital for Union soldiers.

Eunice answered the door wearing a powder blue sweat suit. She had put on a CD of the soundtrack from <u>Hair</u> and it was playing moderately loud. She looked me over from head to toe and indicated with a barely perceptible nod and a broadening smile that she approved of my cotton khaki pants and white polo shirt. She even gave me a thumbs up.

"What did you expect, Eunice? Plaid jacket, high water pants, clip-on tie, sparse bouquet of short-stemmed flowers?"

"With men, you never know. They still sell mesh tank tops, don't they?" I blocked her hand as she reached to unfasten the top button of my shirt.

I watched Linda glide into the room in sync with "The Age of Aquarius." She was average height, very pretty with a big smile, at her ideal weight except for a few pounds in the middle. She was wearing new jeans and sandals with heels. Her pale yellow shirt had an unusual collar and sleeves. I took that to mean it was expensive. The three buttons on the front were open but unrevealing.

"I'm ready for the big date," Linda announced cheerfully. Her voice seemed bigger than it had on the phone, more energetic. The slightly mocking tone immediately lightened the mood. She wasn't making a big deal out of this. Great. "I can't wait, Mitch. Eunice says you're a lot of fun."

"I'm supposed to be fun? Didn't know. I would have worn the clown suit. Honk, honk." I squeezed an imaginary big round nose. "I was going for relaxed and interesting."

I can work with that," Linda said brightly. She looked at Eunice. "Mom, when's curfew?"

"Mitch can't be entertaining past eleven," Eunice said, smirking in my direction. "You two stop back around then. I'll have a dessert ready."

"Nothing too rich or too thin," I said as Linda and I walked out the door.

The girl from the Lone Star State turned out to be a delight. Spending an evening with her was like being on a very nice prom date, where the girl is truly just a friend and you're having one seamless flowing conversation and not trying to impress or entice, not afraid of saying the wrong thing or making the wrong gesture.

The only mild trepidation I had about the date quickly evaporated. I was a little apprehensive about my car. I drive a small black foreign thing, six years old, stick for better response and gas mileage. I imagined Linda driving to pharmaceutical sales calls in a cream-colored Cadillac with matching spotless leather interior. I thought I might notice a brief puzzled glance at my vehicle and feel compelled to explain why a grown man was driving something that is typically purchased as a first set of wheels for a high school kid. Minutes after encountering Linda's relaxed manner and utter lack of pretense, I completely forgot abut any automotive issues.

There was sunlight left when we got to Weston. The antique shops had things we both recognized from grandparents' homes and a few toys from early childhood. We guessed at the uses of rural hand tools, rusted implements with dull silvery sharpened edges. I knew that a big wooden handled sort of machete with a squared off blade was a corn knife, intended to be used for separating green husked ears from stalks.

"I was hoping it wasn't what the farm wives used to shave their legs," Linda said. "Ouch."

A glass case in one store held Civil War era uniforms, weapons and currency. The Confederate bills were much larger than today's dollars. "A guy could take home big money back then," I said. We strolled along some of the red brick neighborhood sidewalks before having dinner at a winery inside an old brick barn that had been a Union hospital. Nice setting. Good food. Okay wine. We talked about the good things in the cities where we lived. We told each other about our occupations. She talked about going to the hospitals in the mornings to meet the doctors coming out of surgery and have coffee with them in the cafeteria. She wasn't at all self-conscious in describing how she sidestepped the advances of the men who purchased her company's drugs. I talked a little about writing jokes, feeding yourself straight lines until one of them leads to a punch line. She shuddered visibly at the thought of facing a blank computer screen and having to fill it with words containing commercial value in order to make a living. I spoke to the feeling of confidence humor writers have, to some degree playing the percentages, so many straight lines to produce a joke, like so many sales calls to get an order.

"What's it like to be funny?" Linda asked out of genuine curiosity.

"It's not something you're especially aware of. Sort of a reflex thing. Not something you know you're carrying around."

"Sure, not a visible thing from afar," she replied with a laugh.

"Unless you're a circus clown."

"Although that look could work for you." Another laugh.

"And the roomy pants would be comfy. One size fits all. And the shoes are kind of a good news bad news thing. Good to be able to float across large puddles, bad for driving a small car. You'd be constantly breaking and accelerating at the same time. You see very few clowns on road trips."

"Hmm. I can see what you're saying. Your logic is flawless and contains a fair amount of originality."

"Deep in a superficial way. The poor man's Aristotle."

"Exactly."

We came out of the restaurant to air that was an ideal temperature, just above sweater weather, perfect for walking. We left downtown and went into some residential areas. There were porch swings on broad verandas and large square rectangular patches of freshly turned earth awaiting garden seeds. In the night illuminated by old-fashioned unbright streetlamps Weston really did seem like a community bypassed by time.

I was content and relaxed, confident that there would be no female hand sliding onto mine as a face with an expectant smile looked up at me. The chemistry between us was complete except for that one little ingredient that created romance. I would not come home from work in a week and find a bulky envelope with a Dallas return address and brochures on fun things we could do together in Texas. No teasing emails. Certainly no scented letters.

The moon was full and the landscape illuminated when we drove back across the Missouri River. I pointed out a hill where it is believed that Lewis and Clark once stood. Linda said she can't imagine enduring all the hardships they did on their trek.

"Merriweather Lewis organized the whole thing," I said, recalling details from a book on the expedition. "Besides all the planning and preparing and enduring, he suffered from acute depression."

"Probably a chemical imbalance. Could have been a candidate for Prozac," commented the medicine seller.

"I think it was mainly being saddled with the name Merriweather."

She had a few more Lewis Clark questions, ones I could easily answer from having had the book from the library in the not too distant past. I gave her a few details about the famous gangland slaying in front of Union Station as we drove past that ornate edifice, and then we pulled into the parking garage for Eunice's place. It was after midnight. I thought it might be too late for me to come upstairs, but Linda persuaded me it was fine.

Linda had a key. She let us in and we saw Eunice on the couch in a padded floral housecoat. On her square glass coffee table there was a tall glass with lots of ice and clear liquid. It looked like water, but Eunice's unfocused gaze and slow movements indicated gin or vodka.

"You're late," Eunice said, good-naturedly and really loud.

"Am I grounded?" Linda asked, not so loudly.

"Are you a ground hog?" Eunice asked, staring at Linda and then at me.

"Hey, I was promised dessert," I said.

"On the, over on the, you know, the counter," Eunice said in a quieter voice. She pointed limply towards the kitchen. Her housecoat opened on one side, revealing most of a breast. She pulled the fabric back over herself without haste. While Linda went to make coffee, Eunice rose unsteadily and took my arm to right herself.

"Down periscope," she said before lowering herself back onto the couch. The bottom half of her garment slide back to expose the entirety of a bare leg. Her hand on my wrist urged me to sit beside her.

"I should help Annie Oakley rustle up some vittles," I said, pulling away slowly but with force. In the kitchen I told Linda that Eunice was probably ready for bed and we should call it a night. She quickly agreed. In keeping with the lack of pressure from the earlier part of the evening, Linda kept a distance from me that indicated there would be no awkward kiss. All that sales rep sidestepping was paying off.

Chapter Eight

Over a period of a couple of weeks I learned some things about the woman Charlie was interviewing. One, she was hired by Punchline. Two, she has the first name of a woman from a bygone era. Irene. Three, she turned down an invitation to go out for drinks with her new boss, Don Harper. Four, she's twenty-nine. Five, she's attracted to me.

The first four I learned from Harper's secretary, Jane Richardson. She's a Kansas City native who started at Punchline the same time I did. We met while filling out forms in Personnel and had lunch together. We've continued eating together every month or so, talking about our personal and professional lives over vending machine sandwiches and sometimes expired yogurt in the company lunch room. Jane was the first person to find out that Kim and I were headed for a breakup.

The last bit of information about our newest accountant was acquired through incident and past experience. It started with a few smiles that drifted back over Irene's shoulder as she walked away from a coffee machine or hallway water fountain. Once I detected the slight stumble that indicates small nervousness.

At first I assumed Irene was doing what the babe with the cell phone had been doing in the Coffee Horse: Tallying up the number of neck craning stares she got from new men she came across. I didn't think it had anything to do with me specifically. It reminded me of high school when I rationalized that the pretty older girls who smiled me in the hallways between classes were soliciting votes for homecoming queen.

Irene's smiles were the first signs, but it was the variety of facial expressions that pretty much gave her away. They included the full arsenal of eye contact ammo that women consciously or unconsciously fire at male targets with the possibility of alerting men to her interest in them. I was attacked with a salvo of upturned eyes staring through a veil of loose hair. I saw the rocket's brown glare of hard piercing looks passing by from twenty or thirty feet away. There were small smiles of satisfaction at receiving an intended smile in return. I occasionally saw half-lidded expressions of swooning submission.

Mostly I knew there was some attraction by one specific look, one I had seen every week for a bunch of months when Megan was in grade school. We had a Saturday morning family ritual where I'd go out early for doughnuts from a nearby family owned bakery.

A high school girl with tight ringlets of dark hair worked behind the counter. The entire time she waited on me, getting a dozen assorted pastries and taking my money, she didn't speak. She just stared at me with blue eyes open to perfect roundness and literally glinting in the bright white bakery light. As time went on her reaction to my presence expanded to shaking visibly from the moment she noticed me in the line of six or so people in line.

I at first thought I was imagining things. Maybe she was just uncomfortable in her first job, a shy girl earning money for gas and clothes. She was just a kid and I was a father. I would have stopped going to that particular bakery if the treats were just for me. However, I couldn't think of a way to explain it at home. What could I say? "You know, there's a young female helper at the bakery who's totally hot for me and I'm afraid she's going to pass out looking at me and hurt herself. How about if we just start having Saturday doughnuts from boxes at the grocery store?" Do I make something up? "I think I'm allergic to those little sprinkles. I've been breaking out in a multi-colored rash every Saturday."

Like most teen-agers in minimum wage jobs the curly girl quit after about a year. I only ran into her one other time. On a weekday afternoon I was coming out of the Nelson Art Museum after visiting their gift shop. I'd picked up a few books to do research for a parody of fine art we were going to call <u>Laughing Impressions.</u> As I passed by a yellow school bus in the parking lot, I heard a girl's high-pitched scream. "It's him! It's him!"

I looked over at the row of windows on the bus and saw the bakery girl pointing as she shouted.

I walked briskly to my car and drove back to work with two thoughts. I felt sorry for the girl who was having such a hysterical and ultimately embarrassing reaction. And I felt extreme gratitude for my own ability to maintain my own equanimity in the presence of beautiful women.

As I recalled by little high school powdered sugar, I thought of a third thing to be glad about: Most women were more like me than they were like the bakery lass. The signals sent by Irene's looks were vague and subtle. She wasn't going to publicly embarrass either one of us. Her being older may help. And she's no doubt been on the receiving end of instant infatuation in the forms of honked horns in passing cars and theatrical winks from men sitting at windows in bars. She didn't need a catcall or a low long whistle to know that she was beautiful and chances are that she didn't want men pointing out in their crude, clumsy ways.

I've always assumed that beautiful women know they're beautiful. One look in a long mirror at the hair, those curves and the lovely face with carefully applied eye shadow and lipstick should make it pretty obvious. It's different with men. For one thing there aren't that many who look that good. The proportion is heavily skewed. Just watch couples come into a restaurant. One gorgeous woman after another comes striding through the door. The men who come in with them or after them tend to be very average in appearance and usually overweight to some degree.

"Irene makes me think of Ann Jensen," Jane said as she cracked open the cellophane on a package of vending machine cupcakes. "Remember her?"

"Sure. Another finance whizzet."

"Such a pretty woman. And tall. Oh my, she looked good in those dark suits she wore in here."

Jane's become a rounder person over the years, moving from slacks and blouses to long loose skirts and bunched sweaters. She says it's from finishing the food on her kids' plates and sharing snacks with her husband during evenings in front of the television.

Jane is one of the few women I know who would describe Ann as attractive. In my experience the women that other women refer to as "pretty" have nice faces and bodies that are not up to swimsuit model standards. Women such as Ann who have it all are usually identified by something unrelated to appearance, a mannerism or unique way of speaking, as though men won't notice if beauty is not pointed out.

"That Ann was almost thirty when she went and got herself married," Jane said. "I heard she turned down lots of men. Seems they were calling all the time when she was trying to work, and lots of 'em just happened to be coming by her desk, out of the way as it was."

I went on business flights with Ann. When she walked down the narrow coach aisle to her seat, men's eyes followed her like they were magnets and she was true north.

"She got married three years ago," Jane recalled. "But you'd know. Heck, you were there."

"That Catholic church over on Holmes. Very ornate. One of the few apparently that hasn't been stripped down and turned into a gymnasium with an altar." Ann and her husband were a couple right out of a wedding photographer's brochure. Matching bright smiles, athletically slender, perfect hair, comfortable with their own very good looks.

"Then they moved away. Montana. Back to where he has family," Jane said almost to herself. She used a plastic knife to scrape off the last of the moist cupcake from its wrapper. "Two brothers and a father and a mother. I heard all this from Melinda, that tiny little thing down in Personnel. He goes fishing or hunting most every weekend. Lord knows what she does up there. In the winter, what would you do?"

After lunch I sat at my desk in the silent inertia of early afternoon and pictured Ann out west, looking at mountains through a sliding glass door, then stepping outside to watch horses galloping high on the slopes before turned her gaze to the east and the place she'd moved from. And I thought about Charlie's brother, Larry. He's a little younger than Charlie but doesn't look nearly as old. More hair, less weight, toned muscles, clear skin without sag or wrinkle. His smile is constant, as though he's always happy. He's kind of Sports Guy. I know him mainly from occasional rounds of golf and joining him and Charlie to watch college and professional golf in sports bars.

The only sort of personal guy to guy conversation I've had with Larry was while we were waiting for his brother at Crazy's before a Chiefs game. His marriage had ended a year before mine. We started talking about the oddness of reverting to our old days of apartment shopping and used furniture buying. He told me about a woman he'd met in the complex of townhouses where he was then hanging his golf shirts.

She was a younger woman who spent a lot of time at the gym and played a pretty good game of tennis. She had been the aggressor, smiling and saying hello from her little front porch when he jogged by, slapping water at him in the little oval complex pool, rolling her hips and looking at his eyes if he drove past as she was walking to the mailbox.

During an early conversation above the noise of clothes spinning in the washers and dryers of the Pioneer Trail laundry room, she told Larry that if he saw blankets on the three railings of her deck on sunny afternoons, he would know she was sunbathing in the nude. Divorce and relocation had been hardships on a guy more interested in reading the sports page than the want ads. His credit cards went to their limits, but he got some new ones so he could escort his lovely predator to dinners on the Plaza, getaways to the Lake of the Ozarks, even a spontaneous Las Vegas run without luggage. After that plane flight and hotel stay, she returned a white dress shirt of his that had found its way into the flight bag she'd picked up at an airport shop. Calling late at night to say it was freshly washed and dried, she offered to bring it over right away. She showed up within a few minutes on his small concrete square of patio and tapped on the sliding glass door. He opened it to find her standing there in nothing but his shirt and the tan she'd picked up lying beside a Vegas pool. They spent the night on the futon in his bedroom. He kept the shirt on a hanger in his closet, not wearing it as long as it retained the scent of her peach scented body wash.

The next day Larry skipped work, didn't even bother calling in sick. He was a latter day French Lieutenant and she was his Woman. He cooked an elaborate brunch while she sat in his robe at the little round table in the little round dining area, reading the paper and moving in vague rhythm to the soft jazz coming from a countertop radio.

In almost no time after that her parents' health fell apart and she moved to Arizona to watch over them, probably to help them out for a long time. She wouldn't be back.

Larry said he seriously considered just packing up and moving. He thought about throwing in what his pick-up truck could hold and taking off. He'd get a place to live and find an okay job. Wasn't Wal-mart always hiring? Then he'd show up at her door and point to the Arizona plates on his truck. He was feeling like a seventeen-year-old who keeps wanting to drive by the house of the pretty girl who had been nice about accepting a date to the prom but told him that her plans to attend college far away meant she couldn't get into a relationship in high school.

Larry had moved past the relationship by the time he talked to me. The smile was intact and unwavering. The incident was just a story to tell, something to bring up in a bar while waiting for someone to show up and a game to start. An interesting episode in an ordinary life.

Well, interesting to Larry. A horror story to me. Semi-proof that a woman could turn a man into the girl at the doughnut shop, exhibiting uncontrolled behavior while clinging to the impossible dream of a good resolution to a ridiculous romance.

Chapter Nine

I was granted a respite from the intriguing, unsettling and possibly intoxicating world of Irene. The long Fourth of July weekend arrived right on schedule. Charlie and I were going with Ted and his friend Porter on an Ozark boating and golf excursion to southern Missouri.

On the Wednesday night before our getaway I had enough pre-event anticipation to take a while falling asleep. I read till late, getting into the waterside mood by reading the fishing trip section of <u>The Sun Also Rises.</u> It's the part where Jake and his good friend are fly fishing in a remote area of Spain, achingly hot in open sunlight beside mountain stream before wading into roiling water cold enough to deeply chill their bottles of beer. The setting was a little more exotic than our cramped lake cabin smelling of inexpensive industrial cleanser and cooled by a pair of straining air-conditioning window units.

Although I'd read the book half a dozen times before, I had a new thought about this section. I started to associate the burning sun with the passion Jake feels for Brett when he's in her presence and the icy water with the war injury that took his manhood and doused the flame. I was contemplating the book in the perfect silence before sleep. And I was remembering, too, a recent newspaper story. It was in the gossipy column in the entertainment section. The people were a movie star couple a few months into their media-documented relationship. He was an ascending star, riding the arc from television to theatrical movies. She had an established cinematic career, a few Oscar nominations, and was the older half of the couple.

According to the few paragraphs that made up the story, the pair never celebrated a six month anniversary. She saw the upcoming Independence Day weekend as an opportunity for the two of them to disappear together into the hilly green world of California wine country where they could ride on horseback to picnic spots beneath broad shade trees, uncork iced bottles of champagne, walk while holding hands through rows of plump grapes, and spend Sunday morning in a luxury suite with breakfast and the Sunday Times on a huge bed, munching and reading in the thick oversized comfort of matching robes. But. But the man's buddies had lined up a white water rafting trip and he thought that sounded like more fun. Okay, end of relationship.

I got a bit of nervous stomach just picturing myself having to make that decision. Duty over desire. Commitment versus shooting down an angry crashing river with a bunch of laughing, wild and crazy guys. I could see me as Abraham being ordered to prove my devotion by taking a sharp knife of self-denial and plunging it deep into the heart of my squirming fun. I wasn't sure which way I'd go. Lucky for me, I didn't have to make a choice. The fun trip was definitely on with no complications or alternative options.

I knew Charlie and Ted were going to be fun. And Porter would be fine. His most appealing trait is basic goodness, unending generosity. He's the guy who actually shows up on Saturday morning on time to help you move after saying he'd show up on Saturday morning to help you move. He's a guy that if you told him that you had guests coming in for the weekend and you weren't sure they'd fit comfortably in your little convertible as you squired them to the Truman Library or up to Weston, he'd just toss you keys to his six passenger Jeep and you'd be set.

Porter's second best quality is thinking it's hysterical to be made fun of. Nobody laughs harder at Porter jokes than Porter. When Ted first introduced him to Charlie and me, he was almost choking with laughter by the time we finished ridiculing his name. "Were your parents trying to nudge you towards railroad baggage handling?" "Do you come from a huge family where, you know, all the good names were taken?"

Porter's the same age as Ted and never married. He's average size and build, decent looking with red curly hair worn short, lacks any single feature that would attract women. He has all his hair, but it's not great hair. His eyes are there strictly as vision tools. They don't have the shadowy hooded brow over them or the sparkling blue twinkle that prompt the girls to react with a tiny smile and a lingering look.

Porter doesn't have the easy wit hooked up to laidback posture that the chicks seem to go for. He wears a thoughtful expression tinged with vague concern. He does try to wear the right clothes the right way, the denim work shirt top button undone, open in an uneven way. Sunglasses on the head, halfway back. Expensive athletic shoes with straight legged blue jeans. But the blue shirt looks a little too big, the sunglasses wrong for his nice guy face, the white Nikes too white, too clean. Nice guys finish last.

Porter and Ted got to know each other when the world's friendliest guy introduced himself in a bar after seeing the Tedster walk up to two women, get immediate laughs and within a few minutes had them scribbling phone numbers on napkins. "I figured maybe the boy could give me some pointers," Porter later told me.

Off and on Porter expresses perplexed dismay over what he sees as women's fascination and infatuation with men who are obviously going to be trouble down the line. He'll point across the bar to a loud talker who's drinking like a landlocked fish, hair too long and wild for anyone holding down a job with good pay and benefits, jeans too dirty for anyone who has a washer and dryer in a home he owns. "Isn't it pretty clear that this isn't the most stable and reliable guy in the world? Yet there he sits with hot chick in tow."

I guess women look at guys like Porter like I look at dinner. I can have a bland meal of baked unseasoned fish with rice, cottage cheese with fruit, raw vegetable like cauliflower or carrots. That cuisine will fulfill the basic requirements of relieving hunger and providing nutrition. I'll have a restful night of sleep with no heartburn.

Apparently to a lot of women Porter is a square of poached perch and men who possess a kind of manic or lazy sensuality are like a Mexican dinner with onions and hot spices. One is a lot more stimulating in the short term, but you're going to be awake in pain later in the night. If you're a laboratory rat, do you skitter into an empty and painless cubicle or do you opt for the one with the food pellet and electric shock? As Kris Kristofferson asked in song,

Is the going up worth the coming down?

This question occupied me during the quiet spaces during our trip south in Charlie's maroon minivan. I hadn't come up with a conclusive by the time we reached our cabin in the middle of a hot cloudless Thursday afternoon. The pine log building sat about a hundred yards off the shoreline of a sizable lake with clear clean water carrying simultaneous currents of warmth and coolness.

The original interior designer of our temporary home might have been Teddy Roosevelt . Stuffed and mounted game were in every room, frozen in poses of stealth or repose. Charlie, Ted and I jumped right in.

"Welcome to the Charlie Manson Motor Lodge, your own private animal helter-skelter shelter."

"You snuff 'em, we stuff 'em."

"No gun too large, no animal too small."

That evening we cooked outside over charcoal on a crumbling red brick with a chimney. We had steaks that we'd hauled down with a case of beer in a plastic cooler. The tourist prices for that basic stuff is crazy at the resort stores. We ate around a smallish formica table with the thin silverware and plastic plates provided. Around sunset Charlie and I took heavy metal lawn chairs down by the water while Ted and Porter drove to an exotic dancer bar with barn siding on a gravel lot off a two-lane highway.

Our waterfront conversation flickered off and on. We couldn't get any momentum going on topics around Punchline, gossip or business. Physical distance reduced the importance and interest of people and issues that ignited lively discussions in offices and meeting rooms just the day before. Charlie confessed to having some envy around my moderate life style and the more active one that Ted lived. He used words like "freedom" and "possibilities." He also stated without sounding defensive that on the other hand he did feel a milt jolt of relief every night when he came home and got a warm response from Margaret to his shouted greetings from the front entryway. I got a sudden image of an old Steve McQueen movie that shows him as a laconic detective who buys a stack of frozen dinners at a corner grocery before going home to a small downtown apartment. The scene is supposed to point out the essential emptiness and loneliness of his life, but from the theater seat where I was watching, it had its appeal.

As night's darkness settled in, Charlie and I relived favorite moments from other vacations, with each other and separately. The mountains of Colorado were a consensus favorite. We were asleep in narrow twin beds long before Ted and Porter came back.

In the morning Ted and I were the first ones up. As the first direct rays of sun burned off the layer of mist over the lake, we sat on the dock, coffee beside us in heavy ceramic cups from the kitchen. We were drinking the good stuff, costs three times what you pay for the brands that your parents considered the expensive ones. But when you figure what it costs to get it in the corner franchise places, it's a bargain, especially if you sip it slowly.

"How was last night?" I asked. "Did you and Portnoy enjoy yourselves?"

Ted smiled the half-lidded smile of the criminally hung over. He was slow to answer, taking a long pull of coffee and setting the cup down ceremoniously before saying anything.

"Shoulda been there," Ted said with a sudden gush of laughing breath. His eyes closed completely and he collapsed into limpness on the water darkened boards.

"Let me guess. Great dancing?"

"Well, the girls moved awkwardly, out of time to the music. Yet somehow it was great. There was something pleasurable in watching them. Hard to pin down exactly what."

Ted looped his fishing line smoothly out over the clear undisturbed water, his arm as loose as a cow's swishing tail. The sinker plopped into the water, creating a bulge but no splash.

"So you like joints like that?" I asked. "It's worth five dollars a beer and a quickly disappearing stack of singles."

"I liked the joint fine. I liked the girls fine. I loved listening to Porter talk to a dancer at the bar. Him in his black polo shirt and white pants and black socks and whiter than white shoes. The dancer in the white lace cover-up, sipping an icy red drink through a swizzle stick and looking past him."

I reached toward my back pocket and said, "I'll pay a dollar for actual verbatim conversation."

"So you'd pay for 'You have beautiful ankles.'" Ted said, again sinking into a boneless chuckling mass on the dock. I took a dollar out of my wallet and stuffed it into his shirt pocket.

"It's a bargain."

"Stage is set at ankle level, so Porter's staring at ankles. Yeah, he's an ankle man. Loves a nice, firm pair of ankles."

We laughed hard, stopped, laughed again.

"Were they real?" I asked.

"Who can tell? Doctors these days, they're miracle workers. Anyway, the dancer and her great ankles leave Porter and his matching clothes and go over to some biker type. Long hair and beard, leather in July. Pretty soon they have become as one on the bench of a booth."

"He probably had nice ankles, too, beneath those big black biker boots."

"You know, I think his name *was* Paul Ankle."

Ted and I were long past being amused about Porter's adventures in dancers by the time he and Charlie joined us with their brown ceramic cups of coffee and their fishing gear. We moved to the shade along the sharply sloping shore as the sun rose to warming height. We tossed lines in for an hour. No luck. By midmorning it was uncomfortably hot even in the shadows of pine and pin oak and we gave it up.

Charlie drove off to an outlet store with a list from Margaret. Ted and Ankle Boy decided to play tennis at courts on a peninsula close by. They invited me to go along and I declined. Tennis is like dating. Two is fine and four creates some interesting dynamics and tensions, but three's not much fun for anyone.

I put on running clothes and went off moderately fast on a trail leading away from the cabin. The heat and exertion felt like they were cleansing me from the inside. Once I'd returned and cooled down enough to stop sweating small streams, I put on swim trunks and walked a few hundred yards to the small section of sandy beach where inexpensive plastic chaises were set about randomly.

There weren't many sunbathers around. A young couple were there with a little girl just starting to walk. The parents held her hands high above her curly haired head and let her stomp gleefully in the few inches of water at the shore. A few older couples in hats with enormous brims sat silently reading or staring into the distance.

I started a routine I'd developed when Megan was old enough to swim in our housing development pool without my holding on and hovering. I'd get in the water and swim hard for several minutes, long enough to get my breathing hard and deep. Then I'd get out and enjoy the respite and the warming golden rays of sun. As soon as I got hot, I'd repeat the ritual.

As I was standing for the third time to slide back into the lake, I noticed a woman walk up with a towel that she spread on the sand. She was young, possibly on summer break from college and vacationing with her parents. She laid on her stomach and listened to music on a tiny headset. She was motionless except for the rhythmic paddling of her feet. A dark even tan ran up her slender legs and across the small round bottom that was left largely exposed by her one piece lime green suit. I tried with limited success not to stare on my journeys to and from the water, and I hoped it didn't seem like my frequent comings and goings were merely pretext for getting passing glimpses.

Turned out she was following my same basic drill of drenching by water and sun. She would glide smiling into the water, drift a short distance, and come up shaking her short straight brown hair vigorously, smile intact, displaying obvious sensual pleasure at the warm cool caress of the water.

We passed once on the sand when she was wet and I was dry. She had the smile still going. She looked not shyly into my eyes and said, "Hi." I was caught off guard. I had expected furtiveness, bordering on avoidance, at the prospect of unwanted attention. I could only give the same one word greeting in reply. I thought of "Wet enough for you?" only after I was up to my knees in the lake.

I knew it was time to go when I felt the first layer of painless sunburn on my shoulders and the inch of forehead skin that used to be protected by hair. I felt a sense of relief. I had avoided the inevitable sharing of the waist deep lake water with the perfect lime of a girl. Once in there together we would either avoid eye contact with heads turned awkwardly away or we would have the spectacle of the man in baggy gray trunks chatting with a beautiful woman half his age as the disapproving oldsters in the big hats looked on from eyes set deep in their faces painted a splotchy white with lotion.

She left at the same time I did, walking ahead of me and veering off to a nondescript American compact car in a graveled lot. She was wearing a t-shirt that came halfway down her backside and gave the illusion that she was wearing nothing else.

When I got back to our rustic abode with its population of stuffed wild animals, I sat on a bench outside the front door with a glass of instant iced tea. It costs about two cents a glass. You can drink for a month for the price of a single can from a vending machine if you're willing to put in the extreme effort of measuring out a teaspoon of brown crystals and stirring it in a glass of water.

I was almost nodding off when Charlie walked up with plastic bags filled with bargains. The Wimbledon hopefuls came back soon after and suggested golf.

As guests at the cabin complex, we were allowed free play a haphazardly maintained nine hole course. It was somewhat worn on the fairways and ragged in the rough, so we allowed ourselves to move the ball around for a decent lie. Surprisingly, the greens were okay, smooth and consistent. I was relaxed from the sun and the swim, from being far away from work in a serene setting, in the company of people who did not rely on me for anything.

I broke forty for the first time in a couple of years. I won big, glass of beer plus a bag of pretzels because my foolhardy opponents pressed on the final hole.

After showering and thoroughly chilling ourselves by sitting directly in front of the loosely rattling window air-conditioner, the four of us drove five miles to a wooden building that housed a restaurant that was known for its pan-fried chicken. We were seated at a middle table in a large dining room with a ceiling of heavy rafters. The menus, the coasters and the t-shirts on the waitresses carried the logo "It's Your Clucky Day."

"I hope it's not like a lobster thing," Ted said. "Where you pick out your meal while it's still alive."

"I think it's more old style gangster," I replied. "I saw a tough guy by the back door with a nylon stocking over his head, a thin rope wrapped tightly around his beefy hands."

"I wonder if that's how they killed the animals in our cabin," Charlie said.

"Now there's a pretty woman," Porter said, his gaze directed past tables of sun-reddened diners.

Ted bent over in his chair until his head was about a foot off the floor. "She's got the ankles," he said. "High and firm, slender, just the way you like 'em, Porter."

"All right, all right," Porter laughed. "That will do."

"And get this," Ted said, still peering from below. "No socks. Just a thin leather sandal strap between you and ecstasy."

When Ted sat back up, I tried to locate the object of Porter's desire. The seated crowd was bobbing like wavy water, animated in conversation and laughter. The clatter of utensils on plates and drink glasses on tables bounced off the beams and hardwood floors. It was the sound of happy vacationing. I surveyed the landscape of bustling waitresses pouring from clear heavy pitchers, carrying trays of food, scribbling food orders.

Porter nudged me and nodded at a waitress who was hurrying past our table. I got just a brief look at the back of her, white shirt and khaki shorts and athletic shoes, tan legs scissoring briskly as she hurried towards the kitchen. I recognized the legs. They belonged to the girl in the lime green swimsuit. When she came back into the dining room with a tray of food and drinks, she looked at me and smiled as her eyes narrowed. She returned with the round tray tucked under her arm, her hips brushing my shoulder as she brushed by another server. A few minutes later she walked with purpose in my direction, stopped abruptly and stooped to reach for something on the floor. She stood up with a restaurant bill in her hand and she slapped in onto the table next to my plate before quickly disappearing. I picked it up and looked it over.

"Not ours," I explained to the other guys. I saw that there was nothing written on it except a phone number and a heart.

I knew the girl in lime was young, and I wasn't even sure if she was of legal age. I decided to keep the bill as a souvenir of a few mildly thrilling beach moments and an affirmation of some level of attraction should I ever need it as a confidence booster. I put it in my pocket and everyone else had forgotten it by the time we finished our expertly prepared dinner of pan fried chicken, fluffy mashed potatoes, green beans with pieces of softly cooked bacon and baking powder that released puffs of steam when opened.

That night in the cabin around the kitchen table we played extremely low stakes poker. I made the dramatic leap from Two Beer Guy to Three Beer Guy. The extra bit of alcohol, coupled with pleasant muscle fatigue, made everything especially amusing: Charlie's constantly referring to two pairs as a small house, Ted calling one bad hand royal flusher, Porter's sincere attempts at bluffing in a game where a stack of chips were valued at a quarter.

The next day was Saturday and brought a repeat of many of Friday's activities. We caught quite a few catfish from the lake that morning, enough to feed all of us that night after Charlie battered and grilled them. He went back to the mall. Porter and Ted played tennis. I ran but skipped the swimming beach. If she were there, I couldn't help but look and I didn't want to offer any kind of encouragement.

On Sunday morning we read the newspaper and went to the golf course midmorning before heading back to Kansas City. The trip involved very little conversation. We traded off driving duties and dozed to low volume classic rock radio, shifting in lazy cadence to very familiar songs. I smiled at "I Need A Lover Who Won't Drive Me Crazy."

Chapter Ten

Twilight was just beginning to fuzz the sunlight when I came through the front door carrying my golf bag and athletic bag bulging with clothes still damp from sweat and lake water. The answering machine blinked insistently. I cringed in annoyance. I've reached the age where letters and phone messages are picked up reluctantly. Good news is rarely incoming. The mailbox brings almost exclusively monthly bills and gaudy advertising circulars. The telephone is there mainly for the convenience of pushy telemarketers, young sounding investment brokers and solemn acquaintances bearing news of personal tragedy.

It was a tart surprise when the phone message blared, "Hey, Mitch, it's Squirrel. Reunion's next Saturday. I'm driving in from Illinois, leave the front door ope, boy. Karen said you sent back the invitation saying you couldn't make it. Wrong. Dinner's at the country club at seven, but some of us are meeting at the West Side at five. I paid you up on supper. You owe me twenty-five nuts."

That last line made me laugh. Squirrel is Randy Krantz. In high school we were always substituting woodland words like nuts and berries for money and cokes and golf balls. Squirrel has the face of a squirrel, round puffy cheeks and prominent front teeth. He's a good guy with a light high pitched voice incapable of carrying any serious anger or threat.

Squirrel had his information correct. I had checked the box on the invitation that read Can Not Attend. Kim and I had gone to my tenth year reunion. Like most of my classmates, I attended alone after my spouse learned what it was like to be largely invisible, sitting with a frozen smile and drink in hand while old friends laughed like hyenas at decades old high jinks. After filling out personal information and job status on the most recent invitation to this graduation anniversary, our thirtieth, I decided I was too old for a night of drinking and loud horse play. Now it looked like I had no choice.

Once I mentally committed to going, I actually started to look forward to driving the three hours to western Iowa on a Saturday morning in July. I hadn't been back since my parents retired to Arizona a couple of years earlier. The warm wind through the car window and the rippling green fields of broad corn leaves would be sentimental scenery. Being in my hometown in summer always makes me feel sharply aching nostalgia for two periods of my life: The dawn to dusk freedom of a non-working boy in a county seat town and the summer before marriage to Kim when we spent nearly every moment together between university classes in Iowa City.

The next morning at work with former classmates in my thoughts, I wasn't thinking of Irene when I ran into her. She was wearing a light blue seersucker suit and thin white blouse with no collar. The sun from the long holiday weekend had turned her skin a reddish brown and added golden highlights to her thick brown hair.

She and I passed in the hallway, initially making eye contact and then smiling with side glances as we went by each other. I felt a small, troubling surge of excitement. It was not something I welcomed. It was the feeling of a person desiring something with a known and experienced negative consequence.

I could detect the subtle sudden stiffness in Irene's walk, a lack of ease in her uncertain smile. I had seen the signs before in this city well populated with beautiful women. At the annual Plaza Art Fair among the tightly packed crowds, cooling off by the tennis courts after jogging in Loose Park, looking up at the crowd at a Royals game, I had exchanged looks with women who are pleased that their extreme good looks have gotten attention. Sensing vulnerability in stunning women always makes me feel sympathy for them, even during the briefest of encounters. I don't know why I feel they should be spared the most minor of rejections, communicated by a smile that conveys only politeness or unavailability. It couldn't happen often and it's not much of a blow.

Why did I feel the tingle of nascent infatuation from Irene that didn't happen when I was around someone also beautiful and stylish at work? That would be Laura. She's an art director who has worked for six years for Charlie. She's in her early thirties, sexy in an athletic way, friendly and relaxed. She has a wide bright smile that makes her eyes light up and her whole face brighten. It's like an instant sunrise.

Last spring I filled in for Charlie at an advertising awards night at a downtown hotel. He was out of town visiting Margaret's relatives and gave me his ticket for dinner and the ceremonies. Laura went home to change after work and I went straight from my desk.

She showed up looking very arty in a black pantsuit and black blouse. Her short black hair was cut at a sharp angle across her forehead. I jokingly called her Yoko Oh No! I asked her if it was difficult to eat with imaginary silverware. She acknowledged that it was but it kept her thin.

After getting scotch and water at one of the two portable bars, we sat at a round table with half a dozen people we knew well enough to feel comfortable around either in conversation or pretty much ignoring. Everyone except me partook liberally from the bottles of wine that came around in the hands of courtly uniformed servers. I remained within the boundaries of Two Beer Guy by having the scotch and then an unfinished glass of chardonnay.

A very young man, too thin for his sport coat, with gelled spiky hair, sat on the other side of Laura and couldn't take his eyes off of her. Turned out to be a recently hired account rep for a medium sized agency. He asked us where we worked and what we did. We seized the opportunity to give each other mild putdowns. "It's all about the writing. Designs are just bland relief between great words, white crackers between sips of fine wine." "Actually, it's all about artwork. We just put in words to make Mitch feel needed."

Punchline was given a few awards during the evening. One went to Charlie and Laura for a t-shirt they had designed for a fund raiser for women's health held at the Nelson. It was a composite of famous pieces by Da Vinci, Toulouse-Lautrec, Picasso and others blended into a single image. By the time coffee and dessert were being brought out, Laura's face bore the half-lidded expression of the slightly buzzed. Beneath the table a silky leg pressed against mine and rubbed softly. I didn't pull away, but I didn't return the gesture. I was glad she switched from booze to coffee. By evening's end she was alert and steady.

When we left the event I made a point of engaging the young account rep in conversation. I gave a farewell to Laura when she stopped at her Jeep and kept talking to our new friend about a few things I 'd learned from my years in the business. I hoped the appearance of being a mentor to the rookie ad guy would make Laura believe I was distracted and not running away, avoiding any chance of an invitation to come up to her place for a nightcap in celebration of the t-shirt award. This situation struck me as different from the possibility of getting essentially the same request from the pool shooting nurse. A proposal from Laura would carry consequences into the workplace, either more invitations or an awkwardness at design committee meetings and run-ins along the corridors. Laura was like the nurse, though, in that the image of her wouldn't linger in perfumed memory after an evening together, the way a few seconds with Irene would.

In fact, being with Laurie that night really made me think of Irene on the drive home. I wondered how I could feel so immediately and powerfully drawn to someone I had never had a conversation with. And I tried to think of ways to get closer to Irene. I could schedule some semi-legitimate budget meetings that she might attend and where I could get to know a little about her from the personality communicated by her voice and attitude.

I could confide in Charlie and have him come up with a reason for the three of us to be at lunch together. I imagined finding a fatal flaw that would dampen an unwanted desire. Perhaps she would be incredibly dull or full of herself . Maybe we would have, not for lack of trying, difficulty keeping conversations afloat. Or she might have a voice like rocks rattling in a rolling mesh cage and a cackling laugh to match.

Actually the voice thing couldn't happen. Like an eleven-year-old schoolboy, full of curiosity and desire, I had called her work number after hours to check out her recorded voice. It was a confection of softness and honey. I felt a sensation I didn't welcome. Heartsickness. A tight and heavy feeling high in the chest. I was hoping like a dieter craving a treat in a bakery window that the first real bite would be no better than bland.

That week at Punchline, in the happy energy at a midmorning's office activity, I felt something unpleasant and very nearly foreign to me: Jealousy. It happened while I was waiting outside Charlie's office as he finished talking on the phone. Down the corridor from his doorway you can see couches and a low round coffee table that make up a small break area. Don Harper, stocky guy of average height, was dressed to bore in his typical dark suit and gaudy tie, gold jewelry on both wrists. He was with Irene.

Harper has a year round tan to go with his dyed brown hair , which he keeps fluffed and swept back to cover a coaster-sized bald spot. I didn't work with Harper much. An afternoon here or there, a few days at budget time. I've spent some business conference time with him in his presence at company days away in settings within driving distance of the office. We go to these locations as a large management group when we're contemplating restructuring or looking at acquisitions that could thrust the mother ship into new currents.

Harper was married for a long time, to a slumped little woman who spent company parties staring at the fruit slices in her drinks. After he dumped her, the Big Harp was wed briefly to a wide-eyed blonde. She was taking scuba lessons at a local pool to get ready for their second anniversary trip to some island in the Caribbean and took a deep dive for the instructor and now they're living the good life on some remote beach somewhere.

The desertion did little to knock Harper off his stride. Just as he had always done when he was married, he picked the prettiest women in conference hotel bars and asked them to cavort with him on the tiny square dance floors. There was ongoing gossip about room keys being slipped into handbags and jacket pockets, about hot tub invitations left under coffee cups.

Although he's a little older than I am, the unfettered Harper ("The unchained malady," Ted once called him.) now pursues very young women, especially the newly hired at Punchline. On weekdays around noon you're liable to see his golden glow accompanying some young lovely in a charcoal suit as they sit down to lunch surrounded by ferns at a Plaza restaurant. You might come across the same scene at a Westport cigar bar after work. In good weather, the perfect Midwest days of May and early June, you could drive by Loose Park and view Harper and his latest little honey overdressed for the park bench setting as they watch intense and skillful tennis being played on the courts there.

Now let me just say that I consider myself a third god in the trinity of empathy along with Walt Whitman and Will Rogers. I know that everyone suffers in this world and one of is perfect. Yet Don Harper is a man I've met and never liked. He does a couple of things that displease this god. First off, he had a nearly drooling way of talking in graphic vulgarity about women. It's his idea of joking with the boys. I once sat in the backseat of conference minivan and heard him fully describe sex involving unconventional orifices, halfway acting it out, as though tricking a woman into the act by pretending to be struck suddenly blind. Funny stuff.

A second irritating thing Harper does, or used to do, is rationalize infidelity. "It's not cheating if you're out of town," he once proclaimed at a picnic table of men during a company picnic. "It's not like you could be with your wife. She's not missing out on a thing. She'll never know. What happens on the road stays on the road."

Personally I prefer to keep my ethics the same way I like to keep my living room: Neat and simple. Situational ethics is just a way to rate situations the way you want them. A mitigating element, something that keeps me from outright hatred of Harper, is his total inability to be witty, entertaining in a clever way, turning phrase, making a humorous yet insightful observation. Nietzche was right when he said you can't hate anyone you feel superior to. He might have known Harper, who could make nihilism seem pretty funny in comparison to his material.

After a few drinks, the normally loud and obnoxious Harper gets extremely loud and obnoxious. He starts shouting out what he thinks are great one-liners. To the waitress who brings him shots of tequila and wedges of lime: "What do I do with the lime? Lick it or suck it? Both sound good to me." He's oblivious to the fact that the only raucous laughter coming from around the booze littered table is his own. Any women present look down and away. Even young male accountants who report to him can only scrape up a limp smile as they lift their heads and sit back in a subconscious move to distance themselves from him.

Back at the Puncline couches with Irene, Harper was laying small stacks of computer paper on a low table. I tried to ignore the two of them side by side, ironically on the loveseat, but Harper's bowling ball of a voice rumbled down the hallway and slammed into me, forcing me to look their way. Irene was smiling, possibly laughing.

Okay, maybe now I could hate him.

Chapter Eleven

As I drove towards Iowa in the warm breezy dawn on a Saturday, I started feeling moderately guilty about my dislike of Don Harper. I just finished my annual reading of <u>Catcher in the Rye.</u> Like the voices of Bob Dylan and Neil Young in music, the narrative voice of Holden Caulfield cuts through to something inside and is thrilling over and over. It was in my head like a moving and memorable song.

I sipped thermos coffee and looked out at clean white farm buildings resting comfortably on summer's deep green blanket. I felt inferior to a sensitive fictional character who could summon compassion for everyone, even the unpopular classmate at prep school who almost begs you to despise him and his disgusting personal habits, petty whining and unearned air of superiority.

Getting closer to my hometown, Chatburn, a county seat town of five thousand, thoughts of Holden gave way to memories of my own high school years, when the time not spent in class or part time jobs was filled with pickup games of outdoor sports and driving very slowly or very fast between the downtown square and the city limits.

By the time my friends and I reached driving age, everyone in our class was more or less friendly. I'd sat near almost everyone in some class or club. The bullies from junior high had tired of the metallic crashing sound of a skinny kid being slammed into a row of lockers and had mellowed into a kind of maturity. I remembered clearing snow from a thickly frozen farm pond so we could all have a Thursday night skating party with a large fire. I recalled walking out in very early spring mornings onto the nine hole golf course as freshly cut blades of grass, soaked with dew, clung to my shoes as Squirrel and I started a day of play that would end when darkness closed the course.

I pictured the various stages of putting together the senior class play. It was called <u>Brian's Dreams.</u> Squirrel had come up with the idea of his writing an original work with me. We began working on it first semester and it was performed in the school auditorium in April. The setting was a high school like ours. Most of the characters grew out of actual teachers and classmates. The basic plot was that a sleepy student named Brian kept falling asleep in history class and having dreams that placed people from the school in historical eras that Miss Tweed had been droning on about just before he nodded off at his desk. We were mainly going for laughs, dropping our friends into famous events. "Et tu, Mary Alice?" Sometimes the scenes brought historical figures into our world. "I regret that I have but one voice to give to my pep club."

In the last act Brian falls into a sleep so profound that he pulls all of the history class into a forever dream in which he marries the homecoming queen in her sash and silver tiara and inherits her father's bank and a mansion big enough to have the whole senior class move in to play basketball in his personal gym and sip magical cherry cokes concocted by the science whiz to keep them all forever young.

The play tended to leave out actual girls who had no hope of being elected any kind of queen. We didn't create a character around Tina, a large girl that was frequently mentioned as the girlfriend of the boy being taunted that particular day in gym class. What I remember most clearly about Tina was her roundness. Her short frizzy brown hair framed a perfect globe of a face. Her curving shoulders and cradled arms formed a kind of large ball on a bigger and round set of hips. I could never look at Tina without thinking of a snowman.

I didn't sit next to Tina until my junior year. I was taking bookkeeping in order to dodge chemistry and geometry. I just couldn't see a future for myself that would benefit from knowing the symbol for zinc or the various mathematical formulas involving pi. Tina sat in the front row and I was right behind her. She dressed in sweaters that matched her skirts, often pastel, and she spoke in an unshy, contented quiet voice that drifted effortlessly over the classroom. The course kept us fairly busy doing simple math and there was little discussion of anything. We greeted each other coming and going.

In senior English we sat side by side. In the ten free minutes near the end of the period when Mr. Quinn shot down to the teachers' lounge for a quick smoke, Tina and I chatted. We spent a little time talking about our assigned reading, usually to agree that it was well-written tedium. I once said, "Okay, Silas Marner had a rough life, but at least he never had to read Silas Marner." When I gave her the paperback copy of Catcher that Squirrel had loaned me, it was the first time we could discuss a novel that excited both of us. We were relieved to discover that there was available literature that we couldn't wait to read. Tina had no interest in sports, local or professional, and I didn't watch television, so many times our conversations consisted of her telling me about her family life while I made jokes. She told me that in the evening she would repeat my humorous comments to her mother while they prepared dinner together.

A week before Christmas Tina told me that she and her mother had just had a tear choked argument. Tina informed her unsympathetic mother that she was too busy with studying for finals and extra rehearsals for the Christmas concert to accompany her to Omaha for their traditional holiday shopping and department store lunch. "Since you ruined my Christmas, I'll ruin yours," her mother said angrily as she stomped into her bedroom. She came back with a brown mailing box from a mail order place. Standing in the middle of the living room, she tore it off the thin cardboard lid and out dropped a pink sweater and matching skirt. "Here's your present a week early," Tina's mom said. "Merry damn Christmas." They went into separate bedrooms to cry. On the following Saturday when they drove to Omaha to shop, over a lunch of Chicken a la King, they cried again.

I was still thinking about Tina when I turned off the interstate and onto the ten miles of two lane highway leading to Chatburn. Before checking into the low white HiWay Motel a few blocks from the country club, I drove the familiar streets for fifteen minutes. I slid slowly past the old vacant high school with its tired red bricks and tall window panes of distorting glass. I went around the downtown square with its stolid courthouse of dull yellow stone. I tried to recall what thriving businesses had been in the storefronts now given over to craft shops and discount stores.

I stopped in front of my family home on the edge of town, high on a hill beneath an enormous sky that stretched to all horizons. The ranch house where my parents had lived until retirement looked young with its light gray vinyl siding and contrasting dark gray shingles. The basketball hoop was gone from the driveway. I could see into the backyard. A small baseball diamond, created informally by batters running to squares of cardboard, had disappeared beneath a neatly kept lawn. So much for going home again.

I checked into the motel and dropped off my athletic bag in a small room fragrant with the light scent of fresh laundry. I emerged into that part of a summer's afternoon when the wind is just beginning to be threaded with strands of coolness and drove down to the country club. The bar area was a large room with floor to ceiling windows overlooking the course. It was almost empty except for a group of people sitting around two square tables pushed together in corner. The only person facing me was a pretty young woman with a bright smile and curly blonde hair.

Figuring I was too late for the class golf tournament and too early for the cocktail hour, I went to the bar to ask about greens fees. It was a handsome afternoon, a Monet vision of shimmering light and blended color. I could be happy playing golf alone at a very reasonable cost. While a ruddy heavyset man at the counter was explaining the cost of golf and reminding me of the soft spikes rule, a hand clamped onto the back of my neck. A second hand cuffed my right wrist and yanked my arm halfway up my back. As my head was forced to waist level, I heard Squirrel's light high voice, a sound too thin to carry hate or anger.

"Numbnuts, didn't you see us all sitting there?" He laughed and released me with an easy shove.

"The only face I saw was on some young chick who couldn't possibly have been with you old fossils."

"Amy. Jim's wife."

"Jim remarried?"

"Brilliant deduction, Sherlock. A couple of years ago. Nurse from Omaha. Met her in the hospital after that tractor flipped over on him. She's a farm wife now."

"Must be hell taking a chicken's temperature."

"Piece of cake compared to livestock enemas."

Except for some gray hair, Squirrel was a well-proportioned heavier version of his younger lanky self. He looked good. I wondered about myself.

Eight people were sitting with drinks at the table. I said quick helloes and pulled a chair to a space next to Amy. Jim smiled and waved briefly from inside his conversation with our intense valedictorian David Harris. They were discussing government subsidies to farmers.

I got involved by asking mostly ignored jokes about soil banks. Only Amy laughed. I talked about tellers in bib overalls making change. "Do you want large or small clods?" I said their ATMs had unusual transaction categories. "Instead of Deposit and Withdrawal, they have Sow and Reap."

"I'll be right back," Amy said, touching my arm before she left. The light white material of her thin summer dress fluttered as long legs carried her to the bar and back with a pitcher of beer and a mug.

"Oh, I should have gotten that," I apologized.

"No problem," she said as she deftly poured my drink into the tilted mug. "You can get the next five."

In the swirl of increasingly loud chatter, Amy and I got to know each other. She had done emergency room work at a large hospital in Omaha. I told her my ex-wife was a nurse, had done some ER work during her training.

"The whole divorce thing, huh? Well, I'm sorry," she said.

"We weren't," I said. Amy's hands settled comfortably into her lap and she looked with concern into my eyes, indicating I could talk about the broken relationship if I wanted to. I shrugged her off. I just wanted the mild beer buzz and the silent music of Amy's smile.

Former classmates drifted in. Two foursomes of boisterous reunion golfers burst in loudly, instantly raising the festive atmosphere. Squirrel and I spent time remembering and reciting strong and lame lines from <u>Brian's Dream,</u> starting with the opening when I stuck my head through the curtain and roared in a parody of the MGM lion. With dinner time an hour away we dispersed to shower and change.

The get-together that night was a pleasant event. I was relieved that the anticipated sharp emotions from seeing so many old close friends didn't materialize. Everyone remained in an upbeat, joking mood. It was nice that everyone was doing okay as far as health and general circumstances. Nobody was there to impress. The occasional soft hand on the shoulder during close conversation was enough physical contact for me. A few times Amy sought me out with a fresh drink and questions to confirm or deny stories that sounded suspicious. "Yes, Amy. There is a Squirrel and he did indeed remain standing an entire downhill block while snow surfing on a school lunch tray."

The only person whose presence brought a small barbed pang to my heart was Beth Atkinson. She clearly liked me in high school, teased me constantly, annoyed me by tapping the bottom of my paper drink cup in the parking lot of the Dairy Sweet. We had one date, prom night when she pressed against me in the backseat of Squirrel's family Buick at the special late night showing at the drive-in. I just made quips about the movie drama and stared over the touching heads of Squirrel and his date. After a pancake breakfast back at the school gym, in the yellow speckled gray just before dawn, I ignored the kiss Beth requested by stopping on a porch step and looking up at me with almost closed eyes. I felt I would be making a vague promise that I would not want to keep.

I became aware that Beth was in attendance just before dinner seating when I was finishing the last bit of my beer and felt a tapping on the bottom of the glass. She was still slender with an ample chest. She still had that very cute impish grin and loose strawberry blonde hair. She was a little too tanned, giving her that hint of desperation that I'd sensed in the old days. Her eyes had a drunken vacancy and she rattled the big ice cubes in her nearly drained cocktail glass.

"Fool me, you kiss," she said in loud whisper as she pulled my face close to hers and let a silky curtain of reddish hair fall across her face.

"Beth, you're looking as easy as ever."

Beth put her hand over the top of her drained drink glass and shook the cubes like dice. "Are you feeling lucky, Mitch? "

"You need a fresh drink. Fortunately, I know where to get you one." I took her glass and went to the bar. I returned to find her sitting next to a small redhead she used to pal around with. I steered the conversation towards the last few years of our lives and volunteered to keep score in a contest of who could match up bored spouses on the fringe of the gathering with the correct former classmates.

While we were in the midst of guessing whether a hunched wary man against the wall was married to April Wellington, Amy appeared and dragged me off to join a dozen people forming a conga line and moving in rhythm to loud disco music in the dining room. With my hands on her shoulders, we moved through the crowd, picking up another twenty people by the time the song ended. Amy gave me a hard hug and floated off with some guy who wanted her as his partner in a slow number.

The rest of the evening was spent in conversations in groups of six or so, followed in the final hour by a game of bridge with David Harris and Jim against Squirrel and me. We played in the bar in the same corner where we'd sat earlier in the day. We kept score for a tenth of a cent a point and kept it light. "Two hearts." "One love."

At midnight the lights came up to signal that the party was over. Amy passed our bridge and plucked an ace from my hand. She threw it on the table and shouted, "Gin!"

"Man, I hate to quit now," Squirrel said. "Just when I could see thirty nuts rolling my way."

Back in my room I was thinking about too many things to go right to sleep. I flipped through the TV channels for a while, seeking and finding confirmation of my belief that cable television was a hollow investment in time and money. Being very awake, I wasn't startled when a light feminine knocking sounded at my door. I imagined a scene five minutes into the future: A man and a woman in a dimly lit bedroom, her bottle of bourbon open on the nightstand next to two glasses from the motel sink, she finds music on the clock radio while he walks down the hall with an ice bucket. That's as far as I got before I opened the door to see Beth. Instead of a liquor bottle in a paper bag, she was holding a black leather overnight bag and a room key.

"Your bridge buddies want you," she said as she muffled a yawn with her key hand.

"They're at the park. A picnic table under a street lamp. By the shelter. They've got cards and beer. I said I'd pass along the message. Now I'm off to bed. Nighty-night, I'm tight, don't reunions bite." She walked away with a loose wave over her shoulder, humming tunelessly. The slight unsteadiness of her walk had her hips moving in a sultry sway.

I played bridge with the group from the reunion. We rotated partners after every rubber. I wondered off and on about life for Amy and Jim on the farm. He's a good guy, patient, always in a good mood. I pictured the hippity-hoppity Amy spending her days on the land when she wasn't working her two days a week at the hospital, pulling heavy denim laundry from the washer and fixing the big meat and potato meals that fuel agriculture, in front of the television where women hosted cooking and decorating programs, Jim slumbering soundly in a comfortable reclining chair next to her. I tried to imagine them going to Omaha for an expensive meal or to attend a dinner theater and I couldn't form a clear image of what they were wearing.

Despite David Harris's superior math skills and determination to come out on top, Jim collected a total of a dollar forty from the three of us and went home the winner. Morning was coming to life as we said our farewells and went to our cars.

Chapter Twelve

On Monday morning I was getting phone messages at my desk when Ted walked in. He moved slowly, a little stiffly, like someone who's been in a car accident and feels worse than he looks. He usually pops his feet onto my desktop, but that day he keeps them flat on the floor. He smiled with closed lips for almost a minute. He lightly brushed imaginary crumbs from his sleeves and shirt front. He adjusted a non-existent tie. He cleared his throat.

"Just a question," he said finally, still smiling as though it took an effort. "Do you think it would be difficult and time devouring, to remove spray painted obscenities from the exterior of a late model, somewhat overpriced white two-door sportscar?"

"Oil or latex?"

"I'm guessing oil," he said evenly. "Thickly applied randomly."

"A bit of Jackson Pollack's technique."

Ted's extended hands made a few looping curves. "Had more of a feminine feel."

"She aches just like a woman. She paints just like a little girl. She was your woman but you done her wrong."

"More or less." His face continued to convey calm and forbearance.

In a way I admired Ted. He did the crime and he could do the time.

No complaints. This is the love life he has chosen. Like an amateur athlete who continues to play sports as he ages, coming into work after a weekend of warring, arm in a splint or leg in bulky Velcro bindings. A little healing and these latter day gladiators return to the courts, the roadways, the tracks.

"You going to need a ride to Charlie's thing tonight?" I called to Ted after he had walked out. A hand appeared in my doorway and gave me a solid thumbs up.

Charlie's thing was a twenty-fifth work anniversary at a big Westport bar. Buffet and drinks. Ted and I were among the first to show up. I got a scotch and water, something other than beer primarily because it was free, and sat with Ted at a high round table. Within fifteen minutes half of the fifty expected guests were there. Irene came in with a date. He was Ben Arlen, a young guy in Personnel. He's one of those unsinkable hopeful types who won't let height, average looks and uninspired personality prevent him from pursuing good-looking women. He's first in line at Punchline to ask out newly hired women. Ben couldn't be nicer, couldn't be more polite or more considerate, couldn't be less threatening. Unfortunately, he couldn't be less successful. A true one date wonder.

I caught Irene looking sideways at me as she came through the door. She had a serious direct expression until she looked back at Ben with a smile. She wore a long light blue skirt and navy blazer, white blouse buttoned to the top. Still, sexy as hell.

After a good crowd had gathered and gotten their first drink, Eunice waved Ted to the small square of dance floor. He held a small portable microphone and did a standard roast of the guest of honor. He joked about how long Charlie had been with the company. "He ushered in a new age. The Bronze Age." He talked about the rise from humble beginnings. "Charlie started out delivering mail and fetching coffee. Now he's in charge of all of Design. Oh, we still make him deliver mail and fetch coffee." He mentioned work ethic and contribution. "Charlie works hard and contributes something every day, so we're willing to ignore the three-hour naps."

Charlie spoke briefly, mentioned several people individually, alternated between humor and sentimentality, ended with a gracious thanks. He had Margaret join him for a quick hug in front of everyone, then they danced on the tan dance floor to a slow number while everyone stood around. The dance ended with crowd applause and then people went back to their tables or to the buffet.

When Ben and Irene slid off their barstools and headed for the food, I did the same. I stood opposite of Irene and started tonging salad things onto a chilled plate. Irene pulled a serving spoon from a bowl of black semi-liquid surrounded by tiny squares of white bread.

"Um, what's this?" she asked.

"I don't know," Ben said with a feeble laugh. "Geez, I don't know."

"Oh, it's great," I said, looking at Irene. "I've got a tub of it at home in the fridge. It's called I Can't Believe It's Not Caviar." Irene leaned towards me with the back of her hand against her smiling mouth. Ben just looked confused.

My feelings at being this close to Irene were just what I had hoped for. On the one hand, there was a pleasant ease at kidding around without feeling it was forced. On the other hand, there was an internal flutter of excitement. It was kind of like serving in a tennis tournament where you're feeling nervous and confident at the same time.

"It's a little salty," I added, drawing out the sibilance and motioning as though I were feeling grit between my fingers. "Plus it takes about twenty of those little bread squares to make a decent sandwich."

My salad plate and I made it back to my table. Ted was on the dance floor, slowly caressing the back of a redhead in a short black skirt and jacket. A few tables from me, Irene listened to Ben without looking at him while he talked on and on. When I caught her looking at me as I surveyed the room, she didn't look away.

Margaret slid into the chair beside me, a plastic glass of white wine in her hand. Charlie walked next to us while being led to the dance floor by a couple of older teen daughters of coworkers. He flipped the back of Margaret's hair as he went by. She smoothed it down with neither amusement nor annoyance.

"God, I'd love a cigarette," she said. "Remember when we used to have cigarettes? Right now I'd really like a cigarette."

"Maybe I'll get you one."

"Maybe I'll let you. It'll be like old times."

"They were good old times."

A slow saxophone instrumental began to play and Margaret swayed in time with it. I liked watching her dreamlike movements. I'd always liked being friends with her, being around her quite a bit. She's taller than average, athletic but still having curves in her hips, alluring in a brief billowy dress on a backyard patio. And like Kim, Margaret was always ready to do whatever the others in our group were up for. It could be bowling, a movie, chattering walks along the Kansas River in the fall. Margaret was bright, a good partner in trivia games on winter evenings near their fireplace. On June trips down to Ozark lakes, her laughter lingered most after everyone's funny comments on events and scenery. In the kitchens of inexpensive cabins she fixed breakfast in bare feet and a thin floral robe.

I got a cigarette from one of the office smokers. Margaret was finishing the last of a new glass of wine when I got back. She set it down resolutely and took my hand to lead me outside. At the sheltered bar entrance I placed the cigarette between her lips and lit it with a match from a little box I'd picked up at the bar.

"You're a sweetheart," she said as she exhaled a languid cloud of smoke. "It's like kissing the past." When she took a long pull on the cigarette I noticed a crinkling of skin above her lip. Suddenly she asked, "Will you take me home?"

Before I could answer she touched my shoulder and took hold of the doorknob. "I'll tell Charlie. He should stay at his party and he's more the dancer than I am. I'll tell him you're taking me home. Home sweet home. Where the heart is."

Back inside I got close enough to Ted and his redheaded love of the evening to give him the universal sign, pointing to the myself and then the door, that indicated I was leaving. He smiled the universal smile that said okay, he had a ride for later. Before Margaret and I walked out, she picked up another plastic glass of wine.

As we drove Margaret quickly finished her drink and then leaned her head against the window and closed her eyes. Rain began to splash in big drops against the windshield. The pulse of the wipers emphasized the silence.

"Don't fall asleep and make me carry you inside," I said.

"I'm awake. Sometimes when I am about to fall asleep, and sometimes in dreams, I get a vision of the four of us. Charlie and you, Kim and me in our ball caps, her hair in a ponytail. We're almost like little girls, giggling. At the lake in your car, that red Nova you used to have. Before Megan came along." The windshield wipers measured out several seconds. "And I just ache. A sharp pain in my chest. A literal heartache." She laughed mirthlessly.

"I know what you're talking about. Familiar territory."

"You never flirted with me," Margaret said in a distant tone, almost to herself. She looked out her rain streaked side window at the dark blurry houses.

"I was looking. We were married."

"I'm talking about flirtation, Mitchy." Her gaze turned to me and her voice lightened. "Flirting with friends is just part of being friends, a compliment, saying you're looking good, girl. Saying your husband is a lucky man."

Margaret's legs were crossed tightly. She slid a hand between her naked thighs. I told her it was the wine talking. She held the stemmed plastic glass to her ear, then she whispered to it from behind a cupped hand, then listened to it again.

"No, it's me talking. Definitely me. The wine is speaking some kind of French I don't understand. Must be from the outer provinces, like Iceland or something. Maybe I shouldn't be talking. I shouldn't be talking about Kim."

"Hey, it's okay."

"Do you dream about her?"

"Hmm, sometimes."

"What are the dreams about?"

"Sex and regrets and anger."

Margaret started to say something, then stopped and slumped forward. She held the weightless wine glass in both hands. I pulled into her driveway, feeling the hump of the curb that Charlie was always meaning to smooth out.

"Do you want to come in, have a little more wine?" Margaret asked. She looked at me with sleepy eyes, then stretched her arms to give me a graceful exit if I wanted to tell her thanks but she was obviously very tired. I said okay. Part of it was wanting the small thrill of anticipating something that really could never happen between us. And partly I was just curious. Margaret was in an unusual mood and I wanted to see where it would lead.

The front entryway leads directly into the living room. Margaret opened a large dark wooden cabinet and switched on softly chorded music from a few decades ago. While she went to the kitchen, I settled into a large cloth easy chair next to the fireplace.

Margaret came back with two large goblets of red wine. She sat on the ottoman in front of me while we listened to Bonnie Raitt sing at a low volume. Margaret absently stroked her brown bare legs.

"I'm sorry I keep bringing up the past, Mitch," she said. "I just seem to miss it so much. Too much really. I don't even know why. Things are fine now. Good, actually. I know I'm acting weird. I have nothing I can really complain about. I only know that being around you brings me closer to then, if that makes any sense." She sipped deeply from her glass. Her eyes reflected the room's faint white light. It was a little chilly after the rain and I thought about offering to start a fire.

"You make perfect sense, Margaret. Everything really was great then or had plenty of time to turn into something great. Everything I remember comes to me in images with a golden glow."

Margaret touched her eyes and went over to lie on the couch.

"Remember playing Trivial Pursuit?" she asked in a voice that was suddenly husky.

"You were good, Margaret. Who knows geography?"

"Former teachers' pets."

"Whatever. You were good. Your team usually won."

"The question was 'What is the leading cause of male mortality?' You said it was slow death by marriage. Made me laugh so much. Do you remember saying that?"

"How could I forget? Kim cited it in the divorce."

Margaret stretched out fully on the couch, her head on a throw pillow, soft brown hair across her mouth. She fell asleep to "Danny's Song." I covered her with an afghan from the back of the couch, then carried the goblets out to the kitchen and rinsed them at the sink before leaving.

Driving away from Margaret in the damp quiet darkness I wasn't tired, but I wasn't sure about returning to Charlie's party. The break had been kind of like getting a phone call during a meal. After the interruption, things didn't look that appealing.

I stopped at the Coffee Horse and sat with a cup of de-caf and a free inner city tabloid. It wasn't yet midnight. Small tables for two in funky shapes were being shared by students from the Kansas City Art Institutes and working couples young enough to stay up late in conversation and still get up for jobs in the morning. Eyes and smiles widened as couple in some sort of love touched each other beneath white tabletops. They were at once patient and urgent about the sex they would be sharing in the deepest hours of the night. I started feeling some of Margaret's nostalgia for a few decades ago.

How perfect it would be to wake up with your lover in a cool sunny bedroom where an open bedroom was allowing a tender breeze to slide silkily over naked bodies partially covered by a simple sheet, your face lightly touching the floral fragrance of her hair, waking up excited about being together in the day ahead. There's something to be said for marrying young, living together in a place of your own like Kim and I did when I was in graduate school and she was getting her nursing degree and we both had okay jobs that required no emotional expenditure.

Irene would stand out in the Coffee Horse. Perhaps the other young woman would envy her natural good looks, the coat from a good department store, the most flattering haircut finally achieved, clear comfort with her beauty and no need to dress in the very latest styles in belts and shoes. I imagined her walking in while Ben sat in his big expensive sedan in the street just outside the entrance. She would pay for a medium mocha with smooth flat dollar bills and leave with a steaming paper cup. She'd turn towards me just before she got to the door and she'd mouth "Call me." Then she'd stumble just a little in nervousness before going out to Ben and staring at me with an expression of longing as the car slid into sparse fast-moving traffic.

I felt like I was poised on the high board and I wanted to have Irene force me to take the plunge. I had a sudden urge to talk to Eunice. It was only a walk of a few blocks to get back to the party. When I got just outside the entrance, I could see the Punchline people through the large windows across the front. The music was no longer thudding against the glass. The party participants were sitting around a table cluttered with glasses and bottles. Ted was gone, having perhaps ascended to hot fox heaven. Charlie was laughing and wearing a triangular hat made from a section of newspaper. Eunice was absently and sleepily smiling through it all. I decided to leave the drunk enough alone.

Chapter Thirteen

The next day was Friday. Casual dress day at work. Cotton khakis and knit shirt for me. I ran into Irene at the water fountain. She was getting a drink after popping a few tablets into her mouth.

"Hangover medicine?" I asked. She looked up with one hand holding her hair away from the small arc of water. I felt the warm honey glow of simultaneous excitement and relaxation that sometimes occurs upon encountering a beautiful woman. It's a more potent intoxicant when the beauty feels equally at ease and interested.

"Allergies," she said, dabbing the corners of her mouth. "Pollen's murder around here." Effortless smile. No nerves. Made it easier for me, in the way a smooth swinging golf partner improves your game.

"Ah, yes, pollen. The silent killer. Well, silent if you don't count the skull busting sneezes." Her laughter was like a stream bubbling over little stones. Her wide eyes flickered blue and yellow light. I looked away to reduce their power to make me timid.

"I think you have to count the sneezes. They're hard to ignore."

"I hope you're not taking those pills on an empty stomach. You should think about an early lunch."

Irene pulled back the sleeve of her white collared shirt and looked at her narrow silver watch. "Is nine-thirty too early?" she asked, looking upward as if calculating. A ringing phone got her attention. It came from a cubicle about twenty feet away. She said she should get it, she was expecting some tax numbers from an outside firm. As she walked away I had to watch the sure strides of her long legs in blue jeans. I spent the next several minutes at my desk trying not to think of Irene's departing and compact behind in the hallway as I did the math on our respective ages at different times and made a mental list of the impracticalities they would bring.

Facing a Friday night with no social plans, I stopped at the library on the way home to look for literary diversion. As I went to the fiction section, I asked myself a familiar question: Why does anyone ever buy a book, purchase a tome, invest in a volume? It's thirty dollars versus free to read any hard cover edition. And there's no guilt because your tax dollars have already paid for the library's collection. Plus you get to keep all those ready books in a neat, organized place that makes them easy to locate. Plus, if you're all confused about where a book might be, who wrote it, what it's called or what it's about, there's an informed, eager person there ready to help. Or go stand in line at a bookstore for the privilege of paying a bunch for the same material. Your choice.

I went to the New Book section, hoping to find something in either fiction or non-fiction that had gotten a strong recommendation in a newspaper or magazine review. Not all that easy. Reportedly, at a recent book convention a publisher delivered a speech in which he lamented the relative rarity of strongly positive reviews at a time when book sales were slowing and costs wee on the rise. Seems to me there was a time not long ago when pleading for easy compliments would not have been an issue. Good fiction was being put out at a steady rate. There were plenty of original, well-written books to read. Then dull repetition set in. Formulaic tales of crime, political thrills and weepy drama. No problem for me. Plenty of classic literature to back and visit, lots of fiction from the past that could provide entertainment and insight.

My dating experiences have some parallels. In the early days of college there were many wonderful pretty girls to take out. I accepted blind dates with no hesitation because odds were good you'd be hooked up with someone fun and interesting, often willing to engage in a heavy make-out session in a dark corner of an off-campus party. Beautiful women were in classrooms, in the downtown bars, at sporting events, in and out of the student union all day long. I haven't gotten that sense in a long time. And in the same way that I envy people who can read all kinds of books and truly enjoy them, I think it must be pretty wonderful to be a man who can date almost any available woman or meet a series of them through a dating service and get thrill after thrill. I fear I'm getting to a stage of life where rather than a constant overlay of contentment, I'll be island hopping from a round of golf to an unexpectedly amusing conversation to a song on the radio that makes me reflexively turn up the volume. Then I'll be not unhappy, but rather in a state of dormancy between the small oases of pleasure.

A good day of jogging occasionally grants me a small vacation into a mildly euphoric oblivion. When you're under thirty, it happens pretty consistently. And under twenty your running can approach an almost dreamlike lack of effort. Everything's clicking, the rhythms are natural. You're only aware of the sensation of happiness tracking through your veins. In your forties it's fairly arduous just to get a few briskly paced miles under your stretch waist band. It can feel as though someone has attached sandbags to your legs and chest. About seventy per cent of the time running requires a strong effort with some difficult uphill stretches. Roughly twenty per cent of the time it's a real struggle and you're not sure you can finish. Ten per cent of the time it's so easy you almost laugh. At my current age, day to day living breaks down to similar proportions.

Over the years when I haven't been able to find something recent to read, I've taken chances on books from the Modern Library's list of the best hundred novels written in English in the twentieth century. I figure even if I don't absolutely love the reading, I'll get context and perspective that will help me appreciate literature in general. Also, it's just fun to see the evolution of literature, the beginnings of symbolism in Knut Hamsun's Hunger. The narrator is struggling against starvation in nineteenth century Sweden. He evades a procession of policemen. At the end the reader sees them as symbols of society's oppression. The protagonist turns away from the city lights at book's end and walks towards the wilderness. In a later work D.H. Lawrence concludes his narrative with a main character who walks towards the city glow and its promise of life more enlightened and fulfilling than the one in the coal mines he is escaping. Still later Eudora Welty in A Delta Wedding has a final scene where a woman is looking up at the night sky and seeing both light and darkness in the equivocal future. Reading these various works makes me feel I'm inhabiting an interconnected universe where all of the attitudes and experiences and perceptions of humanity can be examined and pondered.

I assume and typically discover that acclaimed literary works offer insight as well as craft, and that my view of the world will be altered by the experience of reading in the way that a person will come away with a newly developed sense of grandeur after visiting Paris or the Grand Canyon. And like scientists whose inquiries lead them to expand the scope of the universe by millions of galaxies and billions of years, I find that my somewhat casual reading life of delving into the best of fiction enlarges my literary world, especially with writers like Kafka, and my living world where, for instance, William Faulkner perceives time in a way I had never come close to considering. Like a bedtime reader of the bible, arriving at perhaps sometimes astute and other times incorrect personal interpretations of the written world, the reading has an effect on my life but does not become my life.

I'm content to enjoy the music of the prose and settle for a general, distilled message from the words I've consumed. The New Testament is basically The Golden Rule. Anyone with any degree of seriousness about pursuing literature is compelled to read Joyce's <u>Ulysses.</u> I'm not going to read an encyclopedic amount of criticism and research in order to track down and understand every major and minor literary allusion, historical reference and nit of symbolism. I'm happy to derive whatever pleasure I can and endure the sometimes slow slog through the terrain of tough language and reach an overall conclusion that James Joyce's primary concerns are love and death, embodied in Bloom's sensual wife Molly and deceased little son Rudy, and that the book's title signals that the characters navigating the unadorned streets of Dublin are participating in an epic journey. I may be somewhat wrong at times or even way off the mark, but that doesn't' concern me. I like the feeling that my simple life is profound and that I'm a romantic character inside a saga.

On this particular night in a small branch library off a main road in Kansas City, I decided to pique and reinforce that thrill by checking out Joyce's <u>Dubliners</u> with the intention of rereading its last story first, "The Dead." and its last sentence first, "His soul swooned slowly as he heard the snow falling faintly through the universe and faintly falling, like the descent of their last end, upon all the living and the dead."

The next morning I participated in the definitely non-literary game of tennis at Ted's club. I showed up twenty minutes early so I could have coffee in the food and drink area and watch games being played on the three beige courts below. The club has a lot of members who are solid players, men and women who roll hard topspins and hit with power off the backhand. Like most things, tennis can easily hold your attention for fifteen minutes when executed by skilled performers. And like a lot of competitive events, it holds a certain fascination as you observe the clash of human egos.

In the middle court four guys in their thirties with thick expensive rackets were playing a close match. I watched as one of them blasted a curving first serve about a foot inside the intersecting corner lines. A perfect shot. The receiving player remained frozen in his ready pose and called it out. His opponent at the net challenged the call. The two of them engaged in a high pitched and not especially loud discussion involving disbelieving smiles and slowly shaking heads.

When the server asked what the dispute was about, the receiving player replied, "I called your serve out." He didn't say it actually was out. He just attested to the fact that he had said it was out. He offered to let them take another first serve. After further shaking of heads and smiling of smiles to teammates, play resumed. I supposed that players on both sides were feeling that should they come out on the low side of the final tally, they could rationalize their way to a mental victory by citing cheating or something close to it on the other side.

"More coffee?" a bright voice asked. I looked up to see a pretty woman with blonde hair clipped short on the sides with bangs in front. She was holding two pots, regular and de-caf. She wore an unbuttoned white polo shirt bearing the club logo. The biceps supporting the coffee containers were firm and narrow with a little bulge. Her slightly exaggerated smile betrayed pride in her shining white teeth. I didn't really want more coffee, but I said I did for the small brief pleasure of seeing her strong slender arm reach across the table. She smiled like peach blossoms. She was probably no more than half an hour from the shower.

"Regular," I said. As she filled the white mug, Ted came in and sat down. "I'll need to stay awake while I roll over this guy on the courts."

After accepting her offer to get him a cup, Ted said, "He won't fall asleep as much as pass out. Better dial nine one and then hit the final digit is you see him race to the net. He'll go down for sure."

"I'll do that," she said with an even bigger smile. Then she bounced away lightly in her shorts and shining white shoes.

Ted yawned and stretched. "Too much redhead last night?" I asked.

"That woman at Charlie's anniversary? Turns out she's got a boyfriend. Lives with her but travels out of town a lot. Who needs that? I just can't see myself hanging up when I call and a man answers or sneaking out the back door with shoes and tie in one hand while he's coming up the stairs.

I'd feel like a live version of one of those guys in a fifties men's magazine cartoon."

"Exaggerated tiptoeing across the backyard under a crescent moon. Tough on the calves."

I was already glad I'd come. The atmosphere was like that of a vacation resort. People in athletic clothes were bustling around. The play on the courts was fun to watch. The waitress was a doll. Ted seemed to be in good form.

The blonde returned with Ted's coffee. "Thank you, my dear," he said with an officious and pompous air. "Admirable work. Append a fifteen percent gratuity to the bill and send it along with my monthly charge."

"It's automatic," she said with a laugh.

"Damn straight, and they'll have to come through me if they want to even consider changing the policy."

Ten minutes later we were on the court. The tennis was great. I was pleased to discover that I still had a feel for a younger man's game, could still perform adequately and find it extremely pleasurable. I'd impulsively bought a graphite racket the week before. My old one with the freakishly small head needed to have the brittle strings replaced and without giving myself more than three minutes to think about it, I took one I'd been eyeing up to the register at a discount sporting goods store.

On the court that day I didn't notice that my more expensive equipment was helping me score better. Ted still won sets by comfortable margins, but the overall experience was better. I could place shots more accurately and each contact with the ball felt more solid. After the first set I had lost all anxiety about perhaps wasting a hastily considered investment of a hundred and fifty dollars.

After an hour and a half of intense singles, with both of us lunging for anything even remotely reachable, with both of us dripping sweat in large drops, with legs aching pleasurably, we went back upstairs to have something to drink.

"You're getting better," Ted said casually. "I was really working on that last set. I mean it."

A quick thank you was all that occurred to me to say. I was expecting comments filled with facetious bragging. Besides, I didn't really care about winning. I was content to be on the court more or less keeping up with someone who could hit the ball well. I'd done okay, gotten a good workout and laughed quite a bit. What's a few more points, a couple of close serves that go just in rather than just out compared to all that?

"You mind if I get in some laps on the track while I'm still loose?" Ted asked as he got up. "I'll just be ten or fifteen minutes. Gotta keep the conditioning razor sharp if I'm going to keep playing you."

He was gone before I could say anything. I actually liked that about Ted. He pretty much did whatever he wanted without asking permission from anyone. I liked it because you that any time he spent with you was because he really wanted to be in your company. His sincerity was never false. The benefit for him was the ability to move about freely and still be in relationships.

I was glad to have time alone. Fatigue had completely relaxed me. I was very content to sit and watch four middle-aged men play on the center court below me. It took a few minutes for me to realize that one of them was Don Harper. He held his swept back hair in place with a hat whose enormous bill shielded most of his face. I could tell it was him by the distinctive way his arms swung with limp vigor beside his thick waist as he walked. Also, he was wearing his standard Harper issue huge gold watch.

Harper hit the ball pretty well for a guy who got all this thrust from his shoulders, and he moved okay even though he rarely bent his knees and couldn't turn without obvious effort. He didn't often blow an easy shot. His lack of great mobility would hurt him in singles, with half the court beyond his scope, forget about the corners, he was doing pretty well with his partner. He only mouthed off once in a while and showed little anger when he hit a serve that slapped into the tape at the top of the net or a ball careened off the rim of his outstretched racket.

I was about to go find Ted and see if he wanted to go out for lunch when two tall women in short pleated tennis skirts walked onto the court adjoining Harper's. Even from my perch high above the action, I could tell he was staring at them directly. The rigid bill of his cap was pointed due babe. His partner waited in the ready serve position as Harper just kept looking.

The women were oblivious to any attention as they hit low brisk shots and chattered away. Harper went back to his game but stopped once in a while to look intently when one of the women was facing away from him and bent at the waist to retrieve a ball or kneel to tie a shoelace. Occasionally, if one of them asked him to toss back an errant ball, he'd make a remark that I couldn't quite hear. The girls never seemed amused.

I watched for all this for the same unfathomable motive that makes people pick at a healing scab or poke a tongue into the sensitive area of a tooth. With great immaturity I mentally dressed Irene in a little pink tennis dress with the sides cut out just above the belt and I set her out on the club court to bend and reach and twist for El Dondo, who would observe her movements with animal relish. I pictured office scenes involving the two of them. I got myself fairly worked up imagining Irene bent over at the water fountain and Harper standing close behind her, grinning lewdly while peering at the stretchy material tight across her alluring contours.

"Isn't that Harper down there?" Ted was back. "Must be taking a break from cooking the books."

"More precisely, he's taking occasional breaks from ogling the babes on court three to play a little tennis."

Fashioning binoculars from hands to his eyes, Ted remarked, "Ah, yes, babes off the babeboard bow. Legs, ho."

"That silly big bill on his hat was limp before they showed up."

"Can't say I blame him. Those are some fine looking women."

"A little subtlety would be nice. At least stem the drool waterfall."

"Well, I have to tell you, Mitch, sometimes the subtle approach ain't the best one. At times it's good to show clear intent."

"Intent to behave like an animal?" I was having trouble sounding lighthearted.

Ted shrugged. "They're big girls. They can handle guys like Harper. One cutting look can shut him down completely. And you might consider that a man not blessed with your good looks and reasonably trim form can't wait for the babes to come to him. You might cut him a little slack there, my good man."

Maybe Ted was right. Maybe I was reacting too strongly. Harper was, in fact, just looking. Everybody looks. It might be the straight ahead look, a peripheral glance, a change in direction as though you're going back down a hallway to retrieve something you've forgotten. Whatever. But we all look. Ted had me there.

"And you know, Mitch, sometimes they're just looking to get physical…"

"Okay," I conceded. "But I've always operated under the presumption that to a woman, the physical doing of the deed is the signing of a contract. A non-verbal agreement has been reached."

Ted nodded thoughtfully and then slipped into a trance as he fixated on the babe tossing up serves with balls she got by reaching under her short skirt and feeling around in the thin fabric next to her skin. I thought about asking Ted if ever felt bad about not calling women he slept with, but I let it go.

Chapter Fourteen

One night I came home to find my mailbox containing a single rosebud and a few handfuls of loose petals. No note or letter. Just flower fragments. All right. Good. I'm thinking it'll be fun to think about from a who and why standpoint. A mini mystery. With such scant information, I was free to imagine any scenario I wanted. The first mental picture I formed involved me and a night nurse with a pool cue in a leather case, zooming up a mountain road in a powerful convertible, the radio's rock and roll pounding out a sensual rhythm.

Next I imagined myself in a small secluded lake of clear comfortable water surrounded by lust forest while Margaret sunbathed topless nearby on a weathered dock, a smile on her deep red lips, her gaze hidden by dark sunglasses. I created a back story about Charlie's running off with a new young long-haired secretary. This got him out of the picture. Even in an imagined world I felt the need to resolve issues of loyalty and fidelity before moving in on Margaret.

In my mind I saw myself later that lakeside evening with Margaret in an intimate luxuriously appointed cabin. She was wearing the same snug sleeveless dress she had been wearing a few evenings when I had in reality had dinner at her and Charlie at their house. We sat outdoors in cool candlelit comfort on their screened porch and dined on grilled salmon and asparagus, flavorful slices of juicy tomato and a lemony rice dish.

My hosts updated me on the swinging bachelor next door, a dentist who had installed a heated swimming pool as the focal point of his constant good times with a seemingly unlimited supply of party girls and short term girlfriends. The latest installment of the saga involved two women in their twenties who mistakenly showed up at their house in bikinis with gaudy beach towels around their waists. It was the middle of a Saturday afternoon and the front door was unlocked. While Charlie worked outside in the yard, Margaret was unloading groceries in the kitchen. The girls let themselves in and came to the kitchen carrying twelve-packs of beer. They started to unload individual brown bottles and acted as though Margaret were just another guest attending that day's festivities.

"Hi, I'm Candy," said the first one in. "And this is Michelle. Anything we can do to help?"

"Actually, yes," Margaret said. "One of you can go to the basement to fetch and fold laundry and one can help my husband stain the deck."

This appeared to be the start of a routine that was fairly predictable. A certain make of compact red car starts showing up regularly on Saturday afternoons and is gone by the following morning. Then the car is still in the driveway when Charlie pads out to get the Sunday paper. As things progress, the car is next door overnight in the middle of the week. Then no little red car for a few weeks. This lull is followed by the return of the automobile at about the time of late television news. After half an hour there is the slamming of a car door, the grinding burst of a starting engine and the screaming of tires. Within a few weeks the ritual starts again.

"Fascinating," I said. "The mating habits of the white bellied dental chick sucker in his natural habitat."

"I'm going to have to call it a night," Charlie said, standing up and yawning. "I'm coming down with a cold or something."

"Early to bed, surly to rise," I said. Charlie touched Margaret's hair as he walked behind her. He motioned for me to sit back down as I got up to leave.

"You two go ahead and have dessert. Margaret's made some great cookies. Chocolate chip oatmeal. I'll put on coffee before I go upstairs. You two keep on talking. Just keep the noise level down if you get to laughing or having sex."

"Note to self," Margaret said, pretending to write on her palm. "Quiet sex."

"Appreciate it," Charlie said as he walked away and waved.

In a few minutes Margaret and I moved into the living room. The muted sounds of a television were coming from upstairs. We sat on the couch in the sentimental ambiance of recorded acoustic folk music. When Margaret rose to go to the kitchen, I saw the thin black strap of her bra hanging across her upper arm. The string of garment appeared suddenly, out of nowhere. Women have a magical ability to reveal interest and allure without touching themselves or any part of their clothing. No perceptible twitching or writhing. The lacy red waistband of a thong is visible above the top of low stung jeans. A flash of firm white thigh shows in the open seam of a long wraparound skirt. Like a mound on a relief map, the raised detailed outline of a breast appears beneath a sweater. Just as quickly and magically, at the appearance of a third party, the revelation disappears.

I've wondered if it's instinctive, a reflex like blinking or flinching, stimulus and response or if it's practiced and planned. I'm betting it's instinct. It's all so effortless, as quick as a hand drawn away from sudden intense heat.

Margaret returned with two mugs of coffee in one hand and a small plate of cookies in the other. After setting them down on the coffee table and sitting down , she ran a thumb under the shoulder strap of her dress and leaned back on the sofa.

"Is it warm in here or is it just me?" she asked.

"I'm fine."

"It'll be nicer if I just turn down the lights a little, maybe turn up the music. Charlie's asleep. Who knows what might happen?"

"Are you ending a sentence with a proposition?"

Margaret looked away with a smile as she sat down next to me on the couch. She started to say something, then looked away before speaking. "I wonder if I'm going to cry tonight. You seem to have that effect on me."

"You don't seem sad at the moment."

"I don't know that I ever really am. More just the bittersweet longing. That ever present aching for the old days."

"Remembrance of things past."

"Maybe it's the wine from dinner. Making me feel warm and sentimental."

"Wine. The curse of the weeping class."

"Opiate of the weeple," Margaret said. I raised my cup in a toast.

Faint singing played on the stereo. Margaret took my hands and urged me to my feet. We danced slowly, barely moving away from the couch. She laid her head on my shoulder. My hand rested on her back at the waist. She began to whisper. At first she was singing along with the CD, then she was talking. "We were all young, we had a card table for a dining room table, picnics for birthday celebrations. Not much money. We had so little. And we had so much." Her shoulder strap had slipped down onto her upper arm. I put my hands on her brown shoulders and drew her closer, our cheeks were touching. Her shoulders hunched as she leaned into me, her fingertips pressing against my back.

When the song ended Margaret kissed the corner of my mouth briefly. As we stepped away from each other without making eye contact, she pulled up her dress sleeves and reached down to the coffee table to get her coffee. After a few moments of awkward silence we both started to make comments about the lateness of the hour. I thanked her for a pleasant evening, the dinner and the cookies, wished Charlie well with his impending flu. We parted without a hug.

I drove home wondering how far things could have gone with Margaret if I had pushed them. I have had similar questioning thoughts over the years. The woman at the bar in another city, the rock on her matrimonial band all aglitter, stares in obvious hunger. The coworker in the all day meeting massages your neck and leans forward, her braided hair falling against your ear and cheek, before going to dinner with her husband. I don't think Kim ever behaved that way. Not when we were together. Not when things were good. Something would have been a giveaway. Walking into a kitchen during a party where she moved closer to the man with his arm around her shoulder. An expression with closed eyes during a hello kiss from an old friend. Something.

At home the sight of the rose petals on the dining room table got me back to solving that puzzler. The one woman I couldn't visualize as involved in any way was Irene. I just couldn't conjure the clear image of her furtive self coming up my steps in the dead of night, brown bag in hand, girlfriend in car as the getaway driver. And I couldn't see us on a casual date, joking with a friendly middle-aged waitress at a roadside diner or passing a cigarette back and forth while lying in bed in the dark.

Those seemed like good signs. She was too young, too distant from my world and my routine and interests. I was subconsciously telling myself all that. Deep down I knew it was ridiculous. Not that I haven't been able to attract women from the generation behind me. I've turned down dinner invitations, day trips hiking into the hilly trails of nearby resorts, overnight trips to Chicago. "I've got comps from frequent flyer miles that are about to expire."

No dinner dates for me where there's a second couple or third couple, the men and women are all my ages except for my date, who's drinking beer from a bottle while the rest of us split a bottle of wine. What if my lady companion got carded or referred to by the restaurant staff as my daughter. Like today's gourmet coffee and beer in microbrewery bars, the cost would simply be too high.

I included Eunice in my flowery fantasy. I don't know why. I couldn't go younger, but no problem with older. I had already taken her off the purloined petal suspect list. Actually, Ted had.

"I told Eunice about the rose petals in your mail slot," Ted said as he rubbernecked in an attempt to make eye contact with a leggy blonde seated with an older woman at the New Fredrick bar.

"And she didn't blurt out that it was her," I said.

"Oddly enough, she did not. She laughed in that knowing way of hers."

"Did she have any guesses?"

"I wouldn't say it was a guess. More like the obvious answer."

"But it's not Eunice her own self." My stomach was getting a little jumpy.

"It's not Eunice."

"Well, then, pray tell, what's up?"

"First, let me ask if there was a flyer on your doorknob on the day of the rose petals?"

"Could have been. Some rolled up thing with a rubber band."

"Eunice said you got a flyer for a dating service. They stick the thing on your door and stick rose petals in your mail slot."

"How romantic."

Chapter Fifteen

A dozen years ago Jack Buckley left Punchline to start his own ad agency. He's done pretty well. His offices are on the sixth floor of a newer office building--more stone, less glass than the structures of the '70s. He's got a marble floor in the entrance to his business and, typically, a friendly young lady at the reception desk.

Jack's a good guy. He has an almost Southern relaxed manner and an unforced curiosity about the people he meets. He's my age. Never married. Calls me once in a while. Sometimes it's for golf, or drinks at a bar, or conversation until late at his place. He lives in mid-town in a brick two story Tudor home. He used to invite Kim and me over for parties that would last all night. We usually declined, seeing ourselves as the rare married couple, nursing our drinks and sitting on lawn chairs while everyone else danced and drank and got cozy on blankets beneath pin oaks.

Jack always had an unsubtle eye for Kim. He looked at her with brief wistful glances, never leering or lingering, never anything that I need to call him on. He seemed to be thinking of something whenever he looked, perhaps remembering a woman or an event from a distant past or rekindling a hope for the future.

The last time Jack called me was on Thursday night. He wanted me to stop by his office after work. Okay, fine. Jack's office is large, but no-nonsense. A heavy wooden library table with a computer and phone serves as his desk. A few comfortable leather chairs sit next to sizable square end tables. One wall holds a huge abstract painting from a non-celebrity artist. No photos of himself landing the big one or crashing though a white water wall of foam or standing as part of a charity golf foursome involving a local big shot.

"Do you have any contact with Kim?" he asked after the usual kidding hellos.

"Some. All friendly. Mostly phone messages."

"That's good. Very good," Jack said slowly, regaining that old thoughtful expression that Kim seemed to prompt. He looked out into the distance beyond the floor to ceiling windows. "I landed a big poultry producer. They're in six states and growing. Print and television ads. A budding internet presence. A big account. I can offer you quite a bit of money."

"I'm good financially, Jack. Have trouble spending what I've got. I'd like to work with you. But then I wouldn't be working that much with you. I'd be working with a guy in a chicken suit."

"Tailored chicken suit. Pinstriped feathers." Jack opened a bulky manila envelope. He pulled out an inch of papers and looked at the stack for a few seconds, then he set it down. "I'd love working with you," he said. His mouth puckered into a mirthless smile. "This little business I've got here has worked out fine and all. But I honestly just miss working with you. Good ideas. Such great conversations. And you always got the job done thoroughly to deadline. It's rare, Mitch, that kind of approach to work. We were always laughing. Was it as much fun as I remember?"

"I think it truly was. It was all new. We had endless time in front of us. We didn't think about acquiring wealth. We didn't contemplate loss. Every day was its own enclosed life."

"See, that's what I was talking about. Just talking to you, hearing what you have to say."

"We had energy then."

"We traveled light and lean," Jack said as he lightly rubbed the paunch pressing out his dress shirt buttons. "So much fun to play golf."

We reminisced about a really hot summer Sunday morning on a course near Clinton Lake in Lawrence, the university town twenty-five miles from Kansas City. Wood and streams wind through it. Eagles drift overhead in fall. Deer look out warily from camouflaging brush before treading out warily early in the morning and at dusk to drink the cool flowing water.

That morning the starter paired us with a guy in his thirties and a girlfriend who was maybe five years younger. The guy was a whiter shade of pales and wore a kind of cowboy hat made of straw, the wide brim keeping any speck of sunlight off his face and neck. I could see small white smears of sunscreen on the tops of his ears and along the back of one cheek. The girlfriend didn't wear a hat and she had a very dark tan. Her brown hair was tied up off her neck casually. Loose strands stuck to the thin sheen of perspiration on her face. She had a very white smile that gleamed from her freckled face. She wore a tight white sleeveless top and khaki shorts that went almost to her knees.

The boyfriend shook hands and nodded stiffly when we introduced ourselves. She smiled big and gave a friendly, enthusiastic wave from a few feet away. "Susan," she said. Both of them had expensive brand name equipment, quite unlike the cheap knock-offs I was hitting with. They had good swings, but played inconsistently. Probably didn't get out a lot.

The boyfriend took his game seriously, so he had a rough day. He was obviously pleased when his attempts warranted the occasional "Nice shot" from Jack or me. A low sharp hook or chunky pitch caused him to emit a tight growl of anger and frustration.

On the other hand, Susan smiled and shrugged at her less than perfect shots and commented often on the beauty of the surroundings and the pleasure of the activity. She struck me as one of those women who get some kind of thrill from being with the guys in a typically guy activity, amused at the quips and basking in being the singular object of male attention. She carried a lightweight bag without a lot of accessories hanging off of it. She picked it up effortlessly after each shot. Her white top was soaked through after a few holes and strands of wet hair flopped her forehead. It seemed like a clean kind of moisture, giving off a floral scent as it flowed over her body wash. I was glad she was with us.

Susan became increasingly amused, loose in her walk and gestures, going from smiling to laughing without inhibition as Jack and I lapsed into our usual conversation of mocking conversations and put-downs. "That's short. Maybe you should have hit your driver. Oh, that was your driver." "If you're taking steroids, you should get a refund, weenie arm." "Maybe you should sign up for a literacy course in reading putts."

All four of us walked. Jack and I had our bags on our backs. The boyfriend pushed a contraption with three wheels that looked like a modified drag racer. Big wheels in back, small one in front. I asked the boyfriend if the cart was legal without brake lights. He assured me that if fell well within PGA rules and guidelines. Susan's small smile was almost an apology, and her shrug was a message of helplessness.

When the boyfriend stalked an errant shot into dense greenery beyond the rough, she skipped a little, even with the bag on her shoulder, as she walked between Jack and me. One time while the cowboy golfer was looking for his ball in the woods, Susan hooked her arm through mine and suggested we run off together and leave him to fend for himself.

"Think he could survive on nuts, berries and those huge bottles of water dangling from his cart?" I asked her.

"As long as no drop of sunshine ever hits his skin," she said. We all helped him locate the lost ball, and he chose to hit it from the forest in an effort to save a stroke. The ball came flying out but sliced right back in. He stomped after it, disappearing again.

Susan twirled the ends of her short hair into little pigtails and said, "I feel kind of like Dorothy out here with you strange creatures."

"I'd be the cowardly putter," I said.

"If you only had a game," Jack responded.

At the end of the round I was sorry to lose Susan's company. I had been feeling the happy glow of a good date. I even offered to buy them a pricey drink in the clubhouse. Unusual purchase for me when I'm not paying off a bet. The boyfriend said he had a thing at two o'clock that he really should attend and he easily tossed off Susan's feeble attempt to get them to stick around a little longer. I hated to be deprived of the small ongoing thrill a man can feel for an entire morning when he's in the company of a pretty woman who's glad to be around him, who smiles constantly and is clearly getting a kick out of being in on some guy humor.

As we loaded our bags into Jack's car trunk, he asked, "What do you think he's like in the sack?"

"Don't know, but I'm sure he uses plenty of protection."

"You can't be too careful…well, okay, you can."

I wondered how satisfying Susan could find being with the boyfriend. In the silent moments riding with Jack back to Kansas City, I tried to picture really good moments between the two and I couldn't come up with any. While the car radio buzzed a Royals game, I started to think about another era when I had been around fun-loving woman with an overly serious boyfriend. Her name was Jo. I had just started to date Kim. Jo was her roommate in a suite that had a bedroom and bathroom, plus a kitchen and breakfast nook shared with two other girls.

Jo was a petite dancer and gymnast, cheerleader for the Hawkeyes.

Perky and energetic, usually dressed in some kind of active wear, sweatshirt with matching pants or shorts that showed off her firm smooth legs. She had a boyfriend who was usually busy off studying law, only picking her up occasionally to go to a law school function or sit by him in the library or type his handwritten notes.

I liked getting to Kim's early for dates to hang around a neat, clean, girlie place where the candles were scented and the CD music featured girl groups. Jo was a cookie maker and always offered me some on a plastic dessert plate with daisy designs. She was a free spirit, comfortable walking out from her bedroom in bra and sweatpants or from the shower wearing a towel around her body and one on her head like a turban. She'd even pause for a few minutes to chat before going back into the bathroom to finish dressing.

Once I showed up for a date and knocked without getting anyone to come to the door. Using the key Kim had made for me, I let myself in and called out. Jo's voice came from the bathroom. "Kim called to say she had to stay after class to talk to the teacher about a term paper. She's running just a little late." I was helping myself to ginger snaps on the kitchen counter when Jo said something else I couldn't understand. I went near the slightly open bathroom door and asked her to repeat what she'd said.

"I want you to wash my back," she said with dreamy insistence. I looked in to see her hugging her knees as she sat in the bathtub with sudsy water almost to her shoulders. "There's a sponge in the water behind me." I sat on the tub's edge and fished around for the sponge. I used it to scrub Jo's back thoroughly as she sighed and said it felt good. She called me honey. When I heard footsteps and the clang of the mailbox being opened near the front door I stood up and quickly dried my hands on the thick towel hanging on the sink. I licked cookie crumbs from my lips before giving Kim a hello kiss.

Thinking back on those few watery moments with Jo makes me feel just as I did then. Somewhat excited, warmly content, grateful to life for small unexpected moments of escape and enjoyment in the midst of all the other stuff. Part of the memory is the immediate aftermath when Kim came in with her cheeks slightly red from the brisk autumn weather, looking like sunrise with her yellow overcoat and welcoming smile, and then her cool lips kissing mine as we embraced. We chatted about nothing much as Kim changed into jeans before we headed out to grab a burger and then go sit in the student section of the Hawkeye basketball arena while Jo bounced around in towel, then short robe and big fuzzy pink slippers.

It all blended into perfect happiness. In that regard it was like when Kim and I first moved to Kansas City and we attended lots of Royals games, either with friends or just the two of us. We didn't have a lot of money, and we could park for a dollar and a half, pay a dollar and a half each for bleacher seats, and share a coke for a buck. The team was good then, always contending, adding so much enhancement to the experience just like the omnipresence of Jo in college days. It seemed like we were always happy.

Chapter Sixteen

The phone rang while I was floating in the exquisite concentrated pleasure of good reading. The book in my hands was Annie Proulx's book of short stories. They drew you right in. The dialogue made you feel you were right there in the simple Laramie bar drinking beer from long neck bottles. In the raw wind-carved landscape of mountain and sky depicted and the tragic lives of its inhabitants, there was still a romance in the blue jean dramas of working people looking for love and endurance.

I picked up the phone and heard the voice of Amy, the young nurse from the class reunion. She was in town with two girlfriends and they wanted to go casino hopping.

"We want you to drive us," she said from her cell phone in the car. The radio played country music and her friends were singing along.

"Where are you?"

"The sign off the interstate says Raytown."

"You're fairly close to my place. Who's with you?"

"Darla and Carla."

"Are those their real names?"

"They are in Raytown. You can be our designated driver, chaperone, gambling guide."

"Pull off at an exit and call me from a gas station. I'll find you." I'll say yes to anything that gets me off the couch and out into the world. I'd never go to a bar on my own to meet women. Having married when I was just barely over the legal drinking age, I wasn't experienced at picking up anything in a tavern beyond an illegal beer. Observing behavior over the years had only taught me that most people are there hoping to hook up with someone a level or two above themselves in appearance and that men faced a lot of rejection in the process. That was enough to keep me out of the game.

In the world of movies and fiction men and women in bars are like the beginning of a chess game where the knights and the king and queen pawns are always moved first. In the dark smoky rooms across our make-believe landscape someone asks someone to dance, then drinks are shared and there's a first kiss. After that the story can go in myriad directions.

I've only observed the completion of romantic chess as practiced in real life by strangers one time. It occurred in the early dawn of a parking lot where I was waiting to meet a couple of guys before driving together to a golf course. It was a fairly big square of crumbling asphalt with a bar in the middle of it. The building was a small blocky stucco thing with a window air-conditioning unit. It conveyed a promise of cheap beer and loud music and young crowds. As I sat listening to National Public Radio, a small weathered pickup truck pulled alongside the parking lot's only other car, a big older Oldsmobile with sassy bumper stickers. The driver was a guy in a cowboy hat and undershirt who had both hands and his chin on the top of the steering wheel. His sleepy, nearly closed eyes looked straight ahead. His female passenger had on a lacy black top. Her hair was flat and looked slightly brittle, possibly from hair spray and cigarette smoke from the night before. She forced a long hard kiss on his lips before hopping out of the truck, slinging a big black purse over her shoulder with gusto. She stood and stretched to wave as he drove off in a slow rumble. She was skinny in that way some women are that's leggy and sexy. I could relate to what the guy must have been feeling the night before, but I couldn't have stayed with her all night knowing I'd feel like he looked the next morning when the burgeoning sunlight brought things into realistic practical perspective. She may have had a kid at home, being watched by her mom and the mom's boyfriend who came around once in a while looking for trouble. That was probably his Olds.

I easily located Amy's green Taurus parked at a gas station just off the highway. I waved at them from the open car window and motioned for them to follow me. It was ten minutes from there to Harrah's large complex of hotels, cavernous meeting rooms and limitless gambling opportunities. We parked side by side in a garage with achingly bright white lighting.

"This is Darla," Amy said, pointing to her dark-haired friend. All three women were in their early thirties, average in size, wearing colorful t-shirts and blue jeans. They looked like they could have been related with their small pretty features and sparkling blue eyes. They were attractive in that simple small town way, unaware of their trim beauty, nonpreening with their posture of slightly rounded shoulders and facial expressions that communicated an earnest interest in things outside of themselves. "And this is Carla."

Carla shook my hand loosely as her eyes widened and stayed wide. She didn't say anything.

"I'm Mitch, your guide on tonight's sinful safari." I extended my elbows and bowed slightly. Darla raised her arms over her head and writhed slowly to some silent music. "Come with me and let us seek pleasure." Two Beer Guy was about to become Ten Dollar Guy. I figure if I lose that much in an evening, I've done no more than pay for a few hours of entertainment. The price of a movie. I can't lose. What a great position to be in.

The women wanted to play slot machines. I found some that you could play for as little as a nickel. We sat in fairly close proximity to one another. I ended up next to Amy. I saw her slide two twenty dollar bills into her machine and start wagering fifty cents a pull. I was at the dime level. After twenty minutes I still had half my original ten dollars credit. I cashed out and went walking to stretch my legs and my money. At the roulette table I took some guilty pleasure at not being the guy who lost two hundred dollars in about ten minutes by sticking chips all over the board for the few spins of the wheel that were required to rid him of all he had. I stood outside the live poker area for a while and observed the slumping players keeping their faces expressionless and their nonchalance under tight control.

I wandered back towards the slot machines to see how the farm girls were doing. From a distance I could see Amy and Darla hopping up and down, whooping it up pretty good. Carla merely smiled and sipped a red drink through a tiny straw. Her eyes opened wide again as she saw me walk up.

Turned out that Darla had won four hundred dollars on her machine. She decided to celebrate by upgrading their accommodations from two double beds to a suite. When they got their little black overnight bags and two fifths of whisky from their trunk, I lifted out two twelve-packs of bottled beer and a grocery bag of pretzels and chips. The suite consisted of a bedroom with two large beds and a sizable living room area with a kitchenette and small round table. Darla immediately went to get ice to put in the kitchen sink to chill the beer. Amy found a country music station on the clock radio on the counter and turned it up moderately loud.

When Darla came back, she got a deck of cards out of her bag and announced we were going to play Crazy Eights, with losers of each game being required to take a slug of booze. She put ice cubes in four hotel glasses and filled them with whisky.

"Looks like we're in for some serious drinking," I said as I watched her.

"Hell, honey, I ain't serious about nothing'," Darla said, shaking her little behind as she expertly and steadily dispensed the liquor.

"Now don't get too wild on this stuff," I said to Carla as I handed her one of the tumblers of amber liquid. "You know how crazy you get. I don't, but I assume you do." Her eyes were back to their old wide open position.

"I'll try to control myself," she giggled. Her little laugh was bubbly, like a happy mountain stream sliding over stones. I suddenly like her a lot. And I was feeling good, getting a sense of that feeling of excitement that comes when you're with good-looking women in a fun setting. Thank heaven for lively girls.

"Well, don't try too hard," I said. "Inhibitions can be such a downer."

We gathered around the round kitchenette table and the games began. I won pretty often and didn't knock back too much when I lost and I avoided the beer chasers, so I quickly fell behind the group in terms of sobriety. They started laughing more and harder, moved with more emphasis when they semi-danced to the radio music as they went to the sink for a beer or to the bathroom.

Sometime after midnight Darla found a radio station playing slow music. She put out both hands as she stood in front of me and we moved together to the middle of the room. Our dancing consisted primarily of swaying while we hugged with my cheek lightly leaning on her hair.

"We're taking the bedroom, Mitch," Amy announced suddenly from the doorway by the beds. She signaled to Carla to help her pull out the bed from the sleeper sofa. They worked together in drunken teamwork to put together a loose arrangement of blankets and pillows. Bedtime came pretty quickly after that. The women came out of the bathroom wearing pajama bottoms with their t-shirts and brushing their teeth to wish me good night. I got into my bed with my jeans and shoes lying within reach on the floor and was surprised to feel the room spinning as I closed my eyes in preparation for sleep.

Sometime in the night I felt a body slide in behind me and arms wrap around my neck and chest. A mouth bearing the combined scents of liquor and toothpaste breathed lightly into my ear and whispered, "Hello, baby." I reached behind me to feel a t-shirt and a bare bottom. There were two chances out of three that my bed partner was unmarried. When I turned for a kiss, the small part in the curtains that admitted light from the parking lot allowed me to identify who I was with. We made slow conventional love and fell asleep with the length of our bodies touching.

I awoke in the morning to an empty half of the bed and the sound of hair dryers blasting from the far bathroom. I dressed quickly and went down to the lobby to ask the desk clerk for a disposable razor and a toothbrush. He pulled them from a drawer right below the counter and included a tiny tube of toothpaste. I returned to the bathroom off the kitchen to freshen up. I came out to find the ladies dressed and made up, setting their packed bags by the door. I was already anxious to get back into the routine of my life, the Sunday morning paper and coffee, the running before lunch, a televised sporting event in the afternoon. The magic spell of the night before was long gone. I felt awkwardly stale and unappealing in my freshly showered body and yesterday's clothes.

My companions made a polite request to have me join them for breakfast, and didn't press when I said I had better be going. Amy gave me a little kiss on the cheek and Darla smiled and gave me a little farewell wave, her eyelids at half mast. Carla walked with me out the door and partway down the hall. She stopped me and pulled a little bottle out of her front pocket. "For the morning after," she whispered. "So you don't have to worry about the night before." I gave her a heartfelt hug of relief and appreciation.

I drove home thinking happy thoughts and not feeling any sense of guilt. Maybe my psyche just saw the final stage of the night as a continuation of the good times, maybe I was letting booze count as an mitigating factor. Maybe I was getting old and experiencing changing values. Maybe the randomness of the roulette wheel of chance encounters just came up "Carla" and there really wasn't that much to think about.

I settled comfortably back into the familiar pattern of my life. I was pleased and a little surprised to feel no guilt or obligation to follow up with my partner from the night before. While talking heads put forth vehement opinions on my television screen I considered rearranging my attitude towards gambling, risk versus reward, wealth preservation and a less conservative life style. Then I put on my running shoes and took off into the bursting colors of autumn.

While I was eating a late lunch of spaghetti and sautéed mushrooms and green peppers in red sauce, at a total cost of about two bucks, Megan called from college out in Tucson.

"Hey, old man," There was happiness in her voice as she gave me her standard greeting.

"Hey, kid,. How's it going?"

"Not bad. And you? Found any trophy wife candidates yet?"

"Candidates, sort of. No winners yet. Competitive spots are still available. How's your love life? I'm taking academic excellence as a given."

"Oh, I continue to sleep around." She laughed in the carefree way of the young and unencumbered.

"Well, thanks for the nightmare starter kit. Appreciate it."

"No problem. Actually, I keep pretty busy with school and working at the coffee place, going out with friends."

"That's more like it. But what about Brad, that guy who went out to dinner with us last time I was there? He was nice."

"He's great, but right now strictly in a backburner spot. When are you coming out again? I'm ready to get back up to the Grand Canyon."

"I'm pretty open. Let me know when you get some open time. Just give me three weeks notice so I can get a decent air fare." She and I had been to the magnificent striated stone valley the year before, for an afternoon and most of the next day. It was fall, after the heavy tourist season, sweatshirt weather, high deep blue sky with small puffs of bright white clouds. Walking there had been like stepping into a work of art, like being in Paris of the natural world, like being in love. We climbed down about a thousand feet on a narrow dust trail and seen walls where thousands of tons of tectonic plates had slid across each other. We hiked along the rim where we came across mountain goats in repose and elk migrating through the pines in slow intermittent staccato steps, moving one or two at a time then stopping in rigid poses. We listened to a Dylan CD on the rental car stereo and ate restaurant sandwiches at picnic tables set outside.

"You sound happy, Meg," I told her honestly, feeling buoyant just talking to her.

"I am. Like you say, when everyday life is fine, life is great."

"I'm glad."

"Here's something. My dorm floor is putting me up for homecoming queen."

"Doesn't surprise me. What did you think of it?"

"Not much." She laughed. "I just tried to have fun with the whole thing. During the interview I said my biggest concerns were world peace and rising beer prices."

"I'm not sure I can get behind the world peace one."

"Maybe I should reconsider."

"In any case let me know if you can make it to the full status of riding high in the convertible."

"Will do, although I think I'll lose points on attitude. What are you doing with our spare time?"

"This and that. Some golf and running, tennis with Ted, reading, getting out fairly often. I've started hanging out with Charlie and Margaret a little bit."

"Cool. They're nice. What are you reading?"

"More like rereading. Right now I'm reading Annie Proulx stories. But this year I've been going back through some favorites. I've been taking a leisurely stroll through Cheever stories."

"Okay, you're keeping busy, but when are you coming out?"

"I'll let you know. Is your mother coming out soon?"

"We've got a four day weekend coming up pretty soon. Maybe then. You can have the slot if she doesn't make it."

What a joy Megan has always been. It was so much fun having a daughter who spoke early and well, and had an advanced wit. I was unloading groceries in the kitchen one Saturday noon when she was four and heard her exchange with Kim at lunchtime. "What do you want me to fix you, honey?" "Ham sandwich." "We're out of ham." "Okay, ham and cheese." "I told you, we're out of ham. Now what do you want?" "Ham and tomato." "Okay, that's enough now. No ham. What do you want?" "Peanut butter." "Great. I can do peanut butter." "With ham."

Chapter Seventeen

I was on the elevator at work when Irene stepped on and asked me out. Just like that. She had been giving me the big smiles, eye contact that lingered a little longer than normal for two employees passing in the hall, looking away from small standing groups near the vending machines to watch me walk by.

We exchanged greetings then rode in silence. The elevator stopped. The door opened. Irene calmly extended an invitation. "Look, would you like to go out some night after work, have a drink?" She was assuming interest, as is reasonable from a beautiful woman. It's not like she hadn't been noticed. I had to smile at her nonchalant confidence, asking me out like she was requesting the time of day.

"I'm not doing anything this evening," she said. I liked the lack of pretending to have a busy social calendar that would be difficult for me to get onto.

"Tonight works. We could go across the street. Cup of coffee or a real drink."

"I'll be ready for a drinky drink."

"Drinky drink, okey doke."

"Around six?" she asked as she tugged gently on the end of her shoulder length brown hair. Good sign. Interested, somewhat nervous.

We walked across the street after work to the spacious bar area of an upscale Italian restaurant. It was just right, dark and almost full, no patrons standing in the aisles or two deep at the bar. For the first time in a long time I felt the quiet excitement of being with an attractive woman and having a feeling that it could turn into something.

Irene told me she was from a suburb of St. Louis, had worked after college for a few years at an accounting firm before returning to school for her MBA. She had joined us in pursuit of a work experience that involved more than the counting and accounting of money. Our conversation flowed easily. Up close the details of Irene's beauty were pronounced and obvious. The large eyes, perfect nose, high cheekbones and just right fullness of lips, a distinctive smile just a little off kilter. The brightness in her eyes and a return to occasional hair tugging let me know she was enjoying herself and at least moderate excitement in our being together. I felt a flutter myself, an urge to lean over and kiss those ripe red lips.

She asked me about writing with honest curiosity and envy. Without straining to seem interested, she let me talk about real writers and why I liked them and what they taught me, about art and about life. The only time she looked away a little bit was to pause to allow the sinking in and rumination of something I'd just said. She told me some stories from her professional jobs that were actually fairly entertaining, where she looked a little foolish or inexperienced.

"I've been married," I said. Just laid it out there in case she was wondering. Before it could become awkward to say it. "For many years." Also, although it was screamingly obvious, I wanted to make sure she knew I was fifteen years her senior. I wasn't nervous when I said it. Another good sign.

"Must have been rough."

"It's the past. Our daughter is away at college. Megan. She's out west. She's an adult now. So I'm pretty old."

"You seem like one of those men who will never be old. You give off a certain good humor and youthful energy." Irene smiled even more brightly. She leaned towards me, head bent forward. Her hair fell onto my hand grasping a scotch and water. Exciting. She spied an index card in my shirt pocket. There were handwritten notes on it. Her raised eyebrows and pointing fingers formed a silent request to look at it. I handed the card to her.

"Writing for work?" she asked.

"Well, yes, it is. Some ideas to consider for pages of a humor book. I'll look at them later tonight at home, think about them in the car, getting ready for or going to bed."

"Is that how the creative process works?"

"It's how mine works. Keeps thinking about ideas, sometimes after you thought you were done. Sometimes an answer just pops out. Sometimes not. Patience is definitely a virtue."

I found myself wondering how anyone as beautiful and personable as this young lady had gotten through college, undergrad and grad, plus a few years of working, without getting married. I couldn't stop looking for some previously overlooked physical flaw or off-putting personality trait.

"So you've just been in Kansas City for a few months?" I asked.

"Mmmmm, yeah, a few months, not long," she said with a sleepy expression and a laugh as though I'd said something amusing. She touched my arm lightly with the easy confidence of someone who has never known rejection. "I just got here. Not looking to leave. Sticking around. Kansas City, here I come."

"We've got some crazy little women here, but we can always use a few more."

She fanned out the index cards on the table and stared down at them. "I can't imagine being a creative writer, coming up with things out of nowhere," she said. "Staring at a blank space and having to fill it up with something that people would pay to read, even want to read for free. I'd freeze right up."

I was feeling very good about being with this sweet young lady. It was like being at the first part of a great meal where you've sampled everything and found them delicious.

"I will say that it is nice to have a talent, to be good at something that you enjoy and that can earn you a fine living, pay for the house and car and occasional treat. Also, you get to show off without looking like you're showing off. In that way it's like being beautiful."

"Well, that makes sense," she responded, that looking away indicating that she was processing the information and not just making a polite and expected response.

"I wanted to use an analogy you'd be sure to understand." She took the compliment without blushing or looking surprised, totally at ease with herself. Both of her hands were now touching my arm. I decided to prattle on a little longer. "It's fair and it's unfair. Like being seven feet tall and playing basketball. It's like being born a genius. The fruits of your labor are disproportionate to your labor. It's just the way life is."

"I'm really enjoying this, Mitch. Just having a drink and talking." Her eyes and tilted head asked if I wanted another round.

"I thought a drink would be a good first step. So good for me. Seemed a bit forward to suggest a week in Paris."

"Oh, for sure, that definitely needs to wait until a second date."

"No point in rushing things."

The bar section was now a little more than full. The women and men coming in seemed very young. Definitely more fashionably dressed than I was. Spikier hair. Irene didn't look up at any of them, even the athletically slender men in untucked shirts who stared at her on their way to their friends. She kept her gaze on me. Her fingertips danced lightly on my arm.

"More wine?" I asked.

"Wow, I don't know. Any more to drink and I'll want a cigarette."

"You smoke?"

"Used to in college. A little after that. Now just sometimes when I'm drinking." Irene's deep limpid eyes narrowed slightly into a hard look of seduction as she leaned her head back to expose more of her eager face. Her voice turned into a whisper. "Gives me something pleasurable to do with my mouth." The last word was mouthed silently and followed by a quiet laugh.

"Tease," I accused.

"I prefer the term flirt."

"You're right. Better word." I pointed to the index cards on the table. "Maybe you can help me with these. Just, you know, punch them up a bit." She pulled the reading glasses out of my shirt pocket and put them on, looking over the lenses to avoid an eye stabbing pain from the big magnification, and pored over the handwriting while chewing on a knuckle.

Some women look great from a distance then lose something in the details upon closer inspection. It might be a slight issue with skin or facial features being just a little bit off, not quite coming together. Could be a mouth that simply doesn't invite a kiss. Other women can look quite good seated with you in the car or across the table, their general silhouette just doesn't get it done. Irene had it all. You noticed her right away down a corridor, even one fairly crowded with other people. Up close the attraction remained intact. I was absolutely pulled to her. She literally had a magnetic effect on me. A gravitational pull hard to resist.

This feeling was new for me. Proximity to a beautiful woman doesn't usually give me the roiling in the stomach, tightness in the throat, hesitation in speech. I don't normally get the fear that if I speak, I'll talk too loud, in the volume of sudden love. Now I was afflicted with the early signs of those afflictions.

"I appreciate your editing help," I said. "I'm just a beginner. I've only been doing this for a few millennia. Just getting started."

She handed the cards to me. "Mitch, you know, I really am impressed. You've had to think up enough ideas to fill an encyclopedia. I just put numbers against basic formulas and principles. Standard stuff." She gave my arm a tight squeeze. The waitress asked if we wanted more drinks, and we did.

"You must have a bachelor pad," Irene said.

"Oh, you bet. All leather and pillows and strobe lights and big screen televisions. Very groovy. My smoking jackets are out being de-smoked or I'd let you have the whole experience."

"Wouldn't we be disturbing the stewardesses?"

"Ho, ho, yes, the stewardarrazi, the stewardi, the nubile ladies that put the wild in wild blue yonder. Not to worry about disturbing them. They come and they go. They're in and they're out. They land and they take off. I don't even know their names. I just call them by the cities they come from. Hello, Houston. Good-bye, Denver."

Irene was clearly having fun feeding me straight lines and getting responses. I'd nearly forgotten the exquisite joy of giving pleasure in the form of humor to a beautiful woman. I have a clear memory of the first time I had Kim really laughing hard and uncontrollably. Early in our dating life we attended a movie called <u>The Four Seasons.</u> I kept pretending to be confused about what season was being depicted on the screen. One scene opened with ducks waddling across a frozen pond with a few inches of snow on it. Kim asked me, "Okay, now this is easy. What season is that?" I paused and then said. "Duck season."

"I won't be part of a harem," Irene said.

"Afraid of a little competition? Can't handle fifty other women. Or maybe it's the tents. You don't like camping, is that it?"

"It's the camping. Definitely the camping."

The bar had gotten noisy with the extra people and the volume enhancing intake of liquor. The overhead music was drowned out. Cigarette smoke was noticeable. I didn't want to have a dinner/no dinner decision to make. I had scheduled a burger with Ted to have a legitimate reason to keep the evening brief.

A short thick guy brushed out table as he went to the bar. "Lush hour traffic," I noted. Irene's laugh carried more than amusement. It was like grape wine with hints of peach and walnut and raspberry. Much richer than the everyday stuff. We parted with my promise to call the number she'd written on one of my index cards. I even liked her handwriting.

Chapter Eighteen

A late night phone call from Margaret. "I know it's late," her quiet voice said.

"Not in the Ukraine."

"Thanks for not being annoyed." She sounded tearful and a little bit drunk.

"You're veritably sodden with drink."

"Come over, Mitch. Drive over. I've had just a bit to drink. Can't drive, better not. I want to show you something. You drive over here. Drive to my house."

"Maybe I could drive over."

"Please."

"Where's Charlie? You haven't gotten rid of him, have you?"

"He's playing poker. It'll probably go late."

The late summer night was cool and still, with a slight scent of the delicious fall weather to come. I put on jeans and a hooded sweatshirt. Even though I'd been asleep, I wasn't tired. I was looking forward to the drink Margaret would offer.

My next door neighbors were just getting back from somewhere. They're quiet, willing to say a quick friendly hello and pick up your newspapers when you're out of town. Good neighbors. He's probably around fifty and she can't be much over thirty. They go out walking quite a bit. When they first moved in about six months earlier, candle light swayed in the evenings behind drawn curtains and they spent Sunday mornings leisurely reading the paper on their big stone porch. He drives a larger new car. Hers is smaller and older with a few signs of rust.

Later on he started putting his golf clubs in his car trunk on Sunday mornings and she started planting flowers and small shrubs along the front of their house. The nighttime flickering of light came from a television screen rather than candles.

"Nice night," I said as I passed them on my way to the car.

"Getting cooler," he said amiably. She just smiled and nodded.

"Little bit."

As I pulled out, I saw the dark outline of a man sitting on a porch swing at the house across the street. The small orange dot of a burning cigarette was the only indication of life. He was a big guy who lived alone and rarely left his square of lawn. I'd never seen an unfamiliar car in his driveway. Silhouettes of card players around a kitchen table never appeared in a window. His house never had the vacated look of one whose owner is out of town for a few days. He kept his head down when checking the mailbox next to the street, never looked up and waved if I were pulling in, never asked if I was using anything on the lawn or if I knew a good plumber. I hoped he was happy in his solitude, content in his aloneness, his mind and spirit crowded with memories of exquisite happiness that involved romance which had ended well and brought an undiluted smile to the lips around the cigarette.

Margaret's silhouette was outlined in the front screen as I came into her driveway. She had an open high school letter jacket on over a thin nightgown. She held a beer can against her heart as if using it to soothe a recent bruising.

"I'm sorry to be such a bother, Mitch. I keep bothering you."

"No bother, Margaret. None at all. I always like seeing you."

Her eyes were moist.. "You don't have to say that."

"You had something to show me?"

We went inside. She took a photograph from the coffee table and handed it to me. It was Charlie and Margaret with Kim and me. We were all wearing swimsuits as we sat in a rented motorboat. We were just about to go water skiing.

"By now," Margaret said slowly, "By now I thought we would be going on cruises and off to Europe, not just down to the lake, not just for a few days, but for two or three weeks. But Charlie's off playing poker with the guys and I'm here with my little buddy." She held her beer up and wiggled it. "Want your own little buddy?"

"Beer sounds good."

"We did have fun, didn't we?" Margaret said, a little desperately, when she handed me my drink.

"Always a good time, and I shared your belief in the attaining of modest dreams."

"Everything just ended. All of a sudden."

Margaret pulled another photograph out of the jacket pocket. This one showed Charlie and herself on the crumbling concrete porch of their first house, a two bedroom ranch. They're sitting on metal kitchen chairs and other people are standing around them. The scene is taking place in a neighborhood making the transition from very old residents to very young ones. Margaret's sister, Diane, was visiting from Michigan. Alan, a brand new guy at Punchline at the time, is standing next to her. He would leave for a publishing job in New York within a few years. Kim and I are there with our arms around each other's waists.

Except for Charlie at thirty-one, we were all in our twenties. All of the women have the light first tans of summer, seemingly comfortable in the bodies that stay slender without effort. Staring at the snapshot, I could recall the shampoo scent of Kim's long straight hair and the feel of the sun's warmth rising from the concrete. And I could smile at the remembrance of cross currents of attraction within the group. Half of us are holding cigarettes. Most of us smoked then.

Alan had played tennis with Charlie and me earlier in the day. He was our equal in athletic skill and fairly close in trash talking ability. The picture was taken by a woman walking her spaniel. It was right before we went to the backyard to grill hamburgers and drink no-name beer and eat salads made from fresh produce purchased earlier in the day at the farmers market downtown.

Inside the house after dinner the stereo radio played reel to reel music that was new when we were in college. Its sound and pulse along with the continued drinking pulled us back into an earlier world where we felt we were living a gloriously romantic and even profound life. I know it was only rock and roll, but we liked it. Heavy piano chords, soaring electric guitar, punching harmonica, poetic lyrics. We sat and just listened for quite a while.

Late in the evening Margaret and her sister went out for more beer and cigarettes. They came back wearing each other's halter tops. When Charlie laughingly asked why, Diane answered "Why not?" It's so great when women do things like that, simple fun and simply sexy at the same time.

Charlie set up a screen and slide projector and showed slides of the trip he and Margaret had taken to Mount Rushmore. The audience provided most of the commentary. "America's first rock group." "Yeah, the real Stones." "Is Lincoln going gray or did it just snow?" "How many trees were destroyed to make Washington's his wooden teeth?" "Hey, they put in the wrong Roosevelt. Didn't anybody look at the plans?" "Amazing that they could capture Lincoln's melancholy and genius and empathy when sculpting with dynamite."

We played charades until almost dawn. It was late spring, almost summer. Kim and I would sleep with the bedroom windows open in our rental duplex and wake up late in a space golden with sunlight and smelling like the peonies right outside. I remember thinking then, this is a high point in my life, this is all I need. Kim was apparently hungry for something more, beyond going to job you didn't mind and seeing friends in your spare time, being able to pay the bills and save towards a home of your own for a growing family.

"There's something else I want to show you," Margaret said as she rose from the couch and pulled the letter jacket tight around her. She walked into the dim light of the dining room and came back clutching a small stack of plastic folders to her chest like a schoolgirl carrying homework. "Remember these?" She laid them on my lap and sat down. "I came across them when I was looking for the snapshots in the guest room closet."

I leafed through the typewritten pages. They were scripts for skits and monologues I had written for Charlie when Kim and I had first come to Kansas City. He was part of a group putting on a variety show benefit for a boys' home south of town. He had seen some my early humor writing for Punchline and thought I might be able to work up some material for the volunteer performers. I had approached the request in the same way that I do any writing. People talk about whether writing is done with high or low standards. Really there are just standards. In the skit pieces it was either clever or not. Figuratively speaking, One either made solid contact or one didn't. The ball either went in the general intended direction or it veered off. A golfer either gets on the green or misses. The tap-in for birdie or the rare hole-in-one are beyond your control. You apply talent and effort to get to amusing. Hilarious just happens.

The variety show ran for three performances. Friday and Saturday night and Sunday afternoon. The skits got huge laughs. The evening shows were well-attended. By Sunday afternoon, positive word of mouth attracted more audience members than the hall could accommodate. One skit had the city's celebrities cast in a parody of the Godfather movies. The mayor wakes up in his bedroom next to a smarmy local weatherman and screams to his startled wife that his enemies have put a horse's ass in his bed. Another bit featured historical figures in a living room watching a Chief's football game. Asked when they ran out of buffalo wings, Abe Lincoln intones, "Four scores and seven beers ago."

His wife Mary Todd says to a tipsy Julius Caesar that she hates it when the Chiefs lose because it makes her husband especially dour. After offering his sympathy the Roman leader excuses himself to go to the bathroom because the Boulevard beer is going through him like rain water through an aqueduct. At one point Mrs. Lincoln whips off her top and starts waving it around to celebrate a touchdown, revealing that she is wearing several layers of underclothing.

I did a stand-up act as Robin Hood addressing his band of merry men. "Allan Adale reports good response on his wandering minstrel tour. Women are tossing chastity belt keys onto the stage." "As you all know, Maid Marian used to be called Pretty Mary-O before she requested her current form of address. Now she's asking to be called by a new appellation, Hot Child In The City." "We're having trouble with the whistling arrows we use for communication. I've hired a whistle tuner to keep them on key."

"Mitch," Margaret said slowly, looking me over as though searching for something. "I read them all. Funny stuff."

"Thanks. It was fun. That was a long time ago."

"I was amazed. Especially your monologue. I asked Charlie about the show. He said you brought down the house and the director of the Lyric offered to hook you up with some if his connections on the east coast. He thought you could perform at clubs and write for television. You never followed up."

Kim had been all for our packing up and heading out for the glitter. But it didn't appeal to me, especially being on stage at night in a tight smoky room with an audience of drinkers. I imagined the laughs being alternately too easy and too hard to get. I get no thrill from adulation. No spark. I don't feel the love. I was ready to start a family with Kim. And anticipated quiet thoughtful conversations at dinner, balloons in primary colors on a mailbox to let partygoers know where the birthday child lived, lying in bed at night in contented aftermath. Attainable dreams in a lovely Midwestern city.

"I feel like I'm in the presence of brilliance," Margaret said, still scrutinizing me with meandering eyes.

"You had to stop short of 'genius,' didn't you?"

"Oh, I'll go with genius. It fits."

"Well, whatever. I think my greatest satisfactions are fairly primal. A winter breakfast of jellied toast and scrambled eggs and coffee. The feel of sun and breeze and anticipation on the first tee. Reading <u>Good Night Moon</u> to a two-year-old Megan while she sits safe on my lap in a pink robe and slippers. Little things mean a lot. At least to me."

I took a long swig to finish off the beer she'd given me while I tried to think of something clever to say. No luck. I suggested we end the evening and thanked her for the interest and the compliments. When I left she wasn't sad, just wistful. She smiled without effort when we parted. I tugged on the hem of the letter jacket and said that although her ensemble didn't match, she still looked fetching.

I read for a while when I got home. I finished a recently written memoir book by a talented young author. It was touching, funny and insightful. I especially liked his use of the long established device of something literal throughout that turns symbolic in the end. This work used a balsa wood glider. It was a simple diversion between father and son at various times in the narrative, but in the final pages it came it came to represent their light, soaring, unrestrained spirits.

As I lay on the couch in the comfortable drowse of reading fatigue and visions of Margaret's slender legs pressed against the slight fabric of her nightgown, I started to think about Emma Bovary, the heroine of Flaubert's fictional account of a pretty woman who seeks escape and transcendence above the mundane world through romanticism, attempting to live inside a misty dream. She become a martyr for her personal religion in her reach for ascension, risking and losing her marriage and her son and her life in the obsessive pursuit of an existence on a higher, more fulfilling plane.

Kim may have experienced some of the ennui so prevalent in the French novel. To her I may have seemed like a very close approximation of Emma's husband, a simple country doctor in a small city, a setter of broken bones and a deliverer of babies and not even a real doctor. And there I was, making a living providing copy for greeting cards and illustrated humor books. Not really a writer. The French author compares the husband to a workhorse tethered to a grinding wheel, doing the repetitive work thoughtlessly without complaint or ambition or attempts to flee, content to merely exist.

Kim once accused, "You just want a house with a white picket fence and a backyard with a big garden."

"Wouldn't have to be a big garden," I responded.

"Stop trying to be funny. I'm serious. I need more than that. Megan will be through with high school before we know it. We need to talk about ending this so-called marriage."

"I'm sorry you're unhappy. I really am. I tried. I say that I love you, notice your hair, compliment your cooking, call you from work, surprise you with flowers."

"Check,check, check. You do it all, don't you. What a guy. What a prince. I might as well be married to a computer program. Turn it on and out comes the stuff."

Maybe Kim was right. Maybe I was just going through the motions, satisfied to repeat the circular walk around a grinding wheel of a marriage, no longer seeking fulfillment in love's many splendors, settling for what lay in devotion to duty and commitment. I didn't think that was necessarily the case, but I wasn't sure. For instance, there was the little matter of Kim and Charlie. Their senses of humor were wired the same. Silly puns got tossed back and forth, goofy radio show hosts yakking on our shared car trips made them burst into laughter at the same instant. I never new them to be so intensely amused when they were apart. The two of them flirted openly, sometimes kissed on the lips. I never felt or showed jealousy or upset. Maybe that was part of the problem. What I thought communicated trust may have been seen as uncaring.

I doubt that anything ever went on between them, but I don't know. I might get angry if I found out that something went on, but I might not. I don't mind not knowing. Margaret and I had plenty of little electric moments, the lingering caress or the lengthy thank you hug for a Christmas gift, a mild sexual current that buzzed when the four of us were together for an evening. I saw it as a pleasant side effect to friendship and I never wanted or expected it to go very far. I had never felt intensely possessive of Kim. She has a beautiful bright smile, a lovely and very feminine face, a slender well-proportioned body that moves with an easy grace of swaying hips and long light arms. Maybe I took her for granted and that could have hastened the end of things. I could see that men were looking at her and she never seemed to notice or reciprocate.

When we first started dating in college my guy friends expressed obvious envy. Maybe Kim sensed my lack of jealousy and saw it as a sign of my not fully caring. I wouldn't have agreed at the time, but times have changed.

Towards the end of our marriage Kim would leave the house in the car for several hours. She'd stay out long past the time Megan and I had gone to bed. I never had the urge to call Charlie at home and see if he was in when Kim was out. I would lie in the dark and distract myself with thoughts of projects at work and various mental computations involving short and long term finances. Sometimes I'd agitate myself by replaying incidents where Kim's management of money had precipitated a testy argument. One time she went to an art fair with Margaret while I took toddler Kim to the zoo. Kim paid cash for a framed water color that took out all the money we were to use for groceries during the last week before payday. That led to a juicy fight.

I had to reach back a ways to get to that event. Things had changed so much financially for us between the days of being newlyweds and the bitter final days of being a couple. We started with so little money, barely enough to pay the bills. We only went out to eat at a sit-down restaurant on birthdays and anniversaries. We had our first apartment in the university's brick apartment for married grad students. It was just up the hill from the Iowa River. We'd walk along the waterway for hours, indulging in the laughably cheap habit of smoking cigarettes on the way to a doughnut shop where we'd get takeout coffee and sometimes stopping at a small stand of sheltering trees where we'd lie on soft yellow grass where we cold hear mingled whispers of wind and water, and feel the warm lotion of sunlight on our unclothed bodies as passion and laughter overtook us. Those afternoons seemed to hold all the good things a life can encompass.

Lying in bed at night I sometimes went over incidents where I had to wonder if I had done things wrong. On a Fourth of July when Megan was two, Kim wanted to accept an invitation from Charlie and Margaret to join them at an extravagant fireworks show near downtown at an expanse of flat ground near the World War I museum. Getting there required driving to a shuttle bus area on the Plaza, standing in a long line to be transported to a spot several blocks from the viewing area, which you reached by making a long uphill climb, finding a place among the mass of people with their blankets spread and coolers open, then waiting for well over an hour to see a twenty minute show, which Megan would sleep through.

Kim was more than happy to endure the ordeal, would have done it cheerfully with nary a discouraging word, would have done most of the holding of our limp little sleepyhead. I wouldn't agree to it. I called the whole thing much too impractical. We ended up driving to a display just a few miles away with easy, close parking and plenty of room on the lawn. After just a few bursting bombs of colored lights had been sent into the sky, some freakish jump of sparks caused the whole thing to implode on itself and set off a massive inferno of loud bangs and commingled neon flashes. We left for home as wailing ambulances started showing up. I tried to find some sort of symbolism in it all, but never came up with anything.

Maybe Kim was right about a lot of things. Maybe I was just lazy or lacking in motivation about the marriage and she was the one willing to put a lot of effort into something that had created brilliant exploding thrills for a pretty long time.

Chapter Nineteen

One of the common experiences of business life, even in a smaller company like Punchline, is occasional attendance at daylong seminars. Typically, they take place in a large generic room inside a two-story brick building surrounded by trees of medium height with broad leaves inside a building of a fairly big but not huge city. Half an hour before anything on the schedule happens, attendees help themselves to coffee and orange juice and simple food, usually bagels and slices of melon. The early bird gets the blueberry bagel, while late arrivals are stuck with cinnamon-raisin bagels and the non-fat vegetarian cream cheese. The "light breakfast" is a perfect metaphor for the entire day: Not bad, efficiently provides something of value without making a mess, requiring very little effort from the participants.

On a Thursday morning in early winter I found myself in a suburb of Kansas City in a large plain room just outside the beltway in a setting called Corporate Woods along with Ted and Charlie, Harper and one of his eager young managers. As I chewed my cinnamon-raisin bagel, I looked at the front wall where a PowerPoint slide outlined the day's itinerary. The overall theme was Innovation. Fine with me, although it seems a bit like going to a business seminar where the theme is Business. Isn't innovating just a part of everyday business life? Well, what the hell, I've learned something helpful from any seminar I've been to. And there is some benefit to hearing what the speakers have to say, some ideas to be gained from the discussion in the breakout groups and the question and answer sessions with panelists towards the end of the day.

That Thursday I really enjoyed two younger featured speakers. One was from a company whose main business was camera film, and the other worked at a flashlight company. According to their speeches, both of their firms were struggling to grow while new product teams brought forward ideas that their top management kept turning down. Every year for seven years the highest ranking managers of the film company went to the annual New Product Ideas session and heard about the concept of disposable cameras. Seven years in a row the idea was rejected, usually with the admonition that this was a *film* company and not a camera company. When an overseas company flooded the American market with inexpensive throw-away plastic cameras that created annual revenue of forty million dollars, the speaker's firm scrambled to make up for year of lost profit in a new market.

The guy from the flashlight company told a similar tale. He was an engineer who had been rehabbing a house in midtown Chicago on nights and weekends. He used the company's work lamps and flashlights in the process. He was continually frustrated at not being able to quickly and easily arrange the illuminating devices so that it would shine directly at the precise area he was working on while leaving both hands free. With a small team at his workplace he developed a flashlight with a long handle that could bend into different shapes, wrap around pipes or rafters and stand on its own. The team built a working prototype that tested well with focus groups. Senior management was not impressed. The firm eventually did so poorly with sales of existing products that a whole team of new top management was brought in to run things. They had nothing ready to go so they gave the new bendable tool a try. Within eighteen months it accounted for forty percent of sales.

In companies with a long history of success in a particular field they seem to be largely incapable of the leaps of imagination that upstarts can achieve. The light bulb didn't come from a candle company though its top managers were communicating by telegram, probably on a daily basis, and therefore had exposure to the possibilities of electricity as a power source for decades before Edison. The automobile didn't emerge out of the R & D barn of a horse drawn carriage company even though the Industrial Revolution had produced steam engines that could stamp out buggy parts and people had been traveling on railroads for decades. The personal computer didn't come from IBM. Folgers Coffee never dreamed of selling a few ounces of brown brew and steamed milk for four dollars.

I tend to end up thinking that organizers of business seminars operate under the false notion that people in middle manager and staff positions who attend their sessions need assistance in generating and identifying good ideas. I believe it has more to do with senior managers' inability to be open to radical thought. It might be too threatening to the company and to the individuals running it. It could also have something to do with a modern nation that has stopped placing great value on knowledge and experience, opting instead for hiring and quickly promoting men and women with Master's Degrees in general business, a certificate acquired largely through studying and critiquing case histories of companies in a simplistic fashion isolated from the vagaries and complexities of the real world, with no apparent need to have deep information directly related to the business being evaluated in the classroom. They could be dismantling and reassembling a media conglomerate one day and a waste management business the next without any knowledge of television production or sewage treatment. Observing from a distance, these graduate students may have seen problems and issues as easy to resolve without regard to physical laws, human nature, corporate culture, a complex economy, laziness and the limits of the human mind.

Maybe it has a lot to do with working at a small company, but operating a successful business or launching a new venture that to a large degree actually works has never seemed that complicated or mysterious to me. For example, at some point years ago I spent some time paying attention to the most highly rated television comedies and reading random periodical articles on current trends in humor. It was pretty obvious that there was a trend towards humor that was more reality based, less rooted in the clever twist and the just plain goofy and the cheap scatological or risqué. Largely gone were kinds of jokes that had been around since I heard them as a kid on televised variety shows, things like "My wife decided to try facial mud packs to improve her looks. Worked for a while. Then the mud fell off." And other jokes from the male point of view, like "Just returned from a pleasure trip. Took my mother-in-law to the airport."

After a few conversations with Eunice and Charlie, I asked some of our free-lance writers to go in the realism direction and include some tries from the female perspective. I wrote some myself. One was "Let's get together for our traditional diet lunch---Small salad, diet soda, wedge of cheesecake."

Pretty quickly I had enough material to create a few books and a bunch of greeting cards. Eunice was all for putting out some things at retail. We stuck some in various outlets around the country. I wasn't surprised when they sold really well and became a staple in our product lines.

Still I listened pretty closely to what was being said at the generic room seminar. I don't fall into one of the two typical categories of seminar participants: The Deeply Inspired and the Openly Cynical. The former sit up front, ask a lot of questions and take voluminous notes on paper or laptop computers. The cynics are the largest takers of the free food, sit in the back, doze off sometimes during presentations and account for most of the empty seats in the afternoon sessions. I neither condemn nor applaud either group, as I find rational reasons to embrace and discard both attitudes.

I have gotten some benefit from these things in the form of general tips about setting priorities, dealing with difficult people and tough business situations, general problem solving and, I can honestly say, motivation about persevering against unfavorable odds and not quitting despite repeated rejections and setbacks. The cited examples do give me encouragement, possibilities to consider in my personal and professional life. There's also the continuous improvement thing, making me stop and ponder how I could turn a fine situation into a great one. I enjoy hearing stories of success and lessons learned from failure. I get energy from the enthusiasm of people like the flashlight guy and the camera film guy. I like to be reminded that fresh approaches yield better than average results simply because of their freshness. A lot of think about and none of it unpleasant.

Out of politeness and some degree of genuine curiosity, I paid attention to all speakers introduced by the woman leading the event. She was around forty, very thin, short plaid skirt. Did that sexy thing where women wear a little open necked jacket with no blouse. She had long straight brownish blonde hair framing a narrow face with large expressive, sparkling blue eyes. She looked pretty good as she moved around the podium in her high heels. She spoke rapidly and clearly, punching key words as she rolled along.

Lunch was served in a room as unadorned as the meeting room. The forty of us in the seminar went to a buffet of cold cuts, bowls of salads and chocolate chip cookies. Round tables for six were set around at random. I followed Ted through the food and beverage line before we sat down at an empty table. After a few minutes Harper and his young protégé sat down with us. Don's first words were spoken with a mouthful of food from his heavily laden Styrofoam plate. He said, "I'd like to give our hot moderator a bit of Dondo's ol' Powerpoint, if you know what I mean." His assistant laughed and nodded knowingly. Ted smiled with a kind of politeness. I sipped ice tea and looked away.

The woman moderator came to our table and stood behind an empty chair between Ted and Harper, directly across from me. Her smile and pointing finger were requests for permission to sit with us.

"The pleasure is all me," Ted said, reaching down to slide out her chair. She set down a plate holding a few pieces of fruit and a slice of turkey.

"You're eating light," I commented, then reading her name tag, added, "Kristi."

"Don't want to get sleepy after a big meal. I'd hate to yawn during opening remarks. Leaves a bad impression. Shows a lack of interest."

"If you need a place to sleep, I have an idea," Harper said, leaning heavily towards her. She pretended not to hear his cute remark and changed the subject, saying, "I see by your name tags that you all work at Punchline. I've bought a lot of your books as small gifts. They're very funny."

"Ted and I are in charge of the funny copy, so thanks," I said. "And you're right, we do all work there. We're like the Four Dwarfs. Ted is Trendy, I'm Oldie, the young man is Peppy, and that guy.." I pointed at Harper "...is Pudgy." Looking hurt and angry, Harper took a huge bite from his huge sandwich.

"You're not by any chance Snow White, are you?" Ted asked.

"Not by a long shot, Trendy," Kristi answered. "Not nearly that pure."

"Okay, then," I said. "I was going to warn you about the fruit salad. Mandarin oranges, walnuts, lemon peel, poisoned apples."

We chatted for another twenty minutes. I was curious about Kristi's tolerance for the constant air travel her job required. This led to us all telling our most dramatic story about long delays, frightening weather and lost luggage. Kristi won with a story of the wheels of her jet touching the water of a lake that adjoined a runway in a close call. I noticed that she wasn't wearing a wedding ring. I wondered about her relationship status and whether she had children, but I didn't think it was proper to ask.

Kristi ate her food in small infrequent bites, chewing slowly, dabbing her lips daintily with her napkin. When she was talking and when I was talking, she didn't look at me. If someone else were carrying the conversation, she stared at me with open eyes whether I looked back at her or not. She twisted the simple metal necklace that lay against the bare skin above the V in her jacket. Now and then she held her folded arms pressed against her chest. Harper remained mostly silent in the cold shadow of her disinterest towards him.

A few minutes before the hour Kristi excused herself to prepare for the start of the afternoon session. It began precisely on time and proceeded pleasantly enough. I ended up in a breakout group with a couple of investment people and a middle-aged woman in management at a large chain restaurant. We completed our various assigned discussions in short order and filled the open time by comparing our working lives. Not the worst way to spend an afternoon. The whole thing wrapped up around five.

Ted had picked me up that morning on his way in. He was supposed to have a drink with Harper in the hotel bar and he asked me to join them. I wasn't too crazy about the idea, but what could I do?

The bar was dark and spacious with lots of expensive wood. I figured it probably added an extra dollar to the cost of our drinks. Harper had ducked out early on the day's business and had been sitting in the bar for over an hour. He'd obviously been drinking for a while. His had a kind of vacancy and he smelled of alcohol.

"What a waste of a day," he said right away, cocktail glass tight in his beefy fist. "Well, except for the hot moderator. I wouldn't kick her out for eating crackers in bed." My response to that bit of hilarity was to look at Ted with the classic dull lidded why-are-we-here stare coming from a tilted head. I resumed normal posture when Kristi strode up to the bar with her small black wheeled suitcase in tow. The bartender fetched two bottles of water while she scribbled something while leaning on the heavy cherry wood counter. Then she walked briskly to our table.

"I forgot to give you my business cards at lunch," she said, doling out one to each of us. She quickly and expertly extricated her hand from Harper's clumsy attempt to clutch it. "One for you, Oldie. Here's yours, Trendy. And, of course, Pudgy."

She arranged her purse on her shoulder and straightened her jacket and overcoat before turning to leave. "Call or email me if you have any questions. Nice to meet you."

Her card for me had her handwriting on the back. Harper was watching me as I read "If you ever find yourself in San Francisco call me. I'll show you a good time." There was a smiley face above her signature, which had two tiny hearts for dots.

Harper ordered a double scotch on the rocks from our waitress, a buxom woman in tight black slacks and a white blouse with a red vest. She was neither young nor old. She had medium length permed dark hair and a down home friendly manner. When she brought his drink Harper sat dully while she counted out bills and coins in change. Without offering a tip, he stuffed the money into the pocket of his dress shirt. His vacant stare followed the woman across the room and through a swinging door.

"Aren't you going to tell us what you'd like to do to her?" I asked.

"What?"

"You know, how you'd like to nail her or put it to her or whatever. Let us know what a player you are." The vague sleepy expression on his face snapped to a sharper image. His eyes narrowed to piercing slits, hands clenched into beefy fists. His posture became more upright.

"Why don't you just shut up. You're such a stud and all."

"Hey, hey, hey," Ted said, directing a hand with palm up at each of us. "Let's all just calm down and play nice. There's nothing here that an order of fried cheese sticks can't smooth over. Hell, I'll even pay for a third of the cost. First rule of fried cheese eating is no fighting. What do you say?"

"Harper, someday maybe you'll get a little thing called class. You sure don't have it now."

"Let's go outside and we'll see who has what."

"What, a fight? Me against a drunk. No contest."

"Let's go. Right now," Harper said. He struggled a little stand up. Ted got up also. The burly bartender slung a towel over his shoulder and walked around to the front of the bar. I wasn't worried. Ted and the bartender wouldn't let anything happen as long as I kept things in the room. Knowing that made me more confrontational.

"Let's have it out right here," I fairly shouted, bolting to my feet and spreading my arms in invitation. Ted got between us, a hand on each of our chests. "Let's take a deep breath now," he said. "We're all friends deep down beneath this desire to punch each other into next Thursday. Easy now. Easy." He moved his hands off of us and backed away. "Tell you what. Don, you've had quite a bit to drink. Let me drive your car to take you home. Mitch, you follow us to Don's house. Let's all end this as friends. Come on now."

Harper left to find a restroom. "He lives way out south off Mission Road. Hundred and fifty-first. Third place on the right," Ted said.

"I'll look for the nude statues on the lawn."

"No ogling."

Ted took his keys slowly from his pocket and handed them to me. He put some dollar bills on the table and escorted a returned Don Harper out of the bar. It was fifteen minutes of driving to get to the Harper residence in a suburban development called Patrician Estates, several acres of earth tone two-story homes without distinction. The two of them spent a good twenty minutes inside the house while I listened to the radio with the engine off. The FM station was alternative music. A young guy with an acoustic guitar was singing about a lover who had left him for another. How original. I punched AM and got sports talk. Not broadcasting a competition. Just saying nearly hysterical things about college conference basketball. I ended up opting for silence and the soothing music of pleasant thoughts. I visualized an acceptably attractive woman in a v-necked sweater who kept glancing my way at the seminar earlier in the day. She smiled a few times and ran her fingers lightly over the smooth exposed skin above the front of her sweater.

I got out of the car to move to the passenger side when Ted came out. "Did you put him to bed, make sure he brushed his teeth up and down not sideways, said his prayers?" I asked.

"He wanted to talk," Ted as he started the engine.

"Well, I don't really care to hear what he wanted to discuss. Probably annoy me."

"He wanted to talk about you."

"Hey, if he's offended, that's too bad. He deserves to be offended."

"He wasn't offended," Ted, smiling at the idea.

"Good. I'd hate to live with the all-consuming guilt and self-loathing that would come with knowing he had hurt feelings."

"Not offended. He's jealous."

"He's jealous," I repeated without inflection.

"Of you."

"He's jealous of me."

Ted laughed, then said, "This is going to take all night if you keep repeating everything I say."

"Repeating what you say."

"He sees how women look at you, probably more closely than you do yourself. At work, at the tennis club, out and about. And it makes him feel jealousy. He knows how many women you could have if you had the inclination. You're funny. You look good. You're not...pudgy."

That last bit made me feel kind of bad. No need to be cruel.

"He's only got a willingness to be aggressive towards women and the ability to absorb the shock of rejection. Those are the only two cards he can play. Nothing else. He can only try to force himself onto women in the hope that they will tolerate him for a while."

"He's not jealous of you?" I asked.

"He doesn't measure himself against me. You and he are about the same age. He's watched you for a long time, heard women at work talk about you."

We drove in silence for several minutes. I felt a small pang of regret. Nothing serious. "I still don't like him," I said finally.

"Don likes you. Thinks you're funny and interesting. Got a little tearful talking about you. Said that you and Lynn were the It couple when you first showed up at Punchline. Everyone wanted you at their parties. You didn't come to his."

"I don't even remember being invited."

"I wouldn't tell him that. You might cut him some slack."

"So he really said all that?"

"Well, he *was* drunk."

"Yeah, he was drunk."

"You're repeating me again."

"I am repeating you again."

"You don't realize all the things about yourself that draw people to you."

"Eunice said pretty much the same thing recently. Maybe there's something to that." The car's heater had filled the space with a pleasant warmth. I could have ridden for a long time on Ted's leather seats.

"You don't feel special?"

"I feel like an everyman. A face in the crowd. An incredibly handsome face in the crowd. A chiseled, gorgeous, compelling, movie star quality, one in a ......"

"That'll do."

"I could go on."

"Please, don't."

"Home, James."

"Don't call me Shirley."

"I called you James."

"Okay, then. I left him on the couch."

"He's probably used to sleeping alone."

"I suppose," Ted said. "I felt sorry for him, though. It's just natural to try to attract the attractive. Almost a reflex. Guys like that must go through a lot of rejection. I can't imagine." He stared ahead. Maybe he was imagining. I suddenly remembered a time when I was about twelve at the town's swimming pool, starting to really notice how the older girls looked in their swimsuits and how the water ran off their naked skin when they came up the silver ladders at poolside. Another kid was there that day. I knew him a little. A few giggling girls had been splashing me and ignoring him. Afterwards he was telling me that he despaired of ever being with girls because of his looks. I stared at his face and realized for the first time that he really wasn't very attractive. For the first time in my life I thought of someone as homely. The long drooping nose, close set eyes, rubbery mouth. And he was just a child. A pretty nice kid. I felt pretty sad right away and didn't know what to say. I probably just swam away.

"Okay, Ted, tell you what . You set up a lunch for the three of us. You, me and Harper. Just to have something to eat and to hang out. No big deal. I'll just be friendly and we'll see how it goes."

The following week we had our lunch at a pizza place on the Plaza. The pizzas have unusual toppings like artichoke and feta cheese and meatloaf. Yeah, that's worth paying twice the normal price, I was thinking as I looked over the menu.

"How about if we get a pitcher of beer and split a large pizza with everything on it, a supreme or whatever they call it," Ted suggested. We agreed and that's the order he gave the server. She was a young thin woman with short hair half black and half red. She wore a red sleeveless top that fully exposed a red and black feather that extended up her arm and onto her shoulder. She looked striking. Ted complimented her on her look and made a mild joke about being tickled by the feather. Her response was to smile without blushing.

Don was fidgety and distracted. He seemed to be stifling the urge to say something. I left the floor open by sipping my water with wedge of lemon and looking around. Ted did pretty much the same thing, sitting in patient silence.

"It's nice to get out," Don said. "I usually eat at my desk. Have Marie get me something from a takeout place." Ted shot be a quick let-it-pass glance, a stern look and a smile. "At home it's just me in front of the TV, food on the coffee table."

"We'll have to call you sometime," I offered, smiling back at Ted. "We'll do that next time we have the underwear models over for caviar and champagne. Usually that's a Thursday, unless we're getting back massages from the Italian grape stomping girls." I stretched my back and extended my arms.

"Don't forget the maple syrup breakfasts with the lady lumberjacks," Ted said.

"Some time we'll have to save some syrup to put on food, like pancakes or waffles."

"No hurry," Ted said.

"All sounds good to me," Don said. "It's probably closer to reality than you're letting on. I hear women talk about you two, their voices coming down the hallway or over the tops of the cubicles. 'He's so funny.' 'He's so cute.' 'If he asked me out for a drink, I'd be thrilled.' Whatever you two have, I'd take some."

I was caught off-guard by his candor, the willingness to just put it out there. "Are you sure you're hearing about the right guys? Me, especially," I asked sincerely.

"Don," Ted said soothingly, "As you go through this journey we call life, you'll find that the man we know as Mitch, as great as he obviously is to the likes of you and me, has a bit of a blind spot when it comes to his own level of hotness."

"Okay, kind of hard to believe though," Don said. He studied the thick slice of pizza on the little plate in front of him. He lifted it with a thick hand and bit into the concoction. He ruminated as he chewed and finally said, "I mean, look at your wife."

"I know I did," Ted chimed in.

"Ex. My ex-wife," I corrected. "Had a wife and couldn't keep her."

"At least for a while you had a babe for a wife. I don't mean to be offensive. I hope I'm not. I don't mean to be disrespectful."

"And I don't mean to argue. I'm just pointing out that at least one woman was able to resist my irresistible powers."

"I'm sorry about the divorce. I know it's tough. My second marriage ended after I got back from a long golf weekend in the Ozarks."

Ted perked up. "Hillbilly golf? Collared shirts not required, collared greens are."

I jumped in. "If you take a cart, keep the mule on the cart path."

Ted's turn. "Breaking a hundred means counting that high."

Back to me. "Club of choice is not the five-iron. Tire iron."

Don wasn't laughing but he was smiling broadly and his body posture was one of relaxation. I had a sense that he enjoyed being with us and feeling included. Up close I could see the large pores on his face and the rolling flesh on his chest and stomach pressed against his dress shirt. He turned a little more serious as he described driving up to his house after the golf outing and finding that his wife had hauled away everything except his desk with the computer and a closet of his clothes and the tools and lawn equipment in the garage. He said he had been totally blindsided. Wow. I was hoping the lady in red and black would lay a hand on his shoulder when she put our check on the table. She didn't, but she let Ted linger in touching her hand when he took the bill from her. Don just stared at her.

"One thousand one, one thousand two, one thousand three," Ted said when she left.

"What?" Don asked.

"Look but don't leer. A couple of seconds then look away, smiling. Right, Mitch?" I nodded in agreement. I had never thought about it, but it was exactly how I carried out the drill. Don shook his head slowly in the manner of someone admitting he has a lot to learn.

On the way back to the office I asked him about this quarter's sales, inventory levels and the projections for the year's revenue and I marveled at his ability to remember and mentally organize all those numbers.

Chapter Twenty

In late summer I flew to New York City for the first annual stationery show, a huge convention featuring hundreds of companies and individuals who make and sell greeting cards, calendars and small gifts inscribed with messages. It's endurable . Three days of going up and down aisles looking at products, making notes, chatting with vendors. Just part of the job and not especially arduous. There's time in late afternoon and evening to walk the streets and see the sights. Rockefeller Center with its ice skating rink, the Empire State Building, the Central Park merry-go-round from Catcher In The Rye. Plus, Manhattan is great for cheap good food sold on the street from silvery metal carts. The hot dogs are a small feast for a couple of bucks.

The first time I visited, I was surprised and pleased to discover that the city's so small. One evening I traversed Greenwich Village, SoHo, Little Italy, the theater district and Fifth Avenue. Little Italy is only a few blocks wide, a distance you can cover on foot in a matter of minutes. I had imagined a much larger metropolis, especially given the millions of people who populate it. I brought my Midwestern sense of population density with me. If the city had the sprawling structure of Kansas City, it would have encompassed a huge expanse.

Every trip I take to New York involves walking down to the theater district just before supper time and looking into the ticket outlet offering half price on that evening's performance. It is quite a bargain, but it's not the big deal it used to be. Kansas City gets a fair amount of traveling troupes performing the most popular plays from Broadway. The production values are almost as good as what you'll in the large apple. Once the great dialogue gets written, there is an endless supply of talented actors, dancers, musicians, and singers to bring it all to life.

In my younger days my impression of self was formed partly by televised variety shows and half hour comedies out of the Northeast. My fellow Midwesterners were depicted as hicks from the sticks, rubes and boobs. We were all naïve, unsophisticated, timid, terrified of walking the teeming sidewalks of the big city. I honestly wondered all through my hometown schooling and first year of college what higher level of literature was being pursued by New York students while I was reading Salinger and Fitzgerald, Faulkner and Hemingway, on my way to Kafka and Joyce, Eudora Welty and Flannery O'Conner. I was astonished to discover in early adulthood the Modern Library's list of the top hundred novels written in English and see that I had read half of them, and all in the top twenty.

I was able to take a bit of lighthearted revenge against Gotham provincialism during one stationery show visit. It was at a table on a terrace outside a Manhattan night club, twenty stories up with a view late evening view of the empire state building and the stunning Chrylser building tower. Eunice had left me there with half a dozen employees of the publishing house specializing in books for young adults. While she conferred inside the club with the younger workers' boss about a possible project between our two companies, I was with a crew of editors, personable young men and women in various types of black apparel.

I knew I looked as though I had just come off a golf course in my white polo shirt and inexpensive khaki pants, but my companions didn't seem to notice and I wasn't self-conscious. We were served drinks by a petite long-haired waitress in a tight dress as we looked at the skyline and got acquainted.

During the standard exchange of background information, my new friends learned that I had attended the University of Iowa. They were aware of, and interested in, the school's writing program in fiction and poetry, and the well-regarded writers who taught there. They had heard of the pretty campus with its rolling hills and the quiet river running through it, the stolid stately school buildings carefully preserved for a century and a half. I admit I was surprised at their knowledge of my part of the country and their positive perception of it. I was pretty much expecting a smug superiority and cracks about little old ladies from Dubuque. They asked about certain writers in residence and I was able to give them some fresh insights and personality sketches and authors' thoughts on writing.

The New Yorkers in my midst all had East Coast backgrounds. They asked about my upbringing and seemed to express genuine envy at my boyhood freedom to wander miles from home on any free afternoon, out into sparkling farm country along tree lined creeks or into town to shoot baskets or to swim at the pool among young girls with butterscotch tans. I could ride my bike to the downtown square or play golf until dark on a nine-hole course set in a river valley and surrounded by verdant hills of grass and crops lined up in staggered relief like a Grant Wood version of the reddish purple mountains of Georgia O'Keefe's southwest.

"We think it's a big deal to see a squirrel in Central Park," said a small woman with dark curly hair and a pin on her black dress that looked like a pair of green pastel mints.

I contrasted the obvious display of great wealth in their home city with the less clear manifestation of money in well-maintained farm buildings and hundred thousand dollar planting and harvesting set prominently in front of barns near roads of gravel or tar or simple dirt not much changed since the days of the Oregon Trail.

"Do the well-to-do plow fields by sitting in tractors behind a chauffer in a bib overalls and little flat black cap?" asked a very thin man with large features and a mouth locked in a perpetual smile.

They do," I said. "And the chauffer also wears very white work gloves. One of his duties is to hold the outhouse door open when the owner enters and exits." I pantomimed the gesture of the servant waiting on his employers and bowing in deference.

"Kind of a shitty job," said the thin man, getting a good laugh from his companions.

"Chauffer. No wonder the price of bread keeps going up," said the curly girl.

"It's the overhead," I agreed.

The wind came up suddenly, causing us to place our drinks on cocktail napkins. I told the assembled group about being able to identify types of trees by the pitch and rhythm of the wind blowing through their branches and their unique foliage. Gusts filtering through pine trees is steady and clean, kind of a whistle. Cottonwoods with their soft pliable branches produce a sound that is more full-bodied with rapidly rising and falling in intensity. I talked about the richness of the black moist soil, more valuable and life-sustaining that the richest of coal or oil, that created wealth for farmers.

I described a culture of helping a neighbor before assistance was requested. I told of sitting on my family's front lawn across from a field of ripening green corn as the heavy drops from a hurtling rain cloud stampeded across the broad outstretched leaves and raced toward my way, full of coolness and summer relief.

I relayed the story of a grain elevator manager, new to town and soon known to all those in the county who grew and harvested crops, who quickly became a community favorite along with his energetic wife and two polite children. His lack of experience caused him to check without a safety rope the tons of grain stored inside in deep bins. He stumbled and fell in and drowned in a crushing dry sea. The mood of the town in mourning was palpable for weeks in quieter conversations and in the frequent pauses when people sighed and looked westward to where the big white deadly monolith sat next to the two-lane highway.

Someone asked me about tornadoes. I described going to basements and potato cellars for safety when the dark sky turned a sickly green and the wind screamed like a locomotive. I went on in the severe weather theme to tell them how a hailstorm with frozen stones the size of baseballs could destroy a season's planting in twenty minutes. Winter blizzards left huge drifts that required ropes being strung from farmhouse to barn so that a person doing chores would not get lost and freeze to death a hundred yards from home.

"Kind of makes a subway ride in January seem like no big deal," said a blonde with full red lips and the high cheekbones of a model.

"Wouldn't know. We have a few subways in farm country. We built them and just wondered why." Then I made a leap into a topic that seemed to bring more amusement than interest to my audience. I compared literature to homegrown tomatoes. This earned me the nicknames of "Proust of the Plains" and "Edgar Allen Poor." Great books and red produce contain a double benefit. The tomato is a tasty treat and a nutritional powerhouse. Reading superior fiction is a pleasurable activity with an instructive component, elements of insight and philosophy. That didn't spark a big discussion.

In the distance faint thunder sounded as a black cloud rose up on the horizon. The muted rumbling was in sharp contrast to the sharp cracks I experience back home. "You know," I said. "The Midwest thunder is a lot louder than what you get here and the threat it carries is taken a lot more seriously. Many people are killed by lightning on the fairly flat, unsheltered crop fields."

"With all the big buildings here, I never even think about lightning," said the woman with dark ringlets. "I worry more about freak like frizz from the humidity."

"Totally opposite out in the heart of the country," I replied pausing to sip from a bottle of beer. "Imagine being out in the middle of a flat field during spring planting. You're astride a tractor. No roof. A huge hunk of natural electrical conductor. You're the highest lightning target for miles around and a fast moving storm comes blowing in, sharp bursts of thunder sound like loud rifle shots."

"So you head home," said the Frizz.

" You have to head home. Not on the tractor. You hop off that bad boy and get to the ground. Low to the ground. And you roll. If your dog is out there with you, you have him roll, too. Teaching a dog that maneuver has a history beyond simple entertainment. It's exhausting, your family's worried and…" This is where I lost it and started laughing and pretty soon the New Yorkers were laughing with me. "…the wife and kids come rolling out to help you with bottles of water and shouts of encouragement. 'Knick knack paddy whack' they scream. 'Throw the dog a bone, this old man is rolling home.'"

We all got inside before the rain came. We seated ourselves on burnt orange cloth couches and chairs around a large square marble coffee table. Eunice came out to join us and asked about our lingering laugher, I was asked to repeat the lightning s story.

Later in our hotel bar I had a drink with Eunice. I told her of my surprise at finding out the Manhattan sophisticates had heard of, and even respected, the writing program at Iowa.

"Well, I suppose the Proust is in the pudding," I said.

"Did you say that on the terrace?" Eunice asked, taking a drag on the cigarette she allowed herself out of town.

"No, just thought of it."

"Good, because it doesn't make any sense."

"Has a clever ring to it though, don't you think?"

" Mitch," Eunice said, pausing to put out her cigarette in the ashtray. "You're like the human embodiment of the Iowa writing program to the people you met this evening. You're Midwestern in a cool, informed way, a sort of Fitzgerald or Hemingway. A quick mind with an unpretentious manner. People are amused and impressed."

"That's nice. And nice of you to say to me," I said and I meant it. How generous of Eunice to be talking this way.

"You're like Iowa itself, " Eunice said, waving off the bartender's visual cue asking if we needed another drink. "For one thing, you don't know how attractive you are, how much you have to offer."

I didn't know what to say, even as a joke. I was feeling a lot of affection for Eunice at that moment, but I wasn't looking for a bolstering of my self esteem. I just frankly didn't care much about how people saw me. I remember reading a magazine article on hipness. It said that Bob Dylan had always been perceived as very hip, and now that he no longer cared, he had risen to the level of ultra hip. Well, I guess I was either way up there in some type of cool category or I was well on my way to joining Fred Exley's character in A Fan's Notes in the stands as a mere observer of the action.

"You know, Mitch, I had dinner earlier with a media man. Multi-media man actually. A friend from long ago. From back in the good old golden days. He started out about the same time Lucas and I did. He was syndicating some cartoonists and we used some of their work on greeting cards. He went on to be extremely successful. I see him when I'm in town."

"He's a big fish in a big pond, a whale in the ocean.," I said, making a sweeping hand motion that became a dive.

"I talked about you quite a bit," Eunice said, looking into my eyes for a reaction.

"I hope you didn't give my entire history. There are those narrow-minded types who look down on embezzlement, no matter how justified."

"Lucky for you, the topic didn't arise," Eunice said with a breath of amusement. Then she folded her hands on the table as if in prayer. "I managed to remain on your few good qualities."

"Short conversation."

"Not really. I said in all honesty that I found in you a rare combination of creative talent and business savvy, a pragmatist who comes up with strong commercial writing and ideas for company growth. I did run on, to the point of quoting comments you made in meetings and lines from copy you've written."

"He must have been overwhelmingly bored," I said, pretending to stifle a deeply inhaled yawn.

"Overwhelmingly overwhelmed would be more accurate. I told him about your stint in Los Angeles when you oversaw the script and animation for our Friends and Near Bores characters. You were clear, focused, deadline driven, cost conscious, persistent in a charming way. Even the television writers with their backpacks full of cynicism were impressed. I never told you, but more than a few Hollywood people said you could be successful out there."

"No doubt you were afraid of over inflating my dirigible sized ego." I put my hands on either side of my hand and drew them out to indicate an expanding head.

"Didn't want to lose you is more like it. Didn't want you getting stars in your eyes." Her own eyes sparkled mutely from tears and blue bar light.

"More like smog in my eyes. I can murkily recall the layer of brown acrid cloud sitting like a sludge of frosting on the mountains around L.A. And don't forget the glacial flow of traffic interrupted by the occasional wild speeder and swerving nut job. Not my cup of herbal tee."

Eunice slid another slim cigarette from the pack on the table. I reached for the matches and lit one for her. She drew the smoke in slowly and closed her eyes, perhaps transporting herself to a time when toasty tobacco tasted of youth and sophistication. Her near smile was distant and serene.

"I no doubt prattled on much too long," she said when her eyes opened. "However, I could tell my friend was interested and impressed. He'd like to meet you. Once he did, he would probably offer you something."

"He's that sold on me?"

"Apparently," Eunice said with a small shrug of her narrow shoulders. She held a thumb and forefinger an inch apart. "A tiny number of people have real creative ability."

I leaned forward to peer through the little space. "Now I see."

"People who don't have the spark tend to have one of two attitudes towards those who do. They either think it's easy, just a matter of setting aside some time to do it, or they view it as a rare and mysterious force of massive proportions. My friend is one of the latter."

"I'd probably like him," I mused.

"You like just about everyone. So, yes, you probably would. Well, who knows, maybe I'll throw you two together sometime."

"Eunice," I said, my voice trying to make my sincerity obvious. "This is all very flattering. It really is. I'd enjoy meeting your friend, but I wouldn't be looking for a big change in my small life."

"That's fine." She reached out and patted my hand. "I just don't want you to underestimate yourself. Just once I would like to see you scrape off a few layers of Midwestern humility and give yourself a shot at something. That's all."

"You're a class act," I said, reciprocating the patting of hands.

"You could be passing up some interesting and challenging work, and I'll go ahead and say it, some fascinating women."

"Present company fills that bill quite nicely."

"Thank you." Eunice raised her glass to return the compliment. She put out her cigarette by twisting and crushing it into the ashtray. "Not to throttle a dead horse, but I want to say that my friend is one of those people who doesn't judge writing by format. He doesn't have the typical disdain for greeting cards. Good writing could show up on a kitchen paper towel and it would still be good writing."

"Hmm, Kafka Kleenex? Interesting."

"Mitch, I know you could have gone on to bigger and better things over the years. It's meant so much to me that you stuck around. I know you've had calls from head hunters."

"Some bigger things. Better? I'm not so sure." Molly Bloom could have slept in a queen-sized bed. Little Rudy would still be gone."

"So you don't think…." Eunice let her gaze drift languidly around the room, the dark wood and curved marble bar, the tall windows with a view of a luminous city, stamped tin ceiling that bounced back the mellow sounds of Miles Davis. "You don't think this is better."

"I don't really think about it. I think about how much I like talking to you. And I stand unafraid to underachieve." I hit my palm with a loose fist. "By golly."

"I guess I know that. You never seek to impress." Eunice lowered her head and looked up shyly. "But, Sir Gallant, I profess thou doest impress."

"My Lady doest profess too much." I pointed with a wagging finger to the pack of cigarettes and she pulled out two and handed one to me. We talked about New York for a while. I brought my failure to understand why its citizens tend to cite as a big plus the ability to get takeout Thai food at three in the morning. How often does that come up? And if it does, aren't you probably too drunk to really enjoy it? And I told her about a New York author who had read from a new book at the downtown library that's been beautifully rescued from its former existence as a federal bank building. During the question and answer session he made the statement that "life plus art equals happiness." Being somewhat familiar with his work, I knew that his fiction didn't express that sentiment. They were far less sanguine. And the adults he depicted never demonstrated the possibly redemptive joy of raising children and sustaining a loving relationship with them into adulthood, even though he was quick during his speaking engagement to relay anecdotes about his son and daughter that conveyed exactly that.

"Mitch, tell you what I think," Eunice said at evening's close, pushing herself up from the table with slight two martini stiffness. "I think a good martini plus sleep equals happiness. I'm very happy right now." She gave me a curt salute and walked away.

Later on in my hotel room waiting to fall asleep I was able to imagine a different life for myself by simply embellishing the familiar. I encased the whole thing in the overpowering intoxicating fragrance of the perfume bouquet created by girls at high school prom. For a crisply envisioned prelude I pictured Kim emerging from the bedroom, a New York penthouse bedroom rather than the tiny one in our college apartment. She had just bathed and dressed for a Christmas party, at a downtown Manhattan hotel rather than the large white house of a university professor. It was an image of Kim that came to mind whenever I heard Eric Clapton's "Wonderful Tonight" on the radio. She comes into the living room in a holiday red dress and black high heels, her long straight dark hair soft on her shoulders, a bright smile framed by cranberry lipstick. In my mind she grabbed a long white winter coat and her red purse and extended her hand to me. Later on we emerged from a cab in front of the hotel. I got out first in my gray suit and long black cloth overcoat. Only now it was Irene who was my companion. I reached into my suit coat pocket for my money clip to pay the cab driver before turning to be greeted by a uniformed doorman who directs us to the large ballroom with glittering chandeliers and a live jazz quartet where the company Christmas party is just beginning. Silver-haired men with deep tans and thin young women in colorful dresses that sparkle glide about and greet each other. Irene squeezes my arm as a gesture of anticipation and I take two fluted glasses from the tray of the petite server passing by. Various guests invite Irene and me to their estates on Long Island or the Hamptons for beach parties and weekends of tennis and bridge.

I see myself at a large conference table surrounded by middle-aged men and women in black with expensive haircuts at a tall window looking out over the city. We all have yellow legal pads and either white ceramic cups of coffee or bottled water. The most attractive woman in the room keeps giving me sidelong glances from her expressionless face and crosses her long bare legs frequently. That's when I fell asleep on the hotel bed while cable news droned on at low volume. I woke up eager to get out of town and back home.

Chapter Twenty-one

I was raised in a family of moderately devout Catholics. Sunday morning masses, observance of a handful of holy days throughout the year, and rosaries in the evening during Lent were part of daily life. A wooden crucifix and a portrait of Christ hung on the living room wall. Our church was fifty years old and laid out in the shape of a cross. In my early childhood , before the older structure was replaced with a spacious new one, the church filled to overflowing on Sundays. Late arrivals stood in the aisles or suffered the stifling heat of the choir loft.

During one crowded service in January the priest announced during his sermon that in order to do what we could from our comfortable circumstances in the United States to alleviate the suffering in Africa due to a massive and long lasting drought, our diocese would seek the Lord's intervention on behalf of the starving victims through a novena. This meant that parishioners were to attend mass every morning for ten days in a row and ask God's mercy for the afflicted multitudes on another continent.

Attempting to be dutiful, and feeling especially blessed due to the recent holiday feasting and the presents on Christmas morning, I decided to rise in the dark for the allotted days and trudge twelve steely cold blocks to the church and join the others who would be making a collective plea for a desperate population.

The first Monday I got up and hastily brushed my teeth before dressing in layers of clothing, including a scarf wound tightly around my face, before calling softly into the open doorway of my parents' bedroom that I was leaving for the church. Head down, walking purposefully through a light cutting wind, I said a rosary and offered it to persuade God to provide for the starving masses. Even with thick fur-lined gloves, my hands felt the dull cold of the heavy metal church door handle. I went in just as the priest and two altar boys were striding to the front of the church to begin mass. In the vestibule I pulled back the hood of my parka and lifted off my stocking cap, dipped a few fingers into the holy water font and crossed myself before genuflecting and entering the area that held rows of pews. In the murky light of the few overhead bulbs that were on, the only thing I could see clearly were the few dozen lit candles in red votive holders along a side wall, flickering in silent supplication for the redemption of departed souls.

Standing as the mass started, I counted the scant number of church members in attendance on this first day of the novena. All were elderly. There was one couple and three women by themselves. No need to be in an aisle today. Five altogether.

This was the beginning of my questioning of the seriousness of the faith and devotion of members of my church. I had already had a few doubts, beginning with the divinity of a deity who proved his status by changing water into wine and walking on water. Carnival tricks, in my mind. He also restored the sight of a blind person, but only to prove his special powers, not out of compassion.

After the novena, things pretty much unraveled. A few months later one of my more precocious friends passed me a copy of Catcher In The Rye. The basic humanity and decency, the suffering and musings of an adolescent Holden Caulfield made more sense to me than the scholarly teachings of my organized religion. His observations that we are doomed to lose the people we love and his angst at how badly people treat one another and his touching, naïve wish to shelter little children from the realities of the adult world formed a basis for a philosophy on life and behavior for me.

I began to look to literature to learn about people and life. As with the bible, where interpretations can vary from individual to individual, my learnings from leading fiction were personal and not to be pushed onto anyone else. From MarkTwain's unwashed illiterate hero, Huck Finn, I learned to question the rules and values of culture and society. I also established an appreciation for simple, fairly local adventure and the romanticism it can provide. I identified with Camus' stranger in his feelings of alienation and even confusion about what is going on right around him. John Cheever and Walt Whitman impressed me with their compassion for everyone. I especially noted Cheever's ability to summon a sympathetic feeling towards the upper middle class men with country club memberships who were less than completely faithful and loving towards their wives and distant from their children.

Serious authors, most notably William Faulkner and James Joyce, led me to see my life as more profound that I had previously. I read about the sound and fury of Faukner's feeble brained Benjy and the long deep and shallow and real and surreal thoughts of Joyce's Molly and Leopold Bloom and Stephen Daedalus. I found guidance and inspiration, as well as the pleasure of devouring delicious prose.

The symbols I found in literature meant more to me than the statues and practices I observed in church. For example, in a short story by Eudora Welty, the action takes place in a family home filled with clocks due to her father's occupation as a repairer of timepieces, the reader comes to see that time destroys everything. Reaching this acute understanding that it's all going away made me more diligent about trying to savor the moments available to me each day.

Writers Franz Kafka and Bob Dylan impressed upon me that creativity comes without rules or borders, is basically unlimited, much larger than anything I had earlier imagined. I came to think that opening one's self to the possibilities of art, even in a non-scholarly way, could provide at least partial redemption to those suffering the fate of Emma Bovary.

It was in the writings of Ernest Hemingway and F. Scott Fitzgerald that the aching longings of their heroes in <u>The Sun Also Rises</u> and <u>The Great Gatsby</u> made me fear the consequences of losing at deep love early in life. I came to see that situation as one of the few in life that a person may literally never get over and thought if it as truly tragic, even though the afflicted fictional people never express overt self-pity or hellish suffering.

The guiding priests in my religion of reading were the books of criticism I consulted in the reference sections of public libraries. There were also real-life examples, like the very real love between Scott and Zelda Fitzgerald. On the surface theirs was a thrilling romance. As photographs indicate, they were good-looking in an way that would be attractive in any era.

Witty, talented, adventurous, given to throwing lavish parties, careless with the considerable wealth that Scott's writing generated. Zelda forever impish and wild. How wonderful to be them.

Then Zelda had severe mental problems, had to be institutionalized. Scott would take her out on occasional weekends, perhaps trying to recapture a perfect autumn afternoon on a quiet lake when the whole beautiful world seemed to be theirs and theirs alone or to experience once again a boozy dream of excitement out and about on a Manhattan evening. But those outings didn't go well, and then Scott died young from a heart attack, and Zelda, the former dancer and pretty good writer, stayed in the institution until the place caught on fire and she was consumed in it.

All this seemed a natural outgrowth from a romance that ran smack into reality and destiny. I can't see a picture of Zelda, or any of the very many slender pretty girls with easy laughs that you see everywhere, without thinking of Kim. I often recall Jake Barnes saying "Pretty to think so" in response to Brett's imagining of a love life for the two of them.

A woman from my college days looked at Kim and me as a kind of Scott and Zelda. She dated a friend of mine pretty seriously for a year when I was a senior. He was a tall guy, heavier than the typical lean and lanky undergrad. He had a beard and a quiet, thoughtful manner made appealing by curious intellect and a wry, observant sense of humor.

Sometimes we four went to movies together or drove in one car to beery parties off-campus. The woman's name was Dawn. She was a pretty young woman with long honey blonde hair and a full figure that was something to see in a tight dress.

I was surprised to find out her view of Kim and me as some sort of special couple. The word she used was "glamorous." I couldn't really see that and I only discovered it many years after college. We had lost touch when she and the bearded friend broke up and we all graduated and left Iowa City. She called me shortly after the divorce to tell me she had seen a syndicated newspaper article on the popularity of small humorous gift books. I had been interviewed on the phone for the piece and was quoted a few times and revealed as a writer and editor in Kansas City.

The phone call came at work. Dawn was living in Detroit, doing marketing for a company that distributed records and videos to large retail chains. She said she had felt a perceptible thrill at seeing my name in the paper and instantly pictured the old days in a student apartment living room where everyone had cans of beer and cigarettes with curls of rising smoke, stereo music turned loud. She thought of Kim and me as attractive people who made a great-looking couple, perpetually smiling, always upbeat, always ready for a fun social evening with friends.

She remembered seeing us constantly together, striding across campus with arms linked on sunny afternoons, sitting together in the near darkness of a downtown bar, leaning out from rented horses to kiss in the red and gold autumn, lighting one of our cigarettes from the cigarette of the other. I always pictured everyone as being pretty good-looking in those youthful days and being ready for fun, but maybe I was on the inside looking out and seeing things from a different perspective.

I had small vague recollections of the memories she was talking about. The year we knew her involved a lot of mellow evenings when she and her hairy boyfriend would join us for dark beer and folk singing at a basement bar near campus, playing rudimentary games of bridge at the student union or driving to the countryside for long lazy picnics.

Personally, I saw Dawn as one half of an attractive and appealing couple. He owned a Volkswagon Beetle with the horsepower of a kitchen mixer. When the four of us were all in it on the highway, he would need to downshift if we were going up a hill with any kind of real incline.

Our merry foursome took one longish road trip. We drove to Indiana to watch the university's football team play Purdue. We left in the early morning Saturday darkness and got there an hour before the game. We had camping equipment tied to the roof of the car and after watching the Hawkeyes lose a close game, we hit the road and headed for a lake with campgrounds halfway back. It was the middle of fall, but the weather was pretty warm. After setting up a tent in an area sheltered by trees and shrubs, we went for brief cleansing dip in the lake, at first in underclothes, soon in nothing as twilight turned into a chilly darkness. We ate sandwiches made food pulled from small bags of groceries and sat next to a large campfire and drank instant coffee with whisky and lit cigarettes from twigs ignited by the wriggling flames before retiring to shared sleeping bags after saying our good nights and saying what we would have for breakfast the next morning at the first available truck stop.

"Do you remember a guy from school named Justin Dalton?" Dawn asked after we'd been talking a while. I'd forgotten how everything she said came with a slight current of amusement, almost laughter. It was a pleasure just to hear her voice.

"I do. He was in a couple of my creative writing classes. Nice guy. Like just about everyone else we knew. He wrote very original stories with short paragraphs of just two or three sentences. Very distinctive. Made for a fast read."

"He lives up here in Motor City, vroom, vroom," Dawn said with a high pitched growl. "I know him because his wife works in my building and we're in an aerobics class at the fitness center here. He teaches at a community college. He's published some of his stories in books through the university press."

"I'll apply my massive computer skills towards looking for them online. I thought his stuff was pretty good." I could still recall some of his stories from the undergrad days. One was about a butler who was concerned that the well-to-do friends of his very wealthy employer were stealing steadily from the household. His boss couldn't imagine such things from visitors to his mansion until one day he came down for breakfast to discover that his nefarious pals had absconded with the butler.

"I have to tell you , Mitch, that Mr. Dalton sure remembers you. He thought your stories were terrific. Mainly, very funny. He was reciting some of the lines to me. I was laughing. Then he said you could write some touching things, too. He mentioned a story the class reviewed that was about an Irish family in a tenement. Everyone thought you were raised in a poor neighborhood in New York City. Then you told them you were a hick from some little rural town no one had ever heard of."

"I got a lot of attention for that story. I just sat down one day with a notebook at the student union and it just pored out without much planning. I was really caught off-guard by the reaction from everyone. It was nice to get the encouragement, a strong nudge to pursue something in the way of writing."

"Justin thought you had the makings of a serious writer. Renowned even."

"Renowned? Wow, that's a pipe-smoking level of writer. I hate pipe-smoking."

"And Justin was really jealous of you having the hot girlfriend. He thought you had it all. I guess Kim went to class with you sometimes."

"We were together a lot."

"Loving the constant sexual tension, no doubt," Dawn said, and the laughter just below the surface of her voice burst through.

"Later to be replaced by mere tension."

"Whatever. I've been telling you that you were the cool couple."

"I would have enjoyed knowing that," I said.

"Then you wouldn't have been the cool couple."

"Good point. Well, I'm still surprised. Justin always had a different woman with him, all stylish and beautiful in my recollection." He seemed like a player to me. I wasn't ever jealous. Just pretty much amazed. "And while we're on the subject, Dawn, you were incredibly beautiful and I'm sure you still are. I assumed it was as obvious to you as it was to everyone else."

We spoke for a while about keeping in touch. We exchanged email addresses and compared periods of time when we might be available to spend a day or two in each other's company. Later that evening I would spend a pleasurable fifteen minutes remembering my days of attending creative writing classes, sitting up late at night with music on the headset while I finished the daily writing assignments, reading the work of talented fellow students. I got a fair amount of encouragement from the writers who were there to teach, but I had felt since childhood that any true writing strength of mine consisted of short, punchy, witty bursts unconfined by plot and character. Reading my essays aloud in grade school had generated room-filling laughter. I was later asked to create humorous school spirit posters, write funny filler for the high school paper and even perform my own stand-up material for talent shows and proms. Even the play I had written with Squirrel was primarily one-liners separated by sight gags.

However, talking to Dawn did make me wonder what might have been if I had applied myself to serious writing. Yet I knew that I was not drawn to the confining world of academia, to being a teacher of creative writing and American literature at a small college while I worked on my short story collection in a windowless office shared with a fellow instructor. He and I could play squash over the noon hour and have late afternoon drinks at some little neighborhood place just outside the scope of the bars frequented by our students. I wouldn't be able to travel much on the tight school budget. Much of my perspective on the outside world would be informed by visiting lecturers that I would squire around town in my compact car before they spoke to a half circle of students, some eager and some cynical, the proportions of the two staying constant over the years. I'd teach classic selections along with the occasional new books and force myself late at night to read ten page papers about the same works semester after semester. The beautiful women around me would be almost exclusively students who were around for only a short time before disappearing into the larger world. A few might have an infatuation involving me, and I would resist their interest out of feelings of responsibility and propriety and desires not to look like a fool. As the years passed, I'd become more remote and probably more resistant to trends in literature that I found increasingly difficult to relate to. I guess I prefer being part of the everyday world and letting my writing be graded by the impartial review board of retail sales. And while there's something to be said for wearing your reading chair into threadbare condition from night after night of intense scrutiny of the great works, there's also a point to be made for all the bright yellow afternoons and easygoing rivalry that comes with working at lowering your golf handicap and speeding up your tennis serve. All I was really giving up was something abstract like prestige and some level of adulation.

As a copywriter, I'm immune to the trends of fiction, as well as the changes in personnel at publishing houses and the moving targets set up by various editors at various magazines and small publishers of short story collections. As styles come and go, the success or failure of humor writing is unmistakable. Either the firecracker explodes or it's a dud. People respond to a solid joke no matter when it gets written and presented. It isn't funny for a while, then out of fashion for a period of years or decades, then rediscovered and hailed as a classic. You get a laugh or you don't. No need for an eight-page essay of tortured prose to tell you if it worked and had value.

"By the way, Dawn, are you married?"

"No, never been. Close a couple of times."

"That really shocks me. You have so much going for you." Stupidly, I tried to gauge from the deepness of her voice whether she'd put on weight. The lightness in her voice told me she'd stayed about the same as I pictured a coed in a business suit talking into a cell phone.

"I'm always dating someone. I know it's a cliché, but all the good ones seem to be taken. People tend to be on their best behavior at first, so you learn to wait a little while for the more negative stuff to rise up. I'm not complaining. I have a good life, good friends and a strong relationship with my parents and my sister. We talk all the time and visit back and forth. And I do like my work. The travel is moderate, but when I do go out of town, I'm usually going to a major city and meeting bright, interesting people."

"Sounds nice," I said, trying to muster enthusiasm from somewhere. Her life's outline seemed to be all information, no passion. A little on the defensive side. She sounded like a person trying to make a convincing argument based on a list of things that once added up would equal fulfillment. I had a sudden series of images of romantic and funny and sentimental events in my own life, and I felt sadness for her.

"Right now I'm dating a guy who used to play professional hockey. He does commentary for the Red Wings on radio." As she was talking I was remembering not long ago seeing two youngish women from the office in a casual restaurant on a Saturday afternoon. They were on a double date, getting something to eat before heading out to a bicycle trail. The women looked sexy and fit in tight black shorts and two layers of sleeveless tops. Their dates were wearing long denim shorts and nondescript short sleeve shirts. The guys didn't have much to say as I stood talking to the women while holding my Styrofoam box of takeout fried chicken salad. I achieved my petty, selfish, competitive goal of getting both lasses to laugh and went on my way feeling superior to their companions for the day.

"It's been good to talk to you, Dawn. Makes me feel young." As we said our good-byes and I was pulling the receiver away from my ear, I thought I heard hear a faint "I love you."

Chapter Twenty-two

Eunice had me over for dinner at her condo. It's near the top of the fifteen story structure in the middle of town. From her balcony you can see quite an expanse of the broad, snaking Missouri River. The early fall weather was breezy and warm. We had scotch and water outside as we leaned against a metal railing set atop a low stone wall. The sun was sitting on the horizon below a ceiling of high ruby red clouds.

I was looking forward to sitting down to eat. Eunice's approach to cooking is a few things done well. She prepares just enough for you to have a decent amount without feeling you need to overeat out of politeness. On this particular night she served a creamy chicken pasta dish, steamed asparagus and a garden salad with light clear dressing and walnuts. For some reason almost any green leafy dish with walnuts is delicious.

While we dined, we talked about some new books by some older established authors. I said I was pleased for them that they could still deliver the goods and keep working at their craft in their later years. Eunice seemed less enthusiastic than usual about answering my questions on the state of our business.

After dinner we took big white mugs of coffee back outside and sat on wrought iron chairs with orange pastel cushions and a matching table between them. The evening had cooled and squarish shafts of sunlight were thrust up towards the darkening overhead sky. The moon was a gauzy white and gray circle directly above us. Eunice had put on a pink sweater over her loose satiny white slacks and blouse.

"Beautiful view, Eunice," I said.

"And the sunset is nice, too," she said without a hint of self-consciousness.

"You always look good." I raised my cup in homage to her careful grooming and trim form. "Nature is just providing a nice framework."

"It's funny. I spend so much time out here. I'll have three meals a day at this table when it's warm and clear, even in a breeze. But I never see anyone else outside, other than the occasional guest who's stepped out for a quick smoke."

"I know what you're saying. I'd be out here, just to feel the air and experience the memories it recalls. But most people do prefer the living room couch. Must be the irresistible pull of television."

"Mitch." Her voice was suddenly lower, a little husky. "I might retire soon. I might sell the business and quit working. Cash out. I'm very seriously considering it."

"Wow." I set my cup on the table and leaned back in a slow motion recoil.

"Wow indeed. I'd be careful, do it right. I might sell to a group of employees if they're interested. You and Charlie come to mind right away. Don Harper is a possibility. I'd talk to all of you if you're interested. Do you think you might be?"

"I appreciate your interest and confidence in me. I really do, but I gotta tell you, it ain't me, babe. I have no ambitions to be an owner. I would see it as gaining an abstract reward and acquiring very non-abstract headaches, activities I really don't want to be involved in. Tax issues alone would keep me out of the big office. Thanks, Eunice, but it just holds no appeal for me. I'm sure I can work with anyone who takes over. What will you do if you follow through on your retirement?"

"Travel is always an attractive option," she said, turning and looking into the distance. "And I've been seeing someone. The friend I told you about in the hotel bar in New York at the book fair. He comes here sometimes. Usually I go there."

"Ah, so those frequent flights the last bunch of months weren't all business."

"Only partly. He would consider buying Punchline. There's no risk in it for a corporation the size of his. He'd pay more than fair market value, not that I would be a tough negotiator. It would be a nice little subsidiary for him. He's solid, Mitch."

"You don't have to justify…"

She held a hand up to silence me, then continued, "He's calm and courteous, gracious. He's wonderful to talk to. Informed and open-minded. He listens. We would travel well together. He has good manners. Impeccable, as they say." She paused. "I never realized how important that is to me. The manners." She stood up and walked to the railing. I walked up beside her and put my arm around her shoulder, then drew her close. She let her head rest lightly on my shoulder.

"Eunice, I understand your attitude about manners. I think it's because manners speak to a kind of universal love and respect. Manners come with kindness, not with self-importance or selfishness. I'd like to meet this guy, make sure he's worthy."

"I do enjoy his company," Eunice said, looking up at me to emphasize her sincerity. "I'm not settling. I've more or less given up on expecting what Lucas and I once had. Youth may have figured into that wild alchemy. I don't know." She had to stop for a few seconds, then, "If Paris is unavailable, Zurich will be just fine. More than fine. I'll be happy."

"Would you move to New York?" I asked. The night breeze suddenly blew chilly. Eunice turned up her collar on her sweater and pulled the sleeves of her sweater down around her hands. I put my arms around her.

"I could. It's not really all that important where your home address is. He's quite well-off and I don't mind flying. We could live anywhere and still go anywhere. I might keep this place for a while." She affectionately rubbed the backs of my hands. "I'd still want to have private dinners with personal friends."

"The personal friends would like that." I wrapped her cool hands in mine.

"Frank has friends who…"

"Oh, it's Frank, is it?" I tightened my hold on her and rocked her back and forth slowly. "Sorry. Please continue. What about these friends of Frank?"

"As I was saying before I was so *rudely* interrupted, Frank has friends who bought beach front property in Thailand. They live in Boston and they visit their Asia condo two or three times a year and think nothing of it."

"Perhaps you and Mr. Manners could buy the well-appointed beach condo next door. 'Have a toddie, old boy, before we go off to dig up clams for dinner. Eunice makes the most marrrrr-velous toddies, don't you know. Just the thing after a heated round of competitive croquet."

"Now you're just making fun," Eunice protested laughingly. She pressed herself more snugly into my embrace.

"Having fun. Not making fun. I'm happy for you. And I'm not sure youth is much of a factor. I suppose it's possible that we're always some version of that nineteen-year-old college student who's open to all-consuming infatuation."

"I'll let you know. Look for the email." We were silent for a little while, just looking out at the moonlight reflecting off the distant river and the few dozen stars that had winked on. Eunice said she was cold and was ready to move inside. After we closed the big sliding glass door behind us, she took our coffee mugs to the kitchen for refills and directed me to the living room's white couch with its round pastel orange and peach pillows.

Appearing in the doorway, she held up a bottle of whisky and asked if I wanted my coffee Irish style. "Sure'n that would be grand," I said, not especially wanting to drink, but liking the festive concept of it all. When she came to sit next to me, she was holding to thick clear glass cups with little islands of whipped cream floating on the dark liquid surface.

"Any aspirations to the New York social scene?" I asked .

"Not really interested. Lucas and I used to go to all the Kansas City events. Charity balls, political rallies, annual one thing and another. Same people in different clothes. It was all okay. I don't mind dressing up. Liked it for a while, but not so much anymore."

"No big deal, Eunice. You look great in jeans and a sweatshirt. People mention it."

"Mmmmm, men aren't much interested in women older than themselves," Eunice said distractedly, her eyes almost closed. She raised her cup and blew lightly on the coffee, then took dainty lick of the white fluff. She gave me a hard look and said, "You're what women want, Mitch. Sorry to be so direct, blunt or whatever, but it's true. I don't mean to embarrass you, but there you have it. Oh, there's comfort and serenity in a calm, well-read man."

She forced a small laugh. "It's comfortable. But there's something more, romance and excitement, in a certain look and smile, in someone who makes you laugh, moves through the world with an athletic gait and an infectious easy confidence, makes you want to go places and try things you wouldn't otherwise." She gave another puff of laughter.

"Maybe. I'm not sure I agree. I know an ex-wife who would sees things differently." I sometimes pictured Kim in front of a small stone house in nineteenth century France. She was wearing a white peasant dress and a big gray apron. The beige scarf on her head had a little grime on it. Her raw reddish hands pumped a wooden butter churn. She did not look happy. The sky was almost black in daytime and an ugly smear of gray smoke belched from the chimney.

Eunice looked pained at my mention of Kim, her face taking on a twisted expression. She waved her hand in front of her face.

"I don't mean to get into all of that," she said. "I just feel an urge now that I'm thinking of retiring, a compulsion to say things. Could be silly, but I'm succumbing to the feeling. Some might call it closure, whatever the hell that's all about."

"It's a very natural feeling." I didn't know if it was, but that seemed like the thing to say.

"Mitch, you're the Baby Bear to every woman's Goldilocks. You're not too much one way or the other. You're just right." I leaned over to look at the spiked coffee in her cup and said, "Maybe it's the porridge talking. Powerful stuff."

"Well, no one's been sleeping in my bed."

"Frank could be your bear in shining fur, or something."

"Might be. Politically, we're right together. Our tastes are very close. We each have a sense of humor in our reserved way. I can't picture us ever having a ferocious argument, embattled times. It will be like having frosted cocoanut cake every day. Nothing too outlandish, but always very pleasant." She took a deep drink of spiked coffee, then set the cup down and leaned back on the couch.

"It will probably be nice to relax, give up the day-to-day business, the board meetings, the three-day conferences. Hard to say which will be more pleasant to be rid of, the hobnobbing or the elbow rubbing."

"Definitely the elbow rubbing. Takes its toll." Eunice bent her arm and massaged her elbow. Then she reached for her cup and took a long thoughtful sip. "You know, sometimes when we're together, you and I, and you're just wandering around in a light conversation, you're going somewhere and I am listening. I've thought many times about your comments on James Joyce."

"Decent writer."

"You talked about how in Molly's soliloquy we learn that in her simple rude bed she's had all of the ecstasy, despair, regret, longing, triumph and loss that life can hold. All that on a thin mattress in a plain narrow room. I relate to that." She patted herself just above the heart. "I know where the real journey takes place."

"I'm happy to know you won't miss being the owner of the company. I've always thought you must find it rewarding. You're so good at it."

"Tell you something," Eunice said, standing and taking a few steps, letting her arms float up and tip in the gesture people use to communicate tipsiness. "When you're the owner, even in a company as small and informal as ours, with the abundance of camaraderie and team spirit, the owner is always to some degree an outsider. It's like being the minister of a city church. You don't get invited to the really great parties, the ones that create legendary stories. And at any party you're treated with some degree of deference. You're never one of the gang. Not a big thing, but it's there." She put a hand on the back of the sofa to steady herself. "Here's a golden oldie for you. You used to talk about Faulkner's notion of the permanence of experience, how the past is never really past, all experience being lived at the same time."

"It's an interesting notion."

Eunice stood in front of me with her clenched hands at her neck. Then she reached out and took my hands in hers and led me toward her large tastefully decorated bedroom with its wide bed.

"I want an experience, even just one with you, that I can relive whenever I want. Then I'll move on." She slid off her sweater and closed the door behind us. A large clock radio at the bedside was playing soft jazz. The green glow of digital numbers punctuated white moonlight that was a reflection of the sunlight that had made the early part of the day warm and inviting.

Chapter Twenty-three

The Nelson Gallery of Art is in the heart of Kansas City. It sits at the top of a gradually sloping expanse of lawn framed by trees and shrubbery. The entire property is about fifteen square blocks. A few years ago four badminton shuttlecocks, twenty feet high, were set like randomly scattered toys at various angles on the grass. The presence of the large sculptures transforms the museum grounds into one enormous work of art. The same effect was achieved years earlier when the artist Christo carpeted the sidewalks of Loose Park with shiny silver fabric for visitors to walk on as they literally entered a piece of art and became part of it.

The early stages of love can do the same thing on an individual basis. Suddenly you world is transformed into something of perpetual, ubiquitous light and beauty. When romance first came to life for me in college with Kim, the Iowa university campus, with its quiet river down the middle, its classic stately classroom buildings on a hill, the lively bars directly across the street, the foot traffic between class times of so many attractive young people became a dynamic painting that had drawn me in.

Actual paintings and books of literary quality can give you a feeling that the world you live in every day and the daily experiences you encounter are infused with a kind of profundity, in love or not.

On Saturdays admission to the Nelson is free. If I'm going to the big bookstore n the nearby Country Club Plaza or to a movie in the dark soothing confines of the art theater in Westport, I'm likely to visit the art museum at least long enough to walk through a traveling exhibit or visit favorite paintings. I always drop in on Van Gogh's "Olive Trees." It's a popular piece, easy for everyone to find on the first floor in a small room next to the gift shop. At any time you're likely to see someone standing in front of that painting, eyes six inches from the paint thickly applied with furious, slashing strokes.

I was first attracted and held by the sheer energy pulsating through something so old and motionless. The supplicating black trees and impassioned crimson flowers, like blood mixed with teardrops, black crows in staggering stricken flight, the glittering ground and vibrating shadows. Observing closely, nose almost touching the raised paint, you see that what perhaps the artists himself did not realize until he relinquished himself to intuition and pure energy, that the universe is one thing, a single throbbing and bobbing entity, and every smaller thing is just one infinitesimal part of that one larger body, making hatred of any one person or thing in the universe just a form of pointless self-loathing.

Large truths come through in literature. And they may be things that authors do not know until their striving for portrayal of human existence accurately allows the unintended seeds of truth to grow and blossom. For me , literature is like a music with dinner. . There's a double benefit. Literature offers both pleasure and an instructive component. So much of how I look at the world is informed by the books I've read. It started with The Catcher In The Rye, which I read as a teen-ager for the sheer joy of the narrative voice and came to internalize as a philosophy of a tragedy of life that we move from the innocence of childhood to an adult life where we lose people who are important to us and experience a general insensitivity among humans.

In William Faulkner's The Sound And The Fury the thirty-three-year old idiot, Benjy, lives perpetually with this sister Caddie as a child and an adult, at home and gone from home. Time is a tangle. Faulkner is saying that, as one critic has observed, the past is never gone, it isn't even past. No doubt his living among Southerners still living the tribulations and humiliations of the Civil War shaped his view.

This view of life has helped me to understand why I can think about Kim, and dream about her, with equal measures of tenderness and spite, longing and relief. I'll always have the first night of endless laughing, sweet conversation, the cigarettes after lovemaking as well as the slugs of whiskey after the painful altercations played out like brief dramatic plays with their barely altered scripts at the kitchen table.

I don't know whether to be comforted or disturbed by the knowledge that I will always have Kim as a sweet and spirited college junior completely oblivious to her alluring power over my goofy college roommates as they made their clumsy flirtations. I know I relish memories of football weekends in Iowa City. Rise in the middle of morning , well-rested and eager. Walk the eight blocks to downtown in a flood of sunshine that had burned off the early frost. The sidewalks are bustling. The bars are already loud and crowded with alums from young adults to middle-agers. Get a coffee and chocolate long john at Joe's, sit at the bar between an older couple in school colors and a dressed-up student with a little blonde on his lap as he downs a Bloody Mary. Before noon hook up with friends at an apartment near campus. Drink beer hosed from a keg while a radio blasts the pre-game show. Go to the sorority house to pick up Kim. Wait downstairs in a bevy of soft-haired beauties chattering and teasing in an atmosphere as fragrant as spring. Skip the shuttle bus to the game and walk downhill and across the river, then up the hill to the stadium. Let the flow of people carry us through the entrance and up to the student section. Bench seating. Tight. Everybody's touching. Talk to the people beside and behind us. Thank them for the sips from their small bottles of fruit flavored liquor. The marching band is playing in two long rows, waiting for the players to run past. The drums sound like cannons. The players' entrance brings turns the crowd into a roaring giant. The opening kick-off causes another surge of excitement. Pretty blonde cheerleaders flip through the air and land in the arms of guys with gymnast bodies. Every play is watched closely. Touchdowns create a frenzy of hugs and kisses. After the game join the flow of departing fans, refugees from the fun football wars, heading back across the river for the lull before the nightlife, to the fulfillment of party plans made that morning. Run into another couple Kim and I know, eat dinner with them at a hamburger place that serves mounds of crisp, soft hash browns, linger over coffee and cigarettes until it's firmly nighttime and the parties are starting. Find one where the girls are fun and the guys are funny, the atmosphere laid-back, the music not too loud, some of it suitable for slow dancing, settle into a couch with Kim as a circle of taunting conversation forms in the living room, stay there as the crowd thins out to an intimate few, more subdued and sometimes serious conversations, leave to go where the two of us can spend the night together in a place that seems apart from the rest of the world, wake to bursting sunlight and go back to the hamburger place to see who we'll run into at breakfast.

Chapter Twenty-four

"How much damage did this stalker do?" I asked Ted as we drove together through downtown on the way to retrieve his repaired convertible at a body shop.

"Fair amount. Energetic little thing. Windshield completely gone. Both headlights. Dented hood. Driver's door took a few sizable dents."

"You know who did all that?"

"Oh, I know. Remember the chick in leotards at the tennis club?" Aerobics instructor? The one you wouldn't let me go watch, made me play tennis instead.?"

"You took her out?"

"Several times. Took her out. Took her in. Took her home. Checked her out. Lots of upper body strength in that little chickadee."

"This the damage to the windshield," I deduced.

"As goeth the headlights, so goeth the windshield. Basically, you're looking at clear glass piled on the front seat and floor. It would take a Plexiglass DNA expert to I.D. that puppy."

Wow. I had just moved beyond the tentative flirtatious stage of relationships. Before the Irene deal, occasionally at work, but more often in bars and restaurants, maybe at the library, I'd strive for Level One female interest--women tugging on a loose strand of hair, fingertips brushing across the back of neck, palms stroking thighs. Misread or not, I satisfied and made no attempt to proceed to the talking stage.

Conversations that involved flirtations didn't start out that way. They were tacked on to discussions about the ripeness of a honey dew melon on a produce aisle, a talk with an art director about the amount of copy space needed beneath a calendar photo, a question about the availability and location of a particular volume at the bookstore.

I was at least temporarily content, even happy, with life consisting of facile creativity at work, some sports playing or jogging, conversations of all kinds, reading books of literature or history and periodicals of different viewpoints.

"Okay," I told Ted. "If you don't mind sharing, I'd really like to know a few things. First, how does one go from the first welcoming smile and exchange of phone numbers, the first laughing date to a slag heap of shattered windshield? I'd like to avoid that sequence. Second, I'd like to hear about how you feel as all this is happening and then in the aftermath. Also, again if you don't sharing, who pays for all this? Did you call the police and get a report and talk to your insurance company?"

"Allow me to answer your excellent questions in reverse order. First, I pay for damages. I'm just trying to be fair. I claim it on my insurance as a random at of passion."

"So insurance pays for it all?"

"Not so fast there, Mitchell of Omaha. Not so darned fast." Ted held up a wagging finger. "I pay a sizable deductible."

"You're sure the fitness girl did it?"

"I recognized the handwriting in the spray painted obscenities."

"And you're okay with all of this? You don't feel it's too big of a price to pay?"

"Not really. Call it penance. Assuaging of guilt."

"Assuages?"

"Assuages completely. Absolves my guilt."

"You feels as though you've done something wrong?"

"Mea culpa, mea culpa, mea maxima culpa." Ted touched his chest three times. "Forgive me for I have shagged."

"So," I said as I pondered the situation. "You cheated on her."

"Bingo. First, I talked to a hot bartender when we were out together. Then the serving wench and I were together on the couch when the leotard came through the front door."

"Ouch. You gave her the key to your place and it came back to brand you."

"Like a bovine on the Triple Grrrr Ranch."

"You know, Ted, it's guys like you who give a bad name to lying sons of bitches."

"My apologies to all men everywhere."

"And you never contacted the police."

"Not a word to the authorities. I left a message on her answering machine. Light mention of the cops. Just as a deterrent. Let's keep this a one time thing."

"Have you eve thought of just avoiding this outcome from the beginning, trying to avoid trouble from the start?"

"I'd have to respond in the negative. Thinking about the future can ruin the moment. Takes away the spontaneity."

"I guess," I said without commitment. I thought for a while as we cruised through narrow city streets past stone buildings and crossed the Missouri River on the highway. I asked Ted if the shoe had ever been on the other foot, if he'd been on the receiving end of a traumatic breakup. Turned out he had.

Ted belonged to a fraternity as a student at the University of Kansas. The experience involved a lot of partying, usually kegs of beer set in locations on and around campus. Ted had many brief relationships with coeds he met at fraternity functions that his house sponsored with various sororities or in the crowded bars in downtown Lawrence. There were so many soft-haired lovelies eager for fun and attention, unrestricted for the first time in their lives, loosened by drink, passionate in intimate moments. Meeting them, dating them and moving on was easy. There was always another sparkling fish in the social sea.

It was all pretty much effortless for Ted with his trendy good looks, relaxed self-confidence and easy humor. He described himself as being extremely happy at the time as he socialized constantly, with women or in the company of small groups of men, and seriously applied himself to learning from his courses in journalism and advertising. By most Thursdays he had lined up at least one date for the weekend with one of the many coeds that stream in significant numbers to the big campuses of state universities. Ted loved his life.

At the start of his junior year he was attending the school's first home football game with a woman whose sorority was known for its recruiting of wealthy girls. He was with her that afternoon because his fraternity had set up its available guys with girls from her house as part of the fall semester's social calendar. She was from a prosperous ranch family in the northern part of the state. They owned thousands of acres that included their own private three-hole golf course. Ted had picked her up for the game in his older small car. He felt she was repelled by his lack of money and hid from him behind expensive dark sunglasses that she kept facing the football field, turning occasionally to give very short responses to his attempts at conversation.

When the rich girl icily turned down an offer to share his flask of peach schnapps, he found takers next to him. A boy and a girl on a blind date accepted the metal bottle. She took polite sips now and then while the guy got noisy then sleepy on the free booze. She had the high cheekbones, flawless skin and full lips of a magazine model. She wore her auburn hair simply, parted to the side and hanging straight and loose. Ted spent the game chatting and joking with his new friends while his date stared without expression at the football team's uninspired loss.

Ted told me that in the soothing yellow sunshine of early fall that day, his relaxed attitude toward the inattention of the girl he was with, his moderate partaking of the schnapps and the response of the non-date girl made him especially amusing. The auburn girl seemed to find him hilarious. He turned into a quipping machine and she laughed hard at everything he tossed out. "The peach schnapps doesn't really give you a buzz. More of a fuzz." "My date will be back in a minute. She just went to spit on some poor people." "Look at the mascot. I haven't seen a head that big since I poured my first beer." "I don't know much about football, but I know what I hike." "Looks like your boy is just about out from the peach liquor. Let's just let him take a nice schnap."

The girl's name was Virginia. Her date was a friend of a friend, from out of town and just on campus for the weekend. She was studying to be a teacher. She worked part time the checkout desk of the school library. Later in the week Ted stopped there a few times a day until he caught her sitting behind the heavy wooden counter. He walked up with a book held out and said, "Hey, Gin, check this out."

They started going out once or twice a week. She continued to find him funny, often laughing herself into frozen silence with one hand on her stomach and the other raised in a plea to stop the amusement assault.

Ted was surprised to find that he enjoyed the simple activities that Virginia suggested for their dates. They rode rental horses along lanes where trees were luminescent with glowing yellow and shining orange leaves. They took bicycles along the meandering Kansas River while eagles lazily drifted in the high sky. On rainy days they visited the small museums of art or science on campus. Together they fried chicken and baked pans of thick brownies to supply a picnic basket for late afternoon outings on the shores of Clinton Lake where they could talk until long past sundown.

A few times Ted and Virginia drove the two hours north to where her family lived. He really liked her sister, a few years younger than Virginia and still in high school, very outgoing and planning to study theater at college the following year. He was pleased that Virginia would invite her to join them on walks in the farm fields and drives along gravel roads. She laughed like Virginia and resembled her physically.

Virginia's dad was a quiet man who worked as a mechanic at the car dealership. He had his own kind of sly humor that the family responded to. He'd check out Ted's car and change the oil on Sunday afternoon. His wife rose early six days a week to go to work at the bakery on the town square. She was trim, an energetic older version of her daughters. She served simple, carefully prepared meals and delicious fruit pies and light flavorful cakes. The family's simple square white two-story on a spacious lawn was an oasis of calm and hospitality.

One weekend Virginia drove north to watch her sister perform in a school play. Ted stayed at school to work on a term paper that was due the following Monday. When Virginia got to her parents' house, they had just gotten a call from her sister at the high school to say that there had been a break in a water pipe and the auditorium was under a few inches of water. The play had been postponed for a week.

Virginia decided to drive back to campus and help Ted type his paper. She packed some of her Mother's cookies and took off in late evening. She parked in the fraternity lot and went up to Ted's room while the sound of low rumbling bass stereo music and high pitched laughter of drinking girls came up from the party room in the basement.

Ted had spent the earlier part of the evening in the basement at the party beneath a banner with large letters reading "JELL-O, DOLLY." The themed activities all involved reasons for participants to toss back plastic shot glasses of Jell-o and vodka with plenty of beer chasers. Ted ended up getting pretty well wasted and ended up in his bedroom with a pledge from the sorority in attendance. Virginia walked in with the bag of cookies and a large coffee from a shop on campus to find Ted on the bed with the girl lying across his chest, her top off, both of them snoring heavily. They woke up suddenly at the sound of Virginia's scream and cookies hitting the wall and bed in rapid fire.

That was it. All over now, Baby Blue. Ted tried for several weeks to make contact through phone calls, notes, visits to the school library. No response. Virginia quit her job at the circulation desk. He even called her sister, but she was cold to his excuses and pleadings, and refused to pass on any messages.

While his fraternity brothers were all away at a big formal dance on fragrant balmy evening awash with leafy scents and nostalgia, Ted drank heavily from a fifth of whisky. As music blasted through his room, he pulled the sheet off his bed and took it to a second story balcony and tied one end to a railing post and the other around his neck. He either jumped or fell clumsily, went hurtling through the darkness. A few minutes later he awoke on the ground with a sharp pain in his neck and shoulders.

It turned out the bed sheet was one that had been on his bed for two years. Repeated intense applications of bleach to erase the residue of energetic lovemaking and spilled liquor had greatly weakened the fabric so that the jolt of his falling body had caused it to rip at a rate slow enough to deposit him on the ground fairly gently. There had not been enough force to collapse his windpipe. The only visible injury was a reddish brown bruise around his neck.

"Lucky in life, unlucky in love," I said as we pulled into the repair shop parking lot. Ted felt his neck gingerly as he got out of the car.

"Still hurts," he said.

Chapter Twenty-five

I long ago lost interest in the chronically losing performance of the KC Royals. Too much money for admission and parking to watch sport at its most mediocre. Dates with Irene were most likely to skip athletic events and involve a moderately priced restaurant with a reputation for good food in a modestly appointed space. Mexican, barbecue and Oriental fare were common for us.

Sometimes we ate at the Nelson art museum. It's going through an extensive renovation and admission is free for the duration. Meals are available buffet style at Rozelle court, an Italian patio and columns imported brick by brick and reassembled inside three stories of museum interior. After lunch we visit our favorite exhibits in the permanent collections and walk through the temporary shows. In good weather we stroll out onto the grounds where rows of trees and shrubs frame a downward sloping expanse of green lawn dotted with bulbous bronze animal shapes and a few huge shuttlecocks.

At the museum and elsewhere Irene and I maintain conversations that carry delight and urgency, like the chatter of excited birds early in the morning when the world is peaceful and the food is plentiful in the flush of early summer. Too wound up sometimes to even touch even though we're so strongly drawn to each other that there is an almost palpable magnetic sensation.

In the restaurants or in the quiet darkness of movie theaters we'll touch, light caresses on shoulders and forearms, exchange whispered messages of no importance, lips lightly brushing an ear. At the movies we'll raise the armrest between us and settle in for two hours of relaxed intimacy. On the street or entering departments stores on the Plaza I watch the easy natural sway of Irene's hips, nature's silent siren call. I observe her as she rapidly sorts through a circular rack of dresses, wait just out dressing rooms while she tries on outfits and steps out for to get my assessment. I'd sit on a short bench while the eighteen inches of open space beneath the door of the changing room revealed her bare feet and shapely ankles and the small heap of removed clothing, a nonchalant and provocative striptease.

When we walked in the evening past store windows and people eating at curbside tables across from the shallow waters of Brush Creek, looking for a sidewalk seat to have dessert and coffee, I'd see other men staring at Irene and I'd be so glad to be me, doing exactly what I was doing. I'd think to feel sorry for men who strode by aggressively in groups of three or four, a comfortable number to fit into an older, slightly rusted nondescript compact car, one or two of them angrily glaring at me for my luck at being Irene's companion.

The young guys passing by would usually be a little shorter than average, not particularly athletic, without any of the obvious handsome features that would cause women to place them in the cute category. They're the guys you see at bookstores by the magazine racks, looking intently at the open pages of photos of women in men's magazines, lusting after beauties with perfect bodies and sultry stares. Like men with short arms wanting to pitch in the major leagues and squat men with dreams of NBA glory, the loitering magazine scanners were in pursuit of impossible goals.

I've seen them on the sidewalks of Westport, in concert arenas and ballparks, places were there is a high concentration of truly lovely women in the most flattering of clothes. It's not unusual for the men to be slightly or greatly drunk, compounding their aggression. If you're with an attractive date, you barely notice them until one of them goes out of his way to knock his shoulder against yours in a gesture of hostility, no apology. If you smile in a friendly way to the passing posse or offer a "Hey, guys," it's seen as a taunt and will usually elicit a scowl or even an inappropriate insult.

I imagine these men went through their teens and early adult years without even having an attractive woman meet their interested gaze with a sweet submissive smile and self-conscious tugging of a strand of loose hair.

Lacking natural good looks, these roaming packs of predatory males sometimes try to do too much with their hair. They tend to sport one of two styles. Either it's over the ears on the sides with a wavy bang down to the eyebrows, disheveled and curly, or it's very short on the sides with very fastidiously maintained spiky shoots on top, heavily gelled, sideburns if possible. They appear to be hoping against hope that they will land upon a magical transforming follicle solution that will more than compensate for any shortcomings in body type, personality, cheekbone deficiency or basic intelligence.

The shiny magazines they cherish show them the kind of women they must covet. Not for them are the slightly plump girlfriends with round, pretty faces, quick to laugh at their attempts at wit, who look cute in bib overalls and pastel t-shirts, who will watch with constant attention and endless patience at their showing off at facile sports such as extreme Frisbee and level street skateboarding.

These decent young fellows can't attract and maintain the persistent stare of a waiting young lovely at an airport who feels for some reason inconspicuous and with unself-conscious while looking with aroused eyes at a man reading a paperback book a few seats away. Their visits to beaches on lakes and oceans wouldn't involve women in very small swimsuits stretching their long brown limbs and trying to appear nonchalant behind sunglasses with impenetrably dark lenses.

On evening as I was driving through the Plaza I saw some of these types on an arched bridge spanning the concrete banks of Brush Creek. They were marching in a tight bunch towards the bright lights and leggy blondes of the starry night. I had a flashback to a narrow wooden bridge from my youth. It was a kind of slender floating dock that reached across to an island on one side of a farm pond about a mile from my home. The tiny oval of land was large enough for a weighty weeping willow and a few squat shrubs. The walk across the water was no more than thirty feet. Up to the age of twelve I traversed the bridge many times. My friends and I would scoop up wriggling tadpoles when the weather was warm and we'd build fires in winter after playing hockey with tree branches and ice chunk pucks on the thickly frozen pond.

One day the bridge was just gone. Coming over a low ridge on a Saturday morning during a spring thaw I was the empty expanse between farmland and island. I felt a sudden stab of loss. I was thirteen and aware of changing desires and activities, new sources of interest and pleasure. In that moment of piercing sunlight I had a first realization of the impossibility of absolute continuity. I couldn't return to the balmy afternoons on soft matted grass where I joined other boys in shooting bb's at bottles bobbing on the pond and talked about girls from school.

On the day I saw the young men walking over the creek, I had run into Irene at work. Our shoulders had brushed and we had exchanged smiles in passing. It was at that moment that I realized there was an element of fear in getting to know Irene, taking the first car ride of significant length, feeling the first shared rush of intimacy. It would signal for sure that the bridge to my marriage was gone for good. I had a moment of regret for a time when Kim and I shared an almost unbearably intense romance.

At age thirteen I knew that the strong tug of new desires had as much to do with the remoteness of the island as the disappearance of the bridge. Yet until the weathered, crumbling boards were taken away, I had never really left. I continued to live on the downy brown grass, sunlight warm on my face and naked chest, mint chewing gum fresh in my mouth, dreamily dozing in the bright banter of cherished friends.

Just as I had been the perfect age for a boy to come across a minuscule island of imagined adventures, to enjoy it fully and return each time with fresh excitement, I had fallen in love with Kim at the perfect age for falling in love. I was a junior in college and open to all-consuming romance. Nothing else at the time approached its importance to me. I never tired of her company. I was always thrilled to see her. The entire world exuded the scent of roses. We were young enough to be totally infatuated and old and independent enough to indulge ourselves fully.

At the time there was nothing I would rather do than take a long walk with Kim, just the two of us, any time of day or late at night. We might stroll off campus, past downtown stores, through neighborhoods of family homes, around lakes, along gently curving rivers. We'd meet other couples in downtown Iowa City after sporting events, on Saturday afternoons or weekday nights, and split pitchers of beer while listening to music and making each other laugh and shooting pool on coin-operated tables in an atmosphere of high spirited excitement. Afterwards we'd go off together to lie in quite darkness and wait for sleep to enfold us.

I didn't know if I any longer had the capability to being so devoted to devotion. I couldn't imagine myself walking around anywhere in the midnight hour, being with the same person exclusively for a long weekend, rousing to a touch time after time. And I had to admit to myself that I had grown pretty fond of the noncommittal flirtations and tiny conquests that were taking place steadily in bookstores, the office, bars and the waiting areas of airports. I don't keep a numerical score in my head, but if I did, it would have broken down along the lines of a point for a glance that produce a smile, two points for a look lasting over four seconds, three points for a longing glaze with lips pressed tight to avoid quivering, four points for a fourth look in a two-minute span, time estimated. Game over if she indiscreetly slides back a skirt to reveal a smooth thigh or shifts her clothing to reduce its binding.

Airports are the best arena. Women sitting near huge clear windows or walking down bright side corridors have a searching look in their eyes. Women dress more consciously for travel than men. Their clean hair is full and loose. Clothing colors flatter skin tones. Shoes of questionable comfort lengthen those long legs. Sunglasses provide a degree of anonymity and secret surveillance.

The women come by in a variety of appealing types. There's the handsome woman whose angular face carries the barest hint of makeup, whose simple glasses frame intelligent eyes that promise a conversation as penetrating as any activities of the flesh. There's the Nordic blonde in tights and belted sweater who turns away when you approach, looking at a screen of departure times, the better to reveal a firm backside pressing against stretching black fabric. There's the slender athletic woman who could be a cover model for a running magazine, who pushes herself through shyness to give you a rapid succession of flickering looks. There's the woman with the dark complexion who can roll her curvy hips in a smooth alluring rhythm as she hoists her big leather purse and looks your way.

I could encounter several different air travelers in a matter of minutes and come away feeling flattered, a little triumphant by a delivered and hastily averted stare or a small pursing of interested lips.

At home, around town, in pulsating chaos of a Friday night bar, it's fun to experience the more extended affairs lasting several minutes. I can get a primal feeling of victory in figuratively stealing away another guy's lady for a brief interlude. If he's talking with a buddy or holding forth to a table full and she turns halfway around to continue staring at you, lowering her gaze in an attitude of relinquishing, she is yours, my friend. You win. Extra points if she and the guy are touching at the time. Game, set, match if her wide welcoming eyes are on you while the two of them are kissing.

Swimming laps at a local outdoor pool in summer can create longer liaisons, up to half an hour. If a woman with a tight little body in a red two piece suit is wearing sunglasses and if she wades into the water up to her knees and never gets in deeper, a reflexive finger continually sliding along the back underside of her bikini bottom, splashing water on her reddish brown arms while bending to reveal the pale tops of her breasts, she is in the water to see and be seen. She'll smile as you walk past , either at you or to herself. She might say hello as you're leaving, having gone as far as you can with this woman in the land of young exuberant boys, vigilant parents, pale older couples with lots of reading material and bored lifeguards struggling to remain alert.

It doesn't really matter much if the female attention if partially imagined. You may be largely seeing what you want to see. No big deal. These brief exchanges can carry you through parts of the day that were drifting towards the shores of boredom or an unsettling emptiness. When Kim and I were together in the times when it was good, I never indulged in these little affairs, never had the desire, confined my looks to the briefest of admiring glances. Then in the aftermath, they served as sustaining morsels once the banquet table had been cleared.

I wish many little romantic snacks to the gangs of desperate and peevish young men who possess an exaggerated sense of the possibilities that the dating life holds for them. Like the poor envying the rich or the anonymous longing for fame, the don't know that it isn't *that* great. On the other hand, it is kind of great and their reactions make me appreciate the exquisite joy throughout life in any setting, work or leisure, at home or away, of receiving the smiles and stares of interest from women possessing outward and inward beauty. It's something to savor and be thankful for, a reason to look forward to the potential of each day and not envy other kinds of gifts granted to other people.

I've come to realize some things about those moments of quite intense feelings outside the dressing room, on the street, along the beach, around the airport, the instances of brief successful seductions. They are major events. They carry a lot of complex pleasurable feelings, create memories that endure. I relate them to William Blake's lines of poetry, where he speaks indirectly of the immense romance of an airport encounter when he writes that it is possible "To see the world in a grain of sand, And heaven in a wild flower, Hold infinity in the palm of your hand, And eternity in an hour." And I think about how lucky I am to have been given gifts that are greater than immense inherited wealth or intelligence at the genius level.

Irene and I rode in my sensible gray sedan to Weston on a warm yellow afternoon in early spring. We had on darkly colored t-shirts and blue jeans, white athletic shoes. Thank heaven for the relaxed comfort of a casual America. As informally dressed as we were, we were fine to get into any restaurant that might appeal to us throughout the day.

The sky was light blue with slowly migrating masses of bright white clouds. Off the interstate we rolled across the two lane highway up and down steep low hills best suited for growing tobacco. I pointed the weathered barns that contained stacks of broad green leaves at harvest time.

"Cigarettes were a dangerous enough thing for me to try during that brief infatuation with them in college. I never tried drugs," Irene said. "I'm not much of a risk taker. Kind of a chicken, I guess."

"More like not stupid. Someday your virginal brain will thank you."

"Maybe. I'm not always sure. I became an accountant. I'll have a job wherever I go. Playing it safe."

"You don't like accounting?"

"I actually do like it. Hate to admit it, but I do."

"There you go."

"I don't know. Isn't it just like a support function?"

"Those who can't do, account?"

"Something like that."

"Well, Irene, ol' girl, I'm not much of a taker of chances my own self. Although part of it isn't related to caution or fear. I'm just quite happy with what I have and not looking for a whole lot more."

"Is that true of all aspects of your life?" She gave me a mock sultry stare.

"Maybe not every single aspect." I turned serious, passing a slow hand over the steering wheel. "Look at this day. The very portrait of lovely serenity. A snapshot of happiness made visible. Feel the breeze coming through the slightly opened side window. It carries childhood summers, distant friendships, long afternoons of outdoor sports, long walks with conversation. Who needs anything more?"

"You have a point."

" I personally can't imagine a journey more exquisite or profound than the one I'm on with you today. Really. It's thrilling." Irene leaned away and studied my face, not sure how serious I was being.

"You might be right," she conceded quietly. She reached into the backseat for a ball cap and put it over her pulled back hair, then she rolled the window down farther.

In Weston the three straight blocks of business district have angle parking. All of the slots were full and we parked at one end on a side street. We strolled past small red brick store fronts that once housed business providing the basics---hardware, baked goods, haircuts, furniture, clothing, banking and insurance, supplies for cooking and sewing. Now most are filled with antiques or crafts.

It felt wonderful to be in the company of a beautiful smiling woman. Everything looked better than usual, people seemed friendlier, a small sexual surge accompanied the light touch of a hand. Being on the sidewalk browsing shop windows made me extremely happy. That's why you see a disproportionate number of pretty girls on dates at zoos, in coffee shops, on lake shores. They enhance environment and experience.

"It's weird to see your childhood toys in antique stores," I said to Irene as we stood in front of a glass case that housed faded cast iron little tractors and trucks.

"Maybe you need some new toys," Irene said as she nuzzled a shoulder against my chest. "Something new to play with."

"I thought I'd outgrown toys altogether. You know, when I was no longer a child, I put away the things of childhood."

"Hey, big guy, nothing wrong with a little fun."

We drove away from the little town in the afternoon's last sunlight along a low road running parallel to the river. I pulled into an area with shelters and picnic tables, benches by the water. Irene took my hand and held it tightly as we walked on the asphalt path. I knew enough to pull her close for a warm kiss on her soft moist lips.

"Let's go down by the river," she whispered while I was still close. We found a spot isolated by tall trees with red and gold leafy branches, matted with long brown grass, sheltered from the breeze off the river by low bushes. We sat down side by side. In no time at all Irene was out of her shirt and jeans, arms hugging knees pulled up to her chin, her head turned and requesting a long hard kiss. I used one hand to hold back her fragrant hair and the other to caress her back.

In the afterglow we dozed with arms around each other. My thoughts were peaceful as twilight settled in. As coolness came, we dressed and kissed. We drove in silence through the evening. Irene hummed a love song while I tried not to crave a cigarette.

Chapter Twenty-six

Charlie came by my office midmorning on a late summer Friday. He was laughing as he invited me to his house for supper the next day.

"Why so amused?" I asked.

"It's not amusement. It's joy. Margaret is back to her old fun self."

"Back?"

"She's gotten over losing you and Kim. You've been replaced. She's got herself a brand new baby, Baby."

"Baby?"

"Actually, four brand new babies. Two couples. One's about your age. They just moved into the neighborhood. The other couple is a little older. They've lived here for quite a while. I've started swimming at the Jewish Community Center. That's where I met them. They're regulars, recently retired and trying to stay in shape. We're all having a cookout at our place on Saturday and we want you to join us."

"Wouldn't miss it for the world. You can count on me."

I showed up in the early evening's brightness the next day with a small bunch of flowers. A pot of purple blossoms stood by the front door on the porch. Through a window I could see more fresh flowers on the mantel and on the dining room table.

"Coals for the Newcastle residence," I said to Margaret as I handed her the puny bouquet.

"Sweet'" she said and she rose up to give me a full-lipped kiss on the cheek. She was wearing a little black casual dress and black sandals. Her uneven tan told of sets of tennis played outdoors.

"You look lovely," I told her.

"I feel pretty, oh so pretty," she half sang and waltzed out to the kitchen with the flowers. As she placed them in a small milk bottle, she said, "I can't wait for you to meet the new neighbors. You'll like them."

"I'm sure I'll find them absolutely tolerable. Where's that husband of yours?"

"Out on the patio. Firing up the grill." Charlie appeared at the screen door to the kitchen with a beer bottle in one hand and an empty plate and spatula in the other. Margaret sang a Beatles song. "Someone's knocking at the door, somebody's ringing the bell, do me a favor, open the door." She paused, then went into a high falsetto. "Let him innnnn."

"Thank you, Sergeant Pepper," Charlie said as he came in. "Did you offer a drink to Mitch?" Ogilvy trotted in beside him and came to me for the customary rough patting of the head.

"Beer's fine. I'll have the same as the Beethoven of Barbecue." Charlie acknowledge the appellation with a raising of his drink and a solemn nod.

The doorbell sounded, followed by high-pitched laughter, then chatter coming our way. Margaret went to greet her guests and came back to the kitchen with her elbows interlocking the arm of a thin woman with straight blonde hair and an attractive angular face highlighted by a big smile. Her white dress was similar to what Margaret was wearing. A lanky man in blue jeans and a black t-shirt was right behind them.

"I give you the Pattersons," Margaret said formally with an exaggerated arm flourish. "Terri and Ken." I shook hands with the man first, addressing him as Ken, then turned to his wife and called her Ken. They laughed easily with no hint of awkwardness.

"You must be the famous Mitch," Terri said and offered a warm handshake.

"The limping legend, in the flesh, lots of flesh," I replied. "I hear you are new to Kansas City. From the North. Many rivers. Many fields. The land called Iowa."

Ken pointed dramatically with a straight arm in a northerly direction. "Our land is called Iowa City," he said. He patted his chest a few times and made a sweeping, wiggling motion. "We come in peace. We seek only bounty and peace and the occasional round of golf."

I responded by clasping my hands together and pulling hard on them. "Our bonds shall be strong," I said. "May you find bounty, may you discover peace, may you get rid of that god awful slice."

"Well, well, well, two birds of the odd feather," Charlie said and laughed.

"Speaking of birds, start the chicken, Charlie," Margaret said. "Mitch can help. I'm going to take the Pattersons on a house tour." Charlie responded with a crisp spatula salute and marched stiffly past the counter to pick up a bowl of marinating chicken breasts. As I was accompanying him out the back door, I could hear Margaret telling her guests that I had moved down from Iowa many years ago.

Before we could get outside, the doorbell rang again. Charlie handed me the glass bowl with a look of mock sternness and went to the front door. He came back with a couple who looked to be close to sixty. They were on the short side, a little rotund, and both had very white hair. They were dressed similarly in polo shirts and roomy khaki pants belted just above the waist. They were wearing very new white canvas walking shoes. It surprised me to see Charlie with his arm draped jovially across the other man's shoulders. I wasn't used to seeing him actually touching other people. Even with Margaret, physical contact consisted pretty much of an awkward pat on thigh or shoulder, an occasional brief rubbing of the neck. All three were laughing heartily as they came into the kitchen.

"This is Hans and Hannah," Charlie said. "They've lived in the neighborhood, just a few blocks over, for a long time. I told you we met swimming at the pool at the Center."

"Nice to meet you both. Charlie's on his way to overcook some chicken. Can I fix you a drink?"

"Wine would be wonderful, anything that's open," Hannah said.

"Same for me," said Hans. "Anything alcoholic, actually."

"Ah, sweets for the sweet," Charlie said, provoking another tidal wave of raucous laughter. The three of them went outdoors and I poured two full glasses of chardonnay. As I went out and set them down on the wrought iron table next to the grill, the three amigos burst into ripples of giggles.

"What did I miss?" I asked.

"Oh, that Charlie," Hannah said, wiping her eyes.

"He's Mr. One-liner," Hans said, shaking his head. "He said, 'Boy meets grill.' The guy cracks me up."

The house tour rejoined us. More introductions and then the women went inside to put side dishes onto serving plates.

"Margaret was telling us that you moved here from Iowa City," Ken said.

"Years ago. Easy transition. You'll like it here. Iowa without the winters."

"What could be better than that?"

"Not much," I agreed.

"Longer golf season," Ken said as he made a slow golf swing.

"So you're a golfer. Handicap?"

"Eleven."

"Right with me. We'll have to play sometime."

"I've invited Ken to play a few rounds at my club," Charlie said.

"Oh, the *club*, is it? Well, fine, Ken, but be prepared to conform to some very odd, very strict rules. You have to wear funny shoes. They've got little plastic nails sticking out of the bottom. What's with that?" I had often mentally calculated the cost per round based on initiation fee, annual dues, and monthly food service minimum. Cost was too high for me, especially to play the same course over and over again.

Margaret came out with a metal bucket holding ice and beer. She said cheerily, "Okay, everybody, it's a party. Par-tay. Get down, get funky. Drink up, get drunky."

"Works for me," Ken said, taking the bucket by its wire handle. "What are the others going to drink?"

Margaret growled low and said, "I love a wild party animal."

Dinner took place at a heavy wooden picnic table on the brick patio. It was a little tight, but manageable. Ken and I had a pleasant conversation about working life. He was coming to town to manage a finance group at a utility company. We went over the advantages and disadvantages of big and small companies, discussed the rareness of productive meetings, joked about the tedium of business travel. He had some interesting thoughts on investing.

Margaret and Terri sat side by side, making frequent whispered asides to each other, occasionally exchanging soft high fives and giggling with very little sound. Whenever one of the pair refilled her own wine glass, she reached over and did the same for her friend.

Charlie and Hans carried on a joke-a-thon. Mostly it was Charlie telling and Hans reacting. Hannah looked on for most of it and seemed to be enjoying herself. I thought at one point how great it must be to love the standard jokes, told over and over with their strained premises and predictable punch lines. I felt a bit of envy for the happy trio.

As we were finishing our meal, the wind turned strong and cool. Rain began to fall. We moved inside for coffee and brownies. Margaret pumped up the volume of the big reel-to-reel stereo tape machine in the living room. Songs from years ago, new when Charlie had first shown me and Lynn his monument to high fidelity, filled the room, squeezing out conversation. Margaret started to slowly dance around the room in sliding waltz steps. Terri got up and imitated her. When a lively number started to play, everyone except me got up and formed a rhythmic line weaving in and out of the downstairs rooms. Margaret motioned for me to join. I shouted, "Never drink and dance!" She made a dismissive gesture and led the group once more out to the kitchen.

When the rock and roll snake dancers came back into the living room, I caught Margaret's eye and pointed to my watch. She came over to me by herself and leaned in close as I told her loudly that I had a pre-arranged meeting with Irene at ten to rescue her from a Girls Night Out at a karaoke bar. She nodded in an exaggerated way in sync to the drum beat on the stereo and danced back to her friends.

I went home and fell asleep in bed while reading a thumb-worn paperback copy of Richard Yates short stories. The collection is titled Eleven Kinds of Loneliness. Seems to me to be just the tip of the aloneness iceberg.

Chapter Twenty-seven

On a weeknight I was at a coffee shop in Westport, seated at a small round table by a large window, sipping coffee gone cold and reading "A Soldier's Home" from a book of Hemingway short stories. I was remembering the feeling of romantic melancholy the piece had given me as a college student. I was attracted to the silent suffering of a young military man whose wounds were all invisible and internal, psychological and emotional, creating a sense of alienation from his parents and his community.

As I was lost in reading, the music from the coffee place's speakers was the Byrds, songs I had first heard in college on the jukebox at the student union. I would listen carefully while I smoked cigarettes for thirty-five cents a pack and planned my first dates with Kim. I was thinking that college was a pretty nice place to be.

Hearing jangling electric guitar versions of familiar songs while reading Ernest, drinking flavorful coffee while stylish women of all ages approached the counter and walked out with various expensive caffeine concoctions, I began wondering if I was somehow on the desirable side of life's bookends or if I had come to some kind of full circle, back at my spot in a student mode, just beginning to chart my place in the next phase of participation in the larger world. Maybe that life from twenty-five years earlier had come to an end and it was time for me to move onto some new place, to "strike another match, go start anew."

"Mind if we crash your little party of one?" a voice asked I looked up from my book to see Ted with a very pretty woman wearing a short black leather jacket and a round white cap. It took me a moment to recognize her as Carrie, the nurse from the holiday office party.

"What are a couple of trendy hipsters like you doing in a place like this? Take a wrong turn at Club Hip? You should be in a hot bar with hot music and hot hotties."

"I hate bars, remember?" Carrie said with a smile.

"We're on our way to a movie in the burbs. Way out south," Ted said. "Thought we'd need a couple of beverages to sustain us on our journey."

"A chocolaty, whipped thing, I presume, huh, kids? Basically, a warm melted Snickers in a paper cup."

"Dessert and coffee all in one," Ted replied. "Sugar buzz and caffeine high. Perfection."

"A mere four dollars," I noted. "Who can afford drugs after a fix like that?" Ted pointed directly at me to signal affirmation and turned to go order their drinks. Carrie sat down at the chair across from me.

"So, are you two an item, as they say?" I asked.

"Not so much. Not yet. We'll see. We have a lot of fun together. He makes me laugh."

"But enough about sex. Actually, I know what you mean about Ted. I'm always glad to see him. And for what it's worth, you two do make a very attractive couple."

"Of course, looks are important," Carrie laughed. She tilted her head and struck a dramatic model's pose.

"Almost as important as happiness. Hope you're happy."

"I'm trying. You know, Ted caught me on the rebound. After you dumped me." I thought she was kidding. Her face wore a relaxed lighthearted expression, but it would have been there no matter what her true feelings were.

"Dumped? I didn't even know I had you on the truck."

"Oh, really? I was hoping to get in the cab. You know, you have a lot of the things that women find attractive. You're what's known as a catch. Apparently, you don't know how sexy you are." I had to laugh, partly from being amused and partly from enjoying the compliment.

"You haven't been talking to Eunice, have you?" I asked.

"No, I haven't . How is she, by the way?"

"Well, she's fine, but when you were talking, I had that experience like in the movies where the words were yours and your mouth was moving, but the voice was all Eunice."

"She's a smart lady," Carrie said. She lifted my book from the table to look at the cover. "What are you reading?"

"Hemingway. A story about a soldier who moves back into his parents' home after returning from war."

"Was he wounded?"

"Good question from a nurse. That depends on your definition of wounds."

"Sounds like a good story."

"It is good. Understated. I usually like that."

"No big surprise there," Carrie said and leaned forward to give me a silly look. "That could be your middle freaking name."

"From an ironic uncle on my mother's side." I watched Ted return with two very tall cups of coffee. "So what movie are you two going to see?"

"Come with us and find out," Ted said. "You can hold the popcorn and drinks while we make out."

"We're going to see a romantic comedy, Just About Married," Carrie said.

"Ick-chay, ick-flay," Ted said with a coffee cup hiding his mouth.

I decided to pass. Romantic comedies usually lack two things: Romance and comedy.

"Think about it. Romantic comedy," Ted said. "You might pick up some clever lines to use on fair Irene."

"Irene?" Carrie exclaimed. "Who's Irene?"

"A little Lolita that Mitch is squiring around town. A new hire in the office."

"Ted, what do you know about Lolita?" I asked, hoping to change the subject.

"Only what you told me. You were on your second beer, so you were probably fairly wasted and extremely chatty. Maybe you were just making stuff up, about an older guy on the run with a girl on the verge of womanhood, going from motel to motel, never arriving at a home because once you get to a place permanently, everything heads downhill. So they keep moving, anticipating, never finalizing."

"I said all that. More amazingly, you remembered all that?"

Ted laughed. "You think I could make up all that?"

"Good point, my little friend." Ted excused himself to visit the men's room.

"You're dating someone about my age then," Carrie said calmly, evenly.

"We've had a few dates. She joined the company not long ago. Nothing serious at this point." I held up the Hemingway book. "My date for most evenings."

Carrie took off the white cap and ran a hand through her dark thick hair. Her eyes roamed the room. "Is she gorgeous?" she asked.

"To tell the truth, she is." How did Carrie know? I received a stern look.

"Do you really not know how attractive you are, Mr. Understatement? Modest or just dumb, it's hard to decide. Look, obviously, if you can have any woman you want…"

Ted was back. He held out a crooked arm. Carrie put on her cap and red mittens. She walked out with one hand on Ted's coat sleeve. The other hand was giving me a gesture obscured by the mitten.

Chapter Twenty-eight

I was at work one morning, lost in the time warp of pleasant creative work. I was editing and rewriting copy for various Father's Day formats. We had two t-shirt ideas with barbecue subject matter. "How Do You Want That Burnt?" and "Dad's Grill Work Is Always Well Done." I decided to replace one with a different topic and was deciding between an illustration of Dad on a riding lawn mower that read "All Gassed Up and No Place to Mow" and a drawing of a medieval guy on a putting green with "Eat, Drink and Be Merry For Tomorrow You May Golf."

I was awakened from my reverie by the phone ringing. It was Margaret. "I bopped down to take Charlie out for a surprise lunch, but he's out at the warehouse doing something with somebody or something. So I'm letting you take me to lunch."

"Was I your first choice?"

"Absolutely, Charlie was just, you know, means to an end."

"I understand. Where are you?" With the cell phone still pressed to her ear, Margaret popped her head into view in my door frame and made a lively little dance move.

"I'm close. Beam me up, Scotty."

"So you came in a beamer," I said. Her short angled haircut looked fresh and perfect. She was wearing a thin white blouse tucked into tight jeans. She looked like she'd lost a little weight.

"It's your lucky day, Mitch. You get me. I already left Charlie a voice mail saying we were running off together. It's a done deal."

"Let's do it."

"First some lunch. Italian?"

"Mix of German and English, with a wee bit of Scottish on me dear mother's side."

We went to a little subs and pasta place in Westport. The have good Italian bread sandwiches with pasta salads. It was a perfectly warm and glowing day, high sky with bright little boats of clouds. We sat at the outside patio just off the busy street.

"How are the new friends?" I asked as I took the wax paper off my sandwich.

"Delicious." Margaret said as she ate a forkful of colorful cold pasta.

"The food or your pals?"

"Both. Terri and I are flying up to Chicago for an overnight shopping trip."

"Any museums in the plans?"

"We'll probably stick to clothes and shoes. Maybe take in a play."

"It's good to see you back to your old self."

"I'm old?" Margaret exclaimed with smiling indignity.

"You know what I mean. You're obviously happy." I was glad for her, although I have to admit I had found some satisfaction and validation and a small thrill in her calls late at night. I was guessing that was not likely to be happening again any time soon. "And you're not old. You still have "hot babe" written all over you."

"Temporary tattoos. *Temp-o-rary*. And they're not *all* over." I raised my eyebrows as we exchanged sidelong smiles. Then her expression got a little serious. "I want to thank you," she said.

"Hey, sandwich, side salad and diet coke. What are we talking here, six dollars? After all the terrific meals I've had at your house, it's nothing."

"I was down and vulnerable and you were a good friend. I was confused, a little lost. Something might have happened but you were in perfect control. I appreciate everything."

"It may not be proper to say I was tempted, so I won't say that."

"I even appreciate your saying that, Mitch." She carefully folded up her white food wrapper and took a long sip through her straw. "And now that I'm not quite as self-absorbed, let me ask you, my good friend, how you are. You're fairly damn happy, aren't you? "

"Clams and I chart out at the same level."

"Keeping things simple, if I know you."

"You could illustrate my life with a pie chart and you would only need about half a dozen wedges. Work, Sleep, Socializing, Physical Activities, Reading, Lunch with Margaret."

"And according to Charlie, you have a girlfriend."

"I've had a series of date with a very nice young lady. Not quite girlfriend in the one word sense. More like girl and friend at this stage."

"Good luck with that. Sincerely. I hope it goes the way you want it to, no matter what that is." She looked at me intently for a few seconds as I gazed up at the exuberant sky. "You're looking up at the clouds. You've always been externally focused. So many of us just look inward, viewing the world as a hall of mirrors where we see our own reflection, aware of everything that is right or wrong in our lives and how we're being treated. And," she laughed and lightly slapped my knee, "as long as we're having sex, well, hey."

I didn't say anything, just smiled. I was thinking how I couldn't live the life of Ted, loving them and leaving them. The look of suppressed surprise and hurt on any face for any reason becomes a permanent painful memory for me. I've never forgotten, and can't recall without a twinge of pain, the look on the face of Beth Atkinson when she brought up the subject of prom as we were talking at our desks before the start of English class and I mentioned that I had a date for the spring event, having impulsively asked out a younger girl who made me laugh as I had gotten to know her while we were bagging cookies and brownies at a Thespian Club bake sale in the cafeteria.

I can't remember much about the dance or the date, but I have a clear image of a cue crooked smile dissolving before I turned away abruptly and started joking around with the newly arrived Squirrel.

"I feel like I have a pretty full life. I do fine by keeping busy all the time. One activity after another. Not a lot of meditation. I survive on the crumbs of brief activities and the vestiges of affection."

"Excuse me, on the what of what?"

"I don't know where that came from or what it means. I just had some things pop into my head. I suddenly pictured Kim and the small signs of affection she showed now and then."

"Mitch, are you familiar with the term 'scatterbrained?'" I used both hands to point to my head and then wriggled all my fingers. And my mind was feeling a little scattered. Margaret had gotten me thinking about Beth Atkinson and high school, various young guys and their girlfriends in instantly intense relationships, followed by pregnant brides walking down aisles with grooms set to earn paltry livings. And I was thinking what I had thought in my teen years, that those people seemed to be making partner decisions based on very small pools of availability and a very limited set of possibilities. Until I'd had a chance to get out in the world, at least to college for some years, how could I feel I had not reduced my opportunities too severely?

There was a guy in our class who was a stellar athlete by local standards and an honorable mention on Des Moines Register lists in football and wrestling. He was fairly quiet, indifferent to studies. His stature at school sports gave him access to the prettiest of the non-studious lively girls, a cheerleader and member of homecoming royalty. By spring she was pregnant. They married at a small country church set in a gravel lot just of an oiled county road. The still cold March wind pounded on the white wooden walls. The loose metallic rattling of the sizable furnace fan kicked off and on during the brief standard ceremony and impersonal sermon and surging sobs of the bride's mother.

Squirrel and I knew the bride pretty well from sharing classes with a girl who responded with unforced musical laughter to our ongoing banter and commentary. We often sat in the same row due to the coincidence of our last names beginning with the same letter. Squirrel's family car was one of the few in the sloping parking lot that contained teens. We didn't converse much while driving to and from the service. I was too caught up in fears that such a thing could happen to me at this stage of my young life and I was preoccupied with reassuring myself there were ways to make sure it didn't.

The young couple remained in town. Over the years they avoided class reunions. I heard they had raised a sullen boy whose regular arrests for petty thievery and vandalism gave him a reputation but didn't add up to enough larceny to land him in one of the state juvenile facilities. He dropped out of high school and joined the Navy and was pretty much gone for good. When I thought about his parents, I imagined a woman of middle age in a simple dress under a man's plaid shirt, taking a basket of heavy wet laundry to hang on an outside line, cigarette loose in her mouth as she pinned up white cotton and blue denim clothing with red chapped hands.

I pictured her husband at this county job, doing road and bridge maintenance, taking a break in the cab of a pick-up truck with the door slung open wide, his hands in cloth gloves holding a steaming thermos cap of coffee, his gaze vacant and distant. He would check out of work at the courthouse at four in the afternoon and walk across the street to the VFW or Harold's and sit at the bar with a can of the least expensive beer in front of him on the bar while the dull slap of playing cards measure time like a metronome at a low round table behind him. Around six o'clock he would drive to a home devoid of any reading material other than catalogs for guns and cheap household goods and eat a simple meal comprised largely of potatoes and ground beef.

Such imaginings had kept me from getting involved with Beth in high school. It was mildly electric to talk to girls, especially outside of the classroom at parks or drive-in restaurants, the voltage increased by girls who were older and smugly confident. But I kept my distance. College was a continuation of the same attitude. Dating was more frequent, casual and without commitment. Then I met Kim.

It was a Friday night. I was at my student apartment, a junior rooming with two other guys. They had gone out for the evening. I had come back after playing racket ball at the field house and was working on a term paper for Sons and Lovers. It was early. I planned to look over my notes from the book and maybe do an outline before going downtown and seeing who might be sitting in the booths of the bars that catered to students. The book ends with the protagonist standing at some distance from the night lights of a city, midway between his origins in a grimy impoverished coal mining town and his future as a writer. He surveys the illuminated city and pauses briefly before deciding to walk towards it. I was searching through my index cards for elements of what those lights in the darkness might represent and I was jotting down words like hope, dreams, civilization, romance and knowledge.

I was wearing a headset with ear pieces hooked to a stereo and listening to the wild whisky voice of Janis Joplin. I knew people were coming up the wooden steps to our second story duplex apartment when I felt the familiar vibrations. I went from the living room to the kitchen where a roommate and his short-skirted girlfriend were taking off coats as other people came up the steps. Just before the guests walked in, my roommate pulled quarts of beer and a fifth of bourbon from a paper bag and said, "You've got a date."

It was Kim. Her date for the evening had gotten drunk, peaked very early, and passed out before the group got to our place. She came up the stairs and walked in smiling, looking like one of the dark-haired smiling beauties that get cast in lead roles in romantic comedies. Stunning in a way and still somewhat the cute and friendly girl next door Lucky me.

"What's Charlie doing at the plant?" Margaret asked as drank the last of her diet soda and rattle the ice.

"Beats me. He likes going there. He likes the blue collar feel of the place. Reminds him of his youthful past." Margaret walked with an easy rhythm to a song in her head as she tossed her lunch debris into a big wire outdoor container. "You've got that right," she said.

"He loved working at his Dad's small machine shops, tearing apart and rebuilding lawn mower engines. I don't know why he didn't take over the business."

"Artistic bent, I guess. Pushed toward designing in school maybe. Who knows."

Charlie was ten years older than his wife. They met when he was playing tennis at the Plaza courts one summer and she was working there between semesters at Kansas University. Occasionally he'd ask her to hit with him while he was waiting for his opponents and wanted to warm up. I can picture her as quite a sunlit sight in her little white outfit, racing around the court to return corner shots and stooping to pick up errant balls.

Margaret had just come off a shaky relationship with a boy from school. About the time they were getting pretty serious, he jumped headfirst into recreational drugs. Using and selling. She started to pull away pretty fast, then bolted from him after he had gotten into a brawling fistfight outside a bar on Massachusetts Avenue in downtown Lawrence. A few months later he died in a motorcycle accident, flying up a hilly one way street in the wrong direction in the middle of the night, slamming into the front of a truck and flying off the vehicle that had just recently transported Margaret to classes and bars.

She had told me a long time ago about Charlie's polite requests for drinks and snacks at the tennis food counter and his joking without disrespect on the courts. His maturity and possession of a steady professional job, his encouraging way of encouraging and instructing her fledgling strokes, and later one when he started taking her out to Plaza restaurants, his interest in her studies and his ease at handling himself among the wealthier patrons in Plaza shops, made him quietly appealing.

He was in the process of buying their current house in its rundown state from its longtime residents when they met. Margaret also liked his creative side, his office full of designs in various stages of completion and the little cartoon drawings her put on notes and cards. She loved him truly, found in him a warm and loving companion, had absolutely no complaints. With Charlie and his friends from work she felt that she was part of a witty and attractive group of people who were constantly out and about.

When Eunice and her husband took groups to Plaza restaurants and picked up the check for ten, she felt she had been set down in a world more sophisticated and exciting than she could have imagined while growing up in a town with a single street of businesses in central Kansas. She was grateful for the acceptance and friendship and well-mannered attention from Eunice's husband, enjoying his joy at the fast-flying quips and vivid conversations of the employees he had hired and brought together.

"Got a little extra time?" Margaret asked. She offered to buy me a cup of coffee.

"For you, sure. For you and free coffee, how can I say no?"

"You know I love Charlie," she said as she settled into a comfortable slumped position on the cushioned iron chair. "I surely do."

"Margaret, it's obvious."

"He makes me laugh. One of the most powerful aphrodisiacs known to woman. His love is a big, cozy, warm comforter, a cocoon that wraps around my life without being suffocating. He gives me space and freedom. I still get a little surge of happiness when he comes home." She took a tentative sip of her fresh coffee and looked away. "Excitement comes from other places. It comes from being around bright, beautiful people. Not just the outward beauty, but an inward kind of thing. You and Kim. Even when I was out with Kim. When the two of us walked around the Nelson or went in August to see the butterflies at Powell Gardens or had lunch at some little place up in Weston during Christmas shopping. Or if we decided to have happy hour drinks in little dresses we'd just bought the weekend before. We got looks, sometimes even free drinks sent our way. We were a couple of hot chicks out on the town, getting those looks and those drinks in tribute. I don't want to embarrass you, but I'm going to say that it felt good to feel sexy."

"Well, you weren't deluding yourself, Margaret. You had it all, have it all. Your origins occurred in a small town grown smaller by the depletion of oil under the limestone. Doesn't detract at all from all you've got going for you. You haven't been like that town. You haven't lost a thing over the years."

"And sometimes when it was just you and me, in the kitchen chopping vegetables for a holiday dinner in cold weather or lying on beach towels while Charlie and Kim were off fetching drinks or you and me coming up with movie titles for Charades, well, a little thrill happened and it meant a lot. I just wanted to say something to you sometime. I guess this is the time." Her eyelids fluttered as she looked at me and then away from me and back at me again.

"Margaret, I know exactly, *exactly,* what you're talking about." I considered touching her hand, but her somewhat withdrawn posture and raised knees kept me from reaching over.

"I was happy then, Mitch, very happy. I would never cheat on Charlie. I'm not even tempted. Not even a little. But I did get a rush. And now with these new friends, it's back. Not like before. But it's pretty good. Good enough."

"I'm glad," I said.

Back at work she came inside with me, kissing me with a brushing motion on the cheek in the elevator before going off to see if her husband had come back from the plant. I thought about the beginnings of their relationship for a good while back at my desk. Knowing what I did, I wondered if it had started with her in a state of some desperation, which is never ideal for decision making.

All of my best finds came when I wasn't searching. Kim is the most obvious example. There are many other, pretty trivial ones. One of the best meals I ever had took place after I'd been hiking during an open afternoon at a conference in Colorado. I was with a guy I'd met during one of the breakout sessions and we'd gotten lost and got back to the lodge late in the day, after the event dinner had been served. We took a rental car to the first restaurant we came across, a small old place made of logs with a vinyl siding addition. An elderly woman with gray hair tied up in a loose bun cooked up pan fried chicken and fluffy mashed potatoes and a thick peppery gravy that all added up to heaven on a heavy white plate. <u>Catcher In The Rye</u> got passed to me in eleventh grade study hall and I only opened it as an excuse to delay working on the dreaded and mysterious algebra.

For many years I hadn't required a third or fourth person to supplement my relationship with Kim to keep my daily life interesting and dynamic. Just being with her made any activity a pleasure. An evening car trip of two or three hours, with cigarettes and a thermos of coffee, listening to engaging radio music so much better than today's fare, was something to look forward to and savor. A slow-moving Saturday that began with half an hour of wakefulness in bed, making vague plans for day ahead, light touching and kissing, was a special holiday.

We didn't take many snapshots in our early years. I have some taken by friends and family, kept loose in a kitchen drawer where I shuffle through them when looking for a paper clip or tape to seal an unruly envelope. There are shots of Kim on a model runway in various sun dresses and shorts outfits from a few stints of showcasing new lines of clothing for a department store in Iowa City. She got the job while going through racks of blouses and being spotted by one of the owners.

There are a few black and white pictures of the two of us together as undergraduates. We had been walking hand in hand along the river on a late fall day that was unexpectedly warm. A student photographer was shooting for a class and wanted to get some close-ups of us laughing, kissing while standing and lying down, sitting side by side at the water's edge, hugging with thoughtful expressions. The images showed up in the mail a few weeks later. In a lot of the shots we're stiff and self-conscious, but a few look natural, given a veneer of romanticism by the shades of gray treatment.

I have just a few pictures of Kim in our first home in Kansas City, taken when we first moved in with almost no furniture. She's standing in every one of them. We lived in a duplex in an old part of midtown next to a small rental house with a steady parade of short term renters. The first occupants were a group of male students attending the nearby University of Missouri at Kansas City. Their most memorable achievement was going home for Christmas break and leaving two aquariums of fish. The furnace failed during a huge and sudden drop in temperature and the tanks froze, leaving the fish posing in mid-swim with gapping mouths and wide open eyes.

The college kids were followed by an extremely pale and thin family with a little girl who only appeared in late evening for brief periods on the little front porch. The parents drove through our rented backyard to park in the lawn behind their house. We liked to imagine them as fugitives. One day they were just gone.

They were followed by an extremely fat young couple who seemed to have dried mud perpetually caking their bib overalls, perhaps from constant recreational fishing. They parked their slanted pick-up truck at the curb with the driver side door always open and ready to admit their enormous selves. Right to stereotype, they were jolly. They hauled in big boxes and buckets of fast food and after a decent interval for consuming it, emitted loud sounds of intense pleasure from the open window of their bedroom. We used to joke that we didn't know if the moans and shrieks of ecstasy came from food or sex.

The last neighbors owned a dark short-haired pit bull that was allowed to roam untethered and refused to let us out our front door. He just stood here staring at us, growling low. We had to call the police to come over and get the dog back inside and warn the owners. The situation was resolved for good when the crazy dog injured itself while attacking a running lawnmower. It was all unfamiliar territory to a couple of young Iowa transplants, but rather than being unsettling or disturbing, we found it exotic and amusing. We had jobs we liked and new friends we enjoyed. We felt like a couple of expatriats living in Paris.

After many years of experiencing a sunny outlook on life and love, effortless happiness arising from simply living everyday life, slowly and then almost all at once, a chasm appeared and widened between Kim and me. I hadn't seen it coming. I was totally surprised . I suppose I had been missing signals all along. I knew I was capable of that. In our married student days Kim and I had been casual friends with the couple next door. We said fed their cat when they were out of town, said hello in coming and going, had infrequent meals together.

One day I picked up our mail from the slots near the main entrance to our big red brick building. I opened the envelopes as I walked up the steps to our second floor apartment. I pulled out the contents and laid them on the counter. At first I was confused at a page that outlined the resolution of a bill from an insurance company. Then I noticed the name and address. It was supposed to have gone to our neighbors. The document listed half a dozen sessions for treatment of depression. It was for the wife next door, the outwardly perky young woman with the trim body and welcoming smile that I liked to encounter in the hallway.

Perhaps I had been as oblivious to what was going on in my own home many years later in Kansas City where the days seemed to pass in a continually happy stream punctuated by moments and even hours of deep emotion and hilarity and passion without any need for enhancement by wealth or possessions or fulfillment beyond the easily attainable by aptitude and circumstance and relationships.

When Megan was born, everything seemed to me to stay intact but heightened by her presence. When she turned out to be precocious and sweet with an advance sense of humor, it didn't seem like things could get much better. Later on Kim got quieter and more distant , increasingly interested in spending time with some women she'd met at the nurse's union meetings, eventually seeing a therapist who was right on top of a trend towards women's assertiveness and confrontation and independence.

I don't pretend to know which is chicken and which is egg in deteriorating and then crashing marriages. I could tell that the routine in Kim's personal life that had been satisfying and more than pleasant lost its luster. There wasn't the continued thrill even after experiences repeated many times. It wasn't like the Karen Carpenter album she played over and over in our Iowa City student home. Car trips were just means of getting from point A to point B. In our solid two-story Kansas City home discussions and disagreements sank into arguments of rising volume and barely restrained physicality, and that was probably the point of no return.

Chapter Twenty-nine

Irene's former boyfriend drove into town in the middle of a Friday afternoon. He called her at work and asked her to meet him at the bar of her choice. She picked a little corner bar a few blocks from the office.

"He's a very nice guy," Irene told me. "From a town in Indiana. We dated last year when he got his MBA and joined my firm. Comes from a super family."

She had broken off the relationship, just hadn't felt that spark, that happy glow that starts in the heart and flows throughout you. They had been a couple for less than a year, spending more than a few weekends at the home of his parents in a middle class neighborhood in a city of about fifty thousand.

His mother and father were jolly people, down to earth and hardworking at their jobs and around the house, uncomplaining, grateful to have a place of their own, never putting pressure on any of their three sons to pursue a particular life or career. They laid out bountiful Sunday dinners with two kinds of meat, vegetables from glass jars they had filled up from their backyard garden in late summer, big stacks of bread cut thick. Irene was always happy to visit. The parents had kind hearts and ready smiles, found their pleasure in simple things like long slow drives in the country while licking ice cream cones from the Dairy Sweet and meandering conversations on their broad front porch while sipping lemonade or iced tea.

Irene was immediately drawn to the older couple, their basic goodness and quiet ways of helping out friends and neighbors, their brief prayers of thanks before each meal. She found them endlessly interesting to talk to as they went over their rural childhood and schooling and seasonal social activities. Irene would help out in the kitchen or shop with the mother while the men went off to hunt or fish. The youngest son was still at home, a high school senior with a pretty, cheerful girlfriend. The three females would bake or quilt or pick summer wildflowers along tarred country roads.

Irene admitted to dating the young man longer than she would have if she had not met the family and been exposed to their heartwarming values and innate goodness. The second floor of the family house was spacious and open to balmy summer cross winds and abundant sunshine. The house was sheltered by tall pin oaks and leafy elms. Cooling breezes blew in on even the hottest of evenings, making the bedrooms into refreshing oases where you could air dry after a shower before changing clothes to go out to a movie.

The drive from St. Louis was its own pleasure. Half of it was on two lane highways that snaked past and through little towns, visible for many miles due to narrow triangular church spires rising above the trees, with neatly kept homes on large well-maintained square lawns.

I imagined the old boyfriend's thrill at being in the car with Irene on the four hour drive home. I pictured him endlessly grinning at his good fortune and seeing a newfound image of himself, a guy who could get a babe like Irene for a girlfriend. It's interesting how you can see yourself one way up to a certain point in your life, then have a sudden change that alters that inner perception. Like a shy girl who doubts the beauty encased in her long limbs and perfect features and thick loose hair until she is persuaded by unjealous friends to enter a local beauty contest that she wins or a man who is unexpectedly promoted at his company to a very high executive level due to abilities and a strong character that were more obvious to others than they were to himself.

As for myself, I was not crazy about Irene's getting together with Old Beau. I couldn't see any positive side. But what could I say? I dropped Irene off at the designated bar around six with instructions to return in half an hour as though we were needed to make it to an appointment by seven.

When I did show up to get her, Irene was seated with a guy at a small round table in the middle of the room. She had a half full glass of white wine in front of her and he had a tight grip on a long necked bottle of beer. He was wearing a blue short sleeve shirt with a pocket. He had broad shoulders and firm rounded biceps that pushed up the shirt fabric. The place was fairly full and pretty noisy in a clattery way.

I walked up to the table and introduced myself, shook hands. Irene stood and lifted her purse off the back of her chair.

"Zach, you didn't need to drive all the way over here," Irene said calmly but sternly. "I've got to go now. Mitch and I have to be somewhere."

"You're leaving?" Zach asked with genuine surprise.

"I'm leaving, we're leaving," Irene said. "You had your say. I listened carefully. I hope you feel better."

"I drove all the way over here just to see you," Zach said hopelessly, somewhat dazed. "And you're just going to leave? Goddammit, Irene, sit down and talk to me."

Irene's direct look into my eyes was a prod to get us away quickly. I gently took her arm and guided her to my side so that I was between Zach and her. I said, "We need to run. Got a thing. Nice to meet you. Really need to go."

"Oh, yeah, right, gotta run. Well, run, goddamn, run away." He made a quick gesture with his bottle hand that sent some of the contents out and onto the floor. He sat and glared as we went out to the street.

"He was drinking before I got there," Irene said, eyes wide in aftershock, as we walked quickly to where my car was parked down the street. "He never used to drink that much. He seems changed. I never used to be nervous around him, but this was different."

I thought I might know what had changed. The whole incident made me think of my earliest college days, when boys would follow their hot high school sweeties to the big state school and pick them up several times a week in the lobby of the girls' dormitory. This would go on for some period of weeks until the hometown guys would lose out to some new man with more to offer in whatever categories the girls found more appealing.

I knew these freshman on my own dorm floor, impressed when they introduced me to these fabulous smiling women. The girls would be pretty visible for a while, and then not so much. Then I'd see one girl and then another and another downtown or at the student union with a guy who had an advanced sense of clothing fashion and a noticeably sophisticated haircut along with an air of easy self-confidence that stopped short of arrogance.

Later on at the dorm indoor parties or picnics along the river, the hometown guy would be with a new girl, less full-bodied than the girl from home and not as pretty or sure of herself. I couldn't help feeling sorry for these young men and wished them well.

I recall one guy in particular. He was kind of scrawny and very average looking with no real distinguishing features. He was nice enough, polite in a way that would impress your mom, but had no real wit or really anything very interesting to say. His early girlfriend fell into the gorgeous category. She was Italian, with jet black hair cut at a dramatic angle and features placed perfectly on her high cheek boned face. She was lively with an energetic smile and she dressed to get attention.

The skinny guy introduced her to all of us in the dorm, in a seemingly quick and desperate show of his ability to catch a babe before the inevitable release. Sure enough, within a few weeks, she was seen around campus with a tall handsome law student, a guy who wore nice clothes even to class on Monday and drove a convertible in excellent condition.

I'd see the former boyfriend in the steady company of a mousy little girl who clutched her books and purse tight to her chest as she walked beside him. As far as I knew, he didn't bring her to dorm functions or to nap on his bed while he worked on a term paper.

Once Irene and I were in the car, she let out a long breath. I pulled out into moderate traffic. A large black SUV was immediately close behind us. I could see Zach's stony face in the rearview mirror. "Don't look now. We've got a tailgater."

"Oh, no."

At first I drove the speed limit down past the Country Club Plaza, basically ignoring the guy, trying to let a sequence of stoplights separate us. Didn't work. After sliding through a few yellows turning to red, I still had him on the bumper. I was relieved and impressed that Irene took it all calmly. She touched my shoulder and gave me a tight smile of encouragement.

"He's still with us," I said. "My expert evasive action failed to dislodge our predator."

"By evasive action, I guess you're referring to driving in a straight line at normal speed."

"That would be a roger."

After getting past the Plaza shops I climbed the long looping street that rose into the homes of the city's old money along a wide boulevard. Zach was with us all the way. I continued down the broad street for several blocks before making an abrupt turn into the left lane and onto a side street. No luck. When Zach stopped behind us at a stop sign, he gunned his engine into a loud staccato roar.

"Now he's trying to get our attention," Irene said with slight tension rising in her voice. "I don't know what's gotten into him. He's never been like this before."

"First time for everything," I said. I'm going to try a little harder to shake him. Okay?"

Irene shrugged and nodded her assent. I stuck to primary roads and sped up a little, tried to get other cars between us. I succeeded a few times for short distances, but then he would barrel out and around the intervening vehicles and be right on us again. Still I didn't feel panicky. I had that serenity, false or not, that you get when dealing with younger people in stressful situations, thinking your experience and their hesitation in asserting themselves against an older person gives you some sort of edge.

"Should I call 911?" Irene reached into her purse and came out with a cell phone.

"Give me a little more time. Maybe he'll cool off and we can all just go home."

Just then Zach pulled alongside us and glared down at Irene. She covered the phone with her hands and pushed it into her lap. He stayed right next to us for two blocks, driving in the wrong lane. Big mistake.

At the first intersection I faked a slow sliding stop then suddenly turned away from the black vehicle and took off down a side street. I turned corners at random, ending up in a neighborhood of bungalows and large square stucco homes. I pulled alongside a curb between two parked cars in front of a darkened house and turned off the headlights with the motor running.

"I'm really sorry, Mitch." Irene spoke just above a whisper. "I feel like it's my fault somehow."

"Only for being such an appealing woman. He's realized what he's lost. Seriously. It's hit him hard. He's having a hell of a time dealing with the breakup. Seeing us together probably really provoked him. Proverbial salt in the wound. He may just need time and distance in order to calm down."

Irene leaned across the protruding parking brake for an awkward hug and a kiss. We were sitting back in our seats when the engine roar bolted down the street. It charged hard at us. High beam headlights. Instead of fear, my reaction was anger. Instantly. All fight, no flight. I threw open the car door and stepped out. I told Irene to lock the doors.

The big black monster came to a sliding screaming angled stop a few yards away. Zach hopped down and slammed the door behind him, landing with fists wrapped hard into tight balls. I knew I wouldn't throw the first punch. Let him start. Get charged with assault. Bring it on, tough guy.

I felt calm and even a little curious. I also felt a fair degree of confidence in my ability to calm him down by a passive posture and a nonchalant tone of voice, one of reassurance and no threat. When he said, "Guess you think you're hot shit, don't you" in a voice watery under the weight of heavy tears, I lost any feelings of aggression. He was wounded. He seemed more pathetic than anything. The hurting was palpable. He'd lost the one absolutely gorgeous girlfriend he was likely to have and he knew it. His life stretched before him, gray and monotonous, to a blurred distant frightening horizon.

"Well, you're nothing, man. You're no big deal," he wailed.

"Hey, guy. Let's take a little chill break."

"Take her. I don't care. You can have her. She's nothing to me. We're through."

I felt no urge to taunt him. I learned a long time ago that there is no satisfaction in winning verbal jousts with vulnerable opponents. You just end up feeling like a bully.

"Calm down," I said. "You've been drinking. You're upset. It's cool."

The pull of my voice brought him a few stiff steps closer to me. We locked stares and just stood there six feet apart. I leaned to the lawn side of the curb, planning to fall to the grass if he came at me.

A siren whined in the distance.

"She called 911," I said. "They'll be here in seconds."

Zach thrust his fists hard against his hips and stomped back to his big car. He paused a second with a hand on the door handle before managing to tear himself out of the situation and climbing up and racing away.

Back in my car I asked Irene if she had alerted the cops. "Tried to. No charge. Completely dead."

In eluding Zach, I had ended up with Irene in a midtown neighborhood with tall broad trees and large older homes of two and three stories. We were only a few blocks away from the street where Kim and I had owned our first place. Megan was born during that time, thrusting us into the sleep deprived world of diapers, plastic toys in primary colors and early morning meals served at length with a tiny spoon.

The neighborhood was then transitioning from grandparents long past having children at home to young energetic good-looking singles and couples just starting families. Fitness was part of everyday life. Jogging was a popular inexpensive first step towards health club memberships and workout equipment in basement gyms.

Kim and I quickly became friends with other parents living around us. We got to know a couple down the street after only a few weeks. The husband was a fanatic golfer. He'd played varsity at a small college and had fellow enthusiasts as regular playing partners. Long weekends and weeks of vacation took him to courses in other states as his wife stayed home to chase their very active toddler son around the yard and up the sidewalk. They were from Texas. They'd met in college and moved to Kansas City when he got a job selling pharmaceuticals for a prosperous local company.

She was a honey blonde with long curls and a slow warm way of talking. She wore a one-piece swimsuit in the summer when she mowed the lawn or joined her little guy in races through the sprinkler. It was fairly common to see her racing across the hot cement path by their house in her tight metallic suit, tanned arms pumping as she caught and scooped up the short perpetual escapee she was raising.

A few houses in the opposite direction a fortyish lawyer lived with his very young wife and four-year-old daughter. He worked a lot of hours. They lived in the biggest, most updated house in the area. The family of three sometimes took walks in the small time frame between late dinners and nightfall. Afterwards you could see the light on in his upstairs office.

Sometimes the lawyer would invite me over to watch an afternoon's worth of college or professional football with Megan in tow while our wives went out to shop or eat. We'd play with the children on their thick gray carpet while a muted athletic contest played out on television. He was fun to talk to. He read a fair amount, pretty much from the nonfiction list of best-sellers, and he could convey their information in an interesting way that invited my comments. He had some curiosity about literature and seemed genuinely engaged when I told him about Norman Mailer's Executioner's Song, so fascinating and fast-paced that I was reading it without immediately falling into a deep new father's sleep at night in the otherwise brief interval between sliding into bed next to a table lamp and nodding off.

At the end of our afternoons with the children the living room would be littered with plush animals and puzzle pieces the size of cookies. The kids stayed active and happy, the time went by quickly. Once in a great while I would break my self-imposed fasting from golf and join the lawyer and his buddies for a sunny round on a course somewhere around town. His friends were as welcoming and relaxed as he was, and they didn't make me feel awkward for not joining in their moderately expensive golf betting.

Sometimes during our afternoons together my legal pal would ask to be excused for twenty minutes. A few years earlier he had purchased a used upright piano and had someone teach him by rote how to play five songs by the Rolling Stones. This was his only reason for getting the large instrument. I don't know why he chose piano over guitar, but he went with the big box of sound and I didn't question it. With a wife and child in the house, one or the other of them always wanting or needing rest and quiet, he had little opportunity to indulge his rudimentary passion. I was more than happy to give him the gift of time while he banged out the chords and sang out joyfully. He wasn't awful. It made me almost laugh to share his simple happiness.

The lawyer's wife was curvy and bouncy with short dark hair that slid across her cheek when she tilted her head forward. She dressed very young even for someone of her youthful age, tight jeans and t-shirts, little tops with skinny strings for straps. The lawyer bought her quite a bit of jewelry, and she didn't let it sit idly in a drawer. She never had on fewer than five bracelets on her non-watch wrist and usually had on several thin necklaces of various metals or stones and dark beads.

I liked her for her easy willingness to go ahead and display the gifts that nature and her accomplished husband had given her . What the hell. When she got dressed up to attend a social function involving the law office, putting on a lacy dress of red or black, sometimes ankle length, other times high on her thighs, she'd look stunning when she came through our front door to leave her daughter with us for the evening.

The young mom was quiet but not shy, clever in a way that could truly surprise and delight. She had an easy way with all small children, could relate to them on their level while staying in charge. Her pretty smile was constant, a knowing look that conveyed peace and contentment and gratitude for her situation, being able to stay home with her child all day in a house far beyond the means of most women her age, married to a man who made it a priority to spend part of every well-off day with his family and give her impromptu unrequested breaks from parenting. She didn't aggressively pursue conversation but she maintained a look and pose of approachability and proved herself capable of being interesting on almost any topic anyone might bring up.

The young singles in the neighborhood tended to spend their active hours outside the immediate area. They might have been off using the skis that were sometimes strapped to the roofs of their higher priced compact cars or the bicycles attached to frames hooked onto trunk and rear bumper. They didn't seem to entertain a lot at home beyond the occasional person who would park in a driveway late at night and drive off mid-morning about the time one might complete a lingering breakfast. The unattached neighbors sometimes came to block parties, carrying side dishes purchased at the grocery store and wearing summer clothes that showed off their trim bodies. They tended to congregate near the volleyball net set up in the blocked off street and play with more vigor and competitiveness than the parents among us.

One of them might set up a small beer keg with a stack of big disposable tumblers on it, and that would raise the volume of the shouted coaching and highly physical celebrations of victories. They would be the first to leave, followed by spouses who need to get little ones to bed, leaving the remaining married men and women to sit in webbed lawn chairs to chat about schooling and in-laws and difficulty of budgeting in the problematic world of ear infections and growth spurts and old plumbing.

The only unmarried resident with much visibility was a woman who danced for the Kansas City Ballet. She had parties in her yard, sometimes formal with white tablecloths and servers in bow ties and strolling musicians who played and strolled unobtrusively. The events took place in front of her house, a large stately stucco with a deep sheltered front porch. Her backyard was small with a brick patio and some small fruit trees. The parties were quiet affairs, almost surrealistically so. Groups of three and four people in black attire stood with fluted drink glasses and nodded slowly as they looked at the person in their midst making small relaxed gestures and no sound audible to anyone pushing a stroller by on the sidewalk.

The ballet dancer often used her expansive treeless front lawn for sunbathing. She had an expensive looking white metal chaise with a long light blue cushion. She would wear to tiny pieces of black and lie beneath the vibrating summer sun while she listened to a radio headset. She appeared oblivious to the cars that slowed perceptibly as they drove past.

The married neighborhood men commented on her at block parties and at pot luck dinners during the winter holidays when they were safely beyond wifely earshot. They noticed her in sun tanning attire, bending to fill a big watering can at a side faucet before lifting it with two hands to take to the plants in pots on the edge of her patio. If you were passing by and you made eye contact, she would acknowledge you by smiling and mouthing a silent hello. She was neither standoffish nor flirtatious, but the men were reluctant to be seen chatting with her or even waving in friendly greeting, so she lived among us in a fairly anonymous way.

When Megan got old enough to be mobile and interact with other children and play groups were being formed through direct invitation and notices on the bulletin board at the grocery store, Kim got involved with some moms and kids on the block behind us. She had torn off a phone number from the handwritten page while pushing a cart with Megan as passenger and called to connect with a woman whose daughter was exactly our daughter's age.

The new friend's husband was the co-owner of a barely surviving wine bar in a little street of shops half a mile from our house. The winery wife was very lively, wide-eyed and energetic, spilling out details of her marital life and alarming and amusing incidents in the neighborhood in rapid fire while she cut up chunks of cheese and apple refreshments or poured wine for the moms from half-filled bottles her husband brought home as leftovers as she chatted on about her husband's sexual stamina enhanced by liquor imbibed at work and followed it with a mock swoon and laughter.

The winery wife was a runner. She covered various streets in disparate directions in her late afternoon jogs and participated in charity events. Once a car with a middle-aged man at the wheel had slowly followed her, maintaining half a block's distance. She simply trotted up onto a porch where a workman was painting trim and asked for a drink from his big water jug while the driver sped off. She reported the incident at play group as no big deal and let the cautionary message remain implied.

In the years we lived in the neighborhood, before we left the convenience of a midtown and the charm of older, individually designed houses in order to avail Megan of the quality public schools in the suburbs, I had puzzling encounters with the sugar voiced Texan, the lawyer's wife, the dancer and the runner.

With the southerner I had three versions of the same thing. In the summer when Megan was in bed and Kim was watching television, when there was still some daylight reflecting hazily from a sun not completely set, I would set off from our house on a jaunt of three or four miles. The girl from the Lone Star State lived up a mild incline of half a block around the corner from our house. It was common for me to pass by when I was just taking off and hadn't built up to cruising speed.

The first incident occurred as she was standing between two rounded shrubs near her porch. She was wearing a short shiny robe with a matching fabric belt. Her speedy son was nowhere around. He may have been inside, collapsed in bed after a day of racing around. Her salesman husband may well have been out of town, as he often was, in western Kansas or northern Oklahoma doing the job that often took him away for a few days at a time. On this night my blonde neighbor stood with hands on hips and stared at me as I ran by, with one hand raised up in greeting.

A few days later she was out again at the same time of day, dressed the same but turned away from me. The robe was hitched higher, revealing a crescent of red fabric below the hem. The third time, just before I stopped using that route for evening runs, she was alone by the bushes and she was turned sideways. Again the skimpy robe was raised, held high by the cloth belt, and the front was open to reveal that she was wearing nothing underneath.

On all three occasions I had run past her without saying anything. The last time I sped up. At the time life with Kim and Megan seemed idyllic to me. At the end of my pleasant, well-paced work day I came home to welcoming, smiling females, each interesting and amusing in their own ways, living in the midst of a picturesque section of a good-looking city, surrounded by young people I was enjoying getting to know. I never considered rounding the block and coming back in the opposite direction to see what was going on in the gathering darkness so close to my home. I didn't allow myself to think too much about what might happen if I stopped and said hello.

On one level, as strange as it may sound, it seemed rude not to acknowledge the gesture from the blonde siren and somehow communicate an esteem building compliment. Some small slice of my male brain berated her husband for missing out on the delicious physical attributes of his wife and chastised him for driving her out into the yard for some type of desperate attempt at validation or acceptance or feelings of desirability, for making her behave in what must have embarrassed her once she got back inside and started unloading the dishwasher.

The prima lawn ballerina had an incredibly fit and graceful body. It was obvious as she moved about her lawn, bare feet gliding beneath a silky sleeveless black dress, champagne glass held close to her shoulder. When

I walked by her house holding Meg's hand or clutching a bag with more groceries than I had intended to buy, if she were socializing or catching some sun, she would thrust a firmly set facial expression at me. It was a look of longing and pain, an ache made visible, clearly framed in the dark tight hairdo that was pulled back from her handsome angular face. Sometimes the look lingered, other times it was just a shadow passing across her face.

We never met, got introduced or had a conversation. The only neighborhood functions she attended were her own. If she had a romantic life, she kept it hidden. She may have been lonely, perhaps bored off the performing stage, or she may have found complete or nearly complete fulfillment in pursuit of an arduous art and was only reacting to me as a brief but easy to dismiss reminder that she had foregone the pursuit of a life that could have been hers, one that involved a ready and steady spouse and a little girl who looked at the world with mature curiosity and asked absurd questions that revealed an acutely logical mind.

I saw my lithe neighbor dance professionally only one time, using tickets given to Kim and me by our lawyer friend, freebies from his firm, when a last minute childhood illness prevented him and his teen queen wife from attending. At the end of the ballet, as the cast came out individually to receive singular appreciation, she went to the center of the stage and curtsied in springy ballerina fashion and surveyed the audience. She looked right at me in the sixth row center left and the pained look came to the surface for just a second before being replaced by a wide, sincere smile of gratitude as she blew a kiss to the crowd.

I wondered on the drive home and sometimes later if I reminded her of someone in her past. I found it hard to imagine it had anything to do with irresistible good looks. The occasional high pitched catcalls tossed from a passing car of teen girls in groups of three or more, hurled anonymously along busy residential streets where I was running, had not left me with a self image of male animal magnetism. I guessed the passing whooping young women were mainly seeking release of pent-up boredom induced by the school day they were fleeing.

I knew I would never get close enough to the dancer to have the opportunity to explore the source of her nostalgic looks at me. And I wondered if I ever did speak to her whether the tenuous spider web of relationship would be broken and left to permanently dangle unconnected. It had happened before. On a day at the beach in Ozark country while Kim and Megan went to walk in the blanket of water lying on the hot sandy shore, I was on a blanket trying without success to penetrate a Henry James novel. Oh, well. A very tan busty woman in a white fluffy bikini, a big glistening diamond ring on her hand, spread a towel near me and laid down on her stomach. Soon she had undone her top and tilted her head so that her sunglasses were turned in my direction. She made lots of little shifts in position, raising up on her elbows and pulling back her auburn hair before stretching out prone again. All the while she smiled brightly.

The sunbather was wearing a red and yellow plastic sports watch. Just to see what would happen, I asked in a voice just a little louder than normal if she could tell me the time. She seemed startled. The smile dimmed. Her face became nearly expressionless. I pointed to my bare wrist and said, "Time?"

She held up the large dial of her wristwatch so I could see it, then quickly and expertly fastened her top before turning her head to face away from me. I took from the moment that the rules of whatever was in play forbade an exchange of words and that the end game was brief exchanges of furtive looks of admiration and distant interest.

My private encounter with the lawyer's wife was built on small bits of conversation. It was New Year's Eve. She and her husband were giving a party for the neighborhood and a few people from his firm. The spacious open downstairs of their white stucco was loud with chatter and clinking glassware and ceramic plates and metal utensils bouncing off the gleaming hardwood floors and plaster walls.

The lawyer was drinking a lot from a wide round glass filled with dark amber liquid, perhaps thinking that he would not be driving and his diet soda sipping wife could get up with their daughter in the morning. He glided with exaggerated swagger from one small standing group to another with his ample drink in one hand and an open bottle of scotch in the other, kissing the women in a friendly fashion and loudly whispering mild off-color comments to the men. The upright piano had been wheeled into the living room. Near midnight he announced that he would kick off the new year with a set of Rolling Stones songs. He apologized for their lack of thematic connection to the occasion, but said they would have to do because they were the only songs he could perform and it was his house. Everyone was ordered to join in with gusto.

The lawyer's wife, Cassie, had started giving me attention off and on while she refilled snack bowls and rinsed off dishes in the kitchen sink. She would smile at me in passing, giving me a look with mouth opened beyond what could be considered mere congeniality, frequently placing a hand high on my shoulder and asking me if I needed anything, anything at all.

I spent most of the evening in small gathering of men whose conversation revolved around workplace and sports and housing issues that came up at homes association meetings. I was mildly interested in most of the topics and mostly just enjoyed the festive atmosphere and the sight of so many women looking their best in carefully applied makeup and short glittering dresses with high heel shoes in bright contrasting colors. Off and on I would wander over to the couch where Kim was sitting alone or in sober conversation with some person taking a break from the hubbub, and I'd see if she wanted a refill of her orange juice or a few crackers to nibble on. She'd shoo me away with a weak, contented smile and a little flicker of her fingers.

About the time of the short piano concert, Cassie requested that I help her fetch party hats and horns from an upstairs room. I followed behind her up the steps to a guest bedroom where cardboard party accessories sat in boxes on the bed. Cassie was wearing a red outfit cut low in front with strands of thin gold necklaces laid against her skin.

When I started to pick up a box, she restrained me with a hand on my arm. She relaxed her smile to move into sultry, then she walked around me with an arm around my waist. Sound erupted downstairs as people shouted out "Happy New Year!" Cassie pressed down lightly on the box in my hands until it was back on the bed. "Happy New Year, Sweetheart," she said breathily. She leaned forward with eyes closed and kissed me lingeringly on the lips.

She pulled away without urgency, running a tongue over her deep red lips, when clumsy footsteps sounded heavily on the stairs. Her husband charged into the room, stopped for a second, then pointed to the box I had just set down. He ordered me to bring it downstairs right away before lurching out of the room while shouting, "Hurry up, hurry up, a year of bad luck if we don't put on goofy hats and toot cheap horns." Cassie bounced down the steps in front of me.

The run-in with the jogger involved a little more conversation. She called our home while her husband was tending to his wine business to say she needed to borrow a plunger to unclog the toilet her daughter had filled with armfuls of unrolled tissue. She had just put the little girl down for a nap, couldn't find their bathroom tool and would run over to get it when the child woke up.

I volunteered to walk over to her house and get the toilet water flowing down proper channels. She said that would be awesome, to just come through the unlocked front door and upstairs to where she would be in or around the bathroom, soaking up the recent overflow that had spilled onto the floor when her daughter flushed.

It took me a little while to locate our plunger. For some reason it had been placed on a high shelf in a hallway closet. Once I had it in hand, I did as I was instructed, climbing the cement steps to the two-story clapboard house and going through the frosted glassed front door without making any noise that could waken a sleeping toddler. I could hear classical music coming from a radio turned low and a woman's voice humming in absent-minded accompaniment.

"Ready to plunge right in," I said as I walked into the bathroom. She was standing at the sink, naked except for a bath towel low around her narrow runner hips, looking into a mirror she was wiping with a washcloth. She turned to look at me without expression, pulling her wet hair back from her face, then raising the thick burgundy towel around her damp freckled body and securing it under her arms without opening wide the cloth. She started to speak , but I didn't let her. I set the plunger on the floor and said quickly that she could use it and return it whenever, no hurry, and I went downstairs and out into the afternoon's blinding sunlight.

I think about the women in the old neighborhood from time to time. I feel a mixture of nostalgia and curiosity, and newfound longing now that I no longer have an obligation to a wife. I do miss the early days of adulthood when many women around me exuded joy and sensuality, and smiled constantly with expressions of satisfaction with self and vague desire for another, all of it taking place in a world suffused with its own source of light created from a family life of simple pleasures and freedom from conflict.

I still puzzle about what might have happened if I had made any type of move towards deeper involvement, if I had stepped forward to brush away a strand of hair loose on a cheek or responded to a look of longing with a mirroring look or a wink. I wondered, too, how it would have felt to be around the husbands once something physical had taken place, to look them in the eye, wondering if they had any suspicions about what was going on, whether they had knowledge or at least some sense of what their wives were all about, how I would feel at being the cause of pain and anger and humiliation for these seemingly very decent and personable men.

I had to wonder if the women, these young lovelies with fragrant stylish hair and smooth firm bodies, felt rejected by my lack of aggressive response, or were they affirmed and gratified and completely satisfied just to see me hesitate and vacillate, however momentarily, with interest they could readily assess when confronted with their considerable allure.

The closest I came to any understanding was when I once asked Eunice in a very general way about women coming on to men not their husbands around the neighborhood or at the office. At first a light wave of disappointment swept across her face, to be quickly replaced by a sardonic smile.

"Well, I surmise from your question that you don't think such a thing is possible from me. Otherwise you wouldn't have asked."

"There's your first insight. Not what I might have expected."

Eunice went on to explain that such things tend to be merely affairs of the moment, almost a reflex for some women, perhaps seeking affirmation or a cloudy vision of a romantic future, leftover from girlhood. The actions were not necessarily signals of trouble at home or a wish for anything sustained, didn't carry the expectation or even the desire for follow-up response. They were merely the instinctive actions of men and women in situations where circumstance placed them in proximity, over when over, done and done, to be enjoyed without guilt on the part of one's self without harsh judgment of another. I don't know how much Eunice believed what she was saying. She projected mild boredom with the topic and spoke right away without pausing to give thought.

I am unaware if Kim ever behaved towards other men the way women did towards me. I certainly never saw it. Of course, I noticed men looking at her, sometimes longer and more directly that what might have been considered proper or polite, staring at the long legs beneath a short denim skirt or watching her walk away from a laden picnic table with a flimsy paper plate of food while the rear pocket of her cutoff jeans jiggled just a bit. And if she went to the counter of a coffee shop to get us refills on coffee, it wasn't unusual for trim fashionably dressed customers to chat with her about nothing while giving their best smiles, probably to get a lingering look at her face and perhaps to gauge interest.

I never knew Kim to reciprocate the interest and I didn't really mind that men looked and flirted. It takes two to tango. I knew she had the kind of shape that flattered clothes as she moved with an easy unself-conscious grace that first turned my head. I suppose I assumed she was as overwhelmingly content with our white picket fence life as I was, the steady adequate income that gave us a house in a wholesome neighborhood without prestige or pretension and simple meals shared with our little family, or the likes of Charlie and Margaret, or the lawyer and his wife, as we build solid evenings on with wit and straightforward intelligence and uncomplicated diversions.

I thought Kim was fine with my reluctance to take over more responsibility at work or leave the company for more money or follow through on an entirely different career in the type of entertainment field that some see as glamorous and I just saw as doing my thing in a different arena with meaningless big money and achievement tainted by a phoniness because the success so often came from pandering and acquiescing. Maybe I had my nose too high up in the air to look down and see to see clearly what was happening around me.

"Home again, home again, thank God," Irene said as we pulled into her driveway. The house and yard were dark. Her roommate was out of town for the weekend.

"Everybody who wants a drink, raise your hand," I said.

Irene raised both hands and said, "Make mine a double. Hell, make it an quad."

"Four shots coming up."

Irene pushed around jingly things in her purse in search of her house key. A large dark figure jumped out of the bushes next to the porch.

"Zach!" Irene said sharply.

I stepped between him and her with my palms up.

"Hold on a minute there, Chief."

Zach stepped forward. His fist slammed hard into my temple and I went down on the concrete. For a few seconds I dreamed of myself in a meeting room with several strangers around a very long conference table, everyone talking in low mumbles. Then I was back at Irene's, energy knocked out of me. I couldn't see anything clearly.

I heard Irene calling my name. Not close and not far away. I was able to sit up and look in the direction of the sound, in the thin veil of illumination from a street lamp. Two blurry figures were moving together, struggling towards the street. I put a hand on the low rough stone wall and got to my feet. Blood was running in a trickle into the corner of my mouth.

My head throbbed. I could make out Zach pulling Irene by one arm while she pounded frantically on his shoulder. I collected enough strength to half run down the steps. I caught up with them as Zach was reaching for his car's door handle. I jumped on his back, putting one forearm across the front of his neck and the other behind it, then squeezed hard against his windpipe.

He let go of Irene. "Call the police," I yelled, tightening my grip on Zach. Irene hesitated, then disappeared into the darkness. Zach thrashed around, bucking and twisting, prying on my arms. His foot kicked against the curb and he stumbled backwards. We went down together. Everything ceased. Nothing.

When I awoke, rotating red and blue light were slicing through the night. Static-filled radio conversations crackled nearby. I was lying on a stretcher close to the ground. The faces of two burly young men in medical whites were directly above me. Both had close shaven hair, one blonde, one black. A tight binding was wrapped around my head. Warm wetness was gathering low on my neck.

"You're okay," the guy with golden hair said evenly. "Doesn't look bad. Probably a concussion. We're taking you to Emergency."

"How do you feel?" asked the other attendant.

"Like I lost a fight."

Irene's face appeared between the shoulders of the medical men. Her eyes were wide, her lips tight.

"Well, you got the girl," the smiling big guy pointed out.

"Happy ending," I said. "How's my sparring partner?"

"He hit his head, too. Not as bad as you. Cops have him."

Irene laid a hand lightly on my cheek. "Some neighbors came out and helped, held him until the police got there. I'm sorry, I'm sorry."

I reached up and stroked her hand. Her eyes were red and puffy.

"We need to load him up, Miss," said the dark-haired man.

"Can I ride along?"

"You can follow us. Meet us at St. Luke's Emergency Room. We don't need to race. He's all right."

The two EMTs slid me into the red and white van and closed the double doors. We drove at normal speed without lights or siren, the blonde at the wheel, his partner next to me, studying my eyes.

"Your girlfriend's a looker," he said.

"She is. She's great."

I felt a rising pain in the back of my head. I closed my eyes.

"You still with us, buddy?" I was able to nod. "You paid a price for true love tonight."

I gave him another little head movement as I sensed myself floating on a wave of euphoria, realizing that I was indeed paying a price and it wasn't at all too high. I'd gladly pay more if required. Very gladly. I became suddenly anxious to get to the hospital and be delivered from the white metal womb, to see Irene and tell her about my vast and expanding joy.